DØ2Ø724Ø

What the critics are saying…

"This book is guaranteed to please any reader." ~ *Coffeetime Romances*

"I highly recommend this book." ~ *Fallen Angel Reviews*

"…a wonderful anthology chock full of fun and games." ~ *Sizzling Romances*

"The sex scenes are extremely hot and steamy. When I finished reading them, I needed a glass of ice water." ~ *JERR Reviews*

"For an extra special stocking stuffer this holiday season, make sure R.S.V.P. is added to your Christmas wish list. It's a gift that keeps on giving…" ~ *Romance Reviews Today*

R.S.V.P

Freaturing:

Dominique Adair
Madeleine Oh
&
Jennifer Dunne

R.S.V.P.
An Ellora's Cave Publication, March 2005

Ellora's Cave Publishing, Inc.
1337 Commerce Drive Suite #13
Stow, Ohio 44224

ISBN #1419951769
Other available formats: ISBN MS Reader (LIT), Adobe (PDF),
Rocketbook (RB), Mobipocket (PRC) & HTML

Edited by: *Sue-Ellen Gower, Mary Moran and Martha Punches*
Cover art by: *Syneca*

Warning:

The following material contains graphic sexual content meant for mature readers. *R.S.V.P* has been rated *E-rotic* by a minimum of three independent reviewers.

Ellora's Cave Publishing offers three levels of Romantica™ reading entertainment: S (S-ensuous), E (E-rotic), and X (X-treme).

S-ensuous love scenes are explicit and leave nothing to the imagination.

E-rotic love scenes are explicit, leave nothing to the imagination, and are high in volume per the overall word count. In addition, some E-rated titles might contain fantasy material that some readers find objectionable, such as bondage, submission, same sex encounters, forced seductions, etc. E-rated titles are the most graphic titles we carry; it is common, for instance, for an author to use words such as "fucking", "cock", "pussy", etc., within their work of literature.

X-treme titles differ from E-rated titles only in plot premise and storyline execution. Unlike E-rated titles, stories designated with the letter X tend to contain controversial subject matter not for the faint of heart.

CONTENTS

CAJUN BLUE

By Dominique Adair

Chapter One

The engraved invitation mocked Elle from across the table. She scowled and tried to return her attention to the newspaper article she was reading but it did no good. After a few moments her gaze again strayed to the cream-colored card perched on her tottering To Do pile.

She sighed. That was the problem with To Do piles, they never turned into All Done piles. TD piles were like dishes and laundry—once they were cleared away one only had to wait a few hours for a new pile to begin.

She shoved the newspaper aside then reached for the card. She didn't know why she was dithering over this particular invitation quite so much. It wasn't as if this was her first invitation to a private bondage and discipline party. She'd been a player on the B&D scene for years and had attended many public and private parties.

Elle rubbed the thick cardstock between her fingers. Maybe it was because this party would be her last in her hometown of Columbus, Ohio. Next month she was scheduled to begin her new job in New Orleans, Louisiana as Vice President of Communications for Belle Femme, a million-dollar cosmetics company. Her stomach clenched even as a secret thrill of accomplishment ran up her spine. This was the job she'd trained for and dreamed of all her life.

It also meant her days as a sexual submissive were numbered.

Elle stroked her finger over the raised lettering on the invitation. Her new career would be complex, fast-paced and visible to the public as well as the shareholders of the burgeoning company. Her job was such that a single hint of scandal, let alone one of a sexual nature, could cost her the career she'd worked so hard to achieve.

Her shoulders slumped. That meant no playing for her, not for a long while at least. She was relatively sure there were private B&D clubs in New Orleans but it would take some time to investigate them and determine which ones were discreet and safe enough for her participate. With her new job and future at stake she could ill-afford a single misstep.

She propped the invitation on top of the pile of bills and correspondence. Consequently, this invite would be her last chance to play the game for quite a while. Just the thought of an extended period of celibacy was making her feel itchy, needy. It had been several weeks since the last time she'd played and she was more than ready to indulge herself.

Even though she knew every word by heart, she reread the invitation.

Ms. Scarlet,

You are cordially invited to attend a private party at Master Peter's home in New Albany. The theme is decadence, the color is purple and masks are required.

Prepare to serve and be pleasured.

Master Tyson

Event Coordinator

False names and the use of masks were very common in the underground B&D scene. Not only did it add to the mystery and excitement of the game, it was also used to protect some very public figures. She knew of at least one Senator and several CEOs of multi-million dollar companies who belonged to their group. No one wanted to risk losing their career or family for a few sexual kicks.

Across the bottom of the invitation there was a handwritten phone number and short note.

Please RSVP darling, I have someone I want you to meet! Smooches, T.

Elle grinned. She adored Ty and had from the moment they'd met. He was a friend with a penchant for purple silk boxers, men who were well-hung and women with impeccable fashion sense.

She rose and headed into her bedroom, taking care to avoid the tottering piles of half-packed boxes. He was also well aware that she'd broken off her most recent relationship with Ken, and no doubt had engineered this invitation for one final sexual romp for that reason alone. The parties Ty orchestrated were legendary among the B&D crowd. Known for their enticing themes and everything-goes atmosphere, it was quite a coup to receive an invitation.

Flinging open her closet doors, she stared at the racks of clothing, looking for anything sexy and purple. If she was going to go to this party, she'd definitely want to look her best. Maybe she needed to go shopping?

She'd attended quite a few of Ty's functions, usually with her ex-Master at her heels. She pulled out a purple velvet caftan. If she attended this event, it would be her first without a Master watching her every move.

She tossed the caftan aside and reached for a dark purple leather skirt. It wasn't unusual for a submissive to attend a party alone. She knew several women who'd done so and they'd claimed they had enjoyed the game more as there was no one to tell them where to draw the line. The submissive chose their sexual partners, indulged in whatever behavior turned them on the most, all without repercussions. The evening would be about pleasure, both giving and receiving, and the girls would indulge to their heart's content.

A soft ache blossomed between her thighs and she glanced at her toy drawer. The last few weeks had been hectic and it had been a long time since she'd played and she was more than ready. No, if she was going to attend the party she'd refrain from masturbating. Sexual abstinence would ensure an even more pleasurable evening.

Elle reached for the phone.

* * * * *

Remy "Blue" DeLaughter walked across the crowded terrace toward the bar. Though he'd been raised in a big Cajun family in the heart of Bayou Country, he'd been fortunate enough to receive a college education thanks to a baseball scholarship to one of the Big Ten schools. Consequently he felt at ease no matter where he was or whomever he was with. He was happiest at home in the bayou but the business world felt equally as comfortable. When he'd returned from college, his childhood friends had teased him about becoming a Yankee. His mouth hitched. Most Cajuns thought anything north of Shreveport was Yankee territory.

Blue found an empty seat at the bar and after ordering a drink, he turned so he could watch the festivities. Peter Gallinos, the host of the party, was his business partner and college buddy. Both had played baseball for The Ohio State University and in their senior year had conceived the idea of going into business together. D&G Fisheries of Cocodrie, Louisiana was born less than a year later.

Peter's father was the CEO of the Gallinos Consortium, a family of exclusive restaurant chains. With their business connections and Blue's knowledge of the shrimping and fishing industry in Southern Louisiana, D&G was well on its way to becoming a multi-million dollar business.

The bartender delivered his glass of scotch and Blue took a sip. The ten years since graduation had definitely been interesting. They'd started the business, worked long hours on the fishing boats, battled accountants, the weather and sometimes even each other. Even though they'd made plenty of mistakes, they'd amassed fortunes for the company as well as themselves. One of the first things Blue had done with his money was to build his parents a new house on the family land on the bayou. He swirled the amber-colored liquid around in his glass. They'd come a long way since those early days.

He and Pete had just inked a million-dollar deal with a major restaurant chain and had two more on the table. This completed deal would put them over the twenty million dollar profit mark for the year and they still had four months to go. While Blue was pleased with the progress they were making, he was itching to escape the business world for a while. Now that this deal was signed and sealed, he was leaving for home in a few days. Pete was more than capable of handling the other two contracts and it would be good to be back in Cajun country, though it wasn't quite where he'd pictured himself returning quite so soon.

A year ago he'd hightailed it out of Louisiana to follow a lusty librarian from Fort Myers, Florida. With the exception of business trips, he'd figured he wouldn't live in Louisiana ever again. Mistress Celine was a beautiful redhead who'd possessed a wickedly talented mouth and wielded a leather paddle with the best of them.

He grinned and shook his head. What he'd been thinking when he'd hooked up with her he didn't know. For a few months he'd reveled in her unabashed sexuality and they'd had a good, fulfilling time. Then one morning he'd caught sight of his pinkened ass in the bathroom mirror and knew his time as a submissive was over.

He wasn't wired to be a full-time Sub, he was Dom all the way.

The next day he'd left Florida and returned to Louisiana long enough to buy a house near the headquarters of D&G Fisheries before heading out to hawk his services to the restaurant, fish-buying public. So here he was, nine months later and over a million dollars richer, he was finally prepared to return home.

His gaze moved over the crowd. It had been a long time since he'd come out to play the game. Pete threw B&D parties several times a year, though this was the first Blue had attended in a while.

The house was crowded with well over one hundred guests, and judging from their attire, most were quite wealthy. That was Pete, always rubbing elbows with the rich folk. He grinned and raised his glass. He wondered what his pampered friend would think if Blue showed up on his doorstep with a few Cajuns who'd never ventured out of the bayou in their lives.

Several women walked past, slim purple silk ribbons were tied around their throats signaling their submissive status. The Masters wore black ribbons while those who swung both ways wore red. Almost everyone sported a mask though he'd chosen not to do so as he found them to be bothersome. There was nothing more annoying then kissing a pretty woman only to have their masks become tangled.

A slim blonde sashayed past clad only in a pink leather thong, a matching mask and a slim purple ribbon. She winked then presented him with a pert backside that barely gave a jiggle as she walked.

She was a dish of vanilla ice cream, sweet and tasty but nothing to get excited about, especially for a Cajun who'd been raised on hot sauce at his maman's tit. She was a pretty one, nice breasts, great ass definitely, but ordinary. Blue liked a little more meat on his women and this blonde looked to be in need of a few large helpings of red beans or étouffée. A good wind in the bayou would blow her away. Even the alligators would toss that one back as being too bony.

He preferred his woman to be dark-haired, dark-eyed and very, very curvy. He liked broad hips, large breasts and soft thighs plump enough to cushion a man when he settled in for a long ride. When he fucked a woman, he wanted something to hang onto, not some skinny booty he'd worry about breaking.

Besides, there was nothing better than the sight of a curvy ass turned pink from his hand or a pliable leather paddle.

Heat streaked to his groin and he took another drink, allowing his gaze to move over the crowd once more. Surely there was one woman here who'd meet his criteria?

Blue was ready to play.

Chapter Two

Elle drove through the towering iron gates and onto the Gallinos estate. Gravel crunched beneath her tires as she passed acres of neatly trimmed grass and ruthlessly shaped hedges. It appeared not a single branch, flower or leaf was out of place. She looked up at the towering trees that lined the drive and wondered if the leaves dared to fall and clutter the yard in the autumn.

From the road, only the roofline of the house was visible, lending the property a rarified air that only the wealthy could achieve. It was amazing what money could buy. She drove past the final line of trees then around a soft curve before the house came into view. Her eyes widened and she gave a soft whistle.

Very nice...

She'd known Peter socially for several years but had never ventured out to his house. With its façade of brick, pale limestone and wrought iron details, the sprawling structure looked surprisingly traditional for a man who was well known in the underground B&D culture. A giggle escaped her. What had she expected? Black leather drapes? Maybe some whips hanging from the trees and yards of chain decorating the hedges? She shook her head, amused at her flight of fancy.

The drive flattened out and there was a large parking area right in front of the house. Elle guided her trusty, used Lexus through the impressive rows of cars. Her brow rose when she spied a bright yellow Hummer parked next to a Benz, which was located beside a shiny vintage hearse. She couldn't help but smile at the eclectic mix of cars. That was Ty, always looking to invite diverse personalities to his little soirees. She pulled up to the walkway and stopped her car. Judging from the selection of cars in the lot, this evening would be interesting.

Rows of tuxedo-clad men were lined up shoulder to shoulder along the walk. She'd no sooner put her car into park than a tall, slim man with pale golden hair and a black half-mask approached.

"Good evening, Miss." His voice carried the round tones of the east coast. He opened her door, his white gloves stark against the black of his tuxedo. "My name is Lee and I will be taking care of your car. Please present your invitation to the gentleman at the door and he will assist you from there."

Smiling her thanks, Elle picked up her black satin half-mask and secured it over her eyes before she exited the car. Her stomach felt oddly jittery and her palms were damp. She looked beyond the line of tuxedo-clad men and her eyes widened when she saw the big man who attended the door.

He was dressed in worn blue jeans, the faded denim clung like a lover to every inch of his muscular thighs. He wore a black leather belt and a tight, white T-shirt that did nothing to hide the sculpted terrain of his broad chest and thickly muscled arms. His shiny, straight hair was the color of rich cocoa and it was neatly tied at the nape of his neck with a thin black ribbon.

She sucked in a noisy breath when she realized this man wasn't wearing a mask. His body alone would've gotten her attention as he was built for sin, but it was his beautiful face that cinched the deal. His skin carried a faint olive cast and his eyes were the perfect shade of melted dark chocolate. His nose was even and his mouth firm, commanding. This was a man who was used to giving orders and having them followed.

Her gaze assessed the entire package. Dark hair, beautiful mouth, big hands, slim waist…yum! He had the look of a man who knew his way around a woman's body and he would derive as much pleasure from giving as receiving.

She blinked. Where had that come from? Disturbed by the direction her thoughts had taken, Elle looked away from the doorman. She leaned down and tweaked the hem of her skirt into place. She was here to indulge her darker nature and find sexual release, not fall into bed with the first man she saw for a bout of wild monkey sex, no matter how handsome he was. She straightened.

Besides, he was a hired hand required to man the door, not an invited guest. What was the chance that this man was an experienced Master?

No chance, Elle.

Her car door slammed shut as the blond got behind the wheel of her car then drove away, removing her last line of defense. Straightening her shoulders, she approached the door, her chin held high and her gaze directed anywhere other than the man who stood before it. She fixed a smile on her face and was about to pat herself on the back for pulling herself together when the gravel shifted beneath one stiletto heel and she stumbled. A brunette in an immaculate tuxedo took her elbow and helped her regain her footing. With flaming cheeks she gave her helper an embarrassed nod and continued up the walk.

Silly girl! You'd think you'd never walked in heels before tonight.

Even though her purple suede trench coat covered her from shoulder to knees, she didn't miss the bold look the doorman gave her. When their gazes met, a slow, lazy smile curved his amazing mouth and her belly clenched. That heated look alone evoked images of damp, tangled sheets and hungry kisses. Skin against skin, fingers entwined, fucking this man would be like taming a wild horse—the ride would be wild and possibly dangerous but well worth the effort. Her breasts ached and her breathing grew shallow.

Whoa, Elle-girl, slow down now. This is not what you're looking for.

Her lips firmed and she returned his bold gaze with one of her own. Plain vanilla sex was easy to come by for an assertive, self-assured woman such as herself, but indulging her B&D fetish in total safety was not. She'd come to this party for a final chance to pander to her chosen submissive lifestyle, not to have amazing sex with the hunky doorman. Besides, he looked good but he probably had the voice of a chipmunk on steroids—

"Good evening." His voice was low, resonant and it carried more than a hint of the Deep South.

Damn, even his voice was perfect.

Mustering an impersonal tone, Elle tried to ignore the slow heat that slipped under her skin when she stopped beside him. "My invitation." She held the ivory card toward him.

His liquid chocolate gaze dropped to the card. "That, it is." She shivered when he took the invitation, his broad, thick fingers brushed hers. "What is your name?"

Her brow arched. She'd never been asked for her name at a party. "Isn't it customary to remain anonymous?"

His gaze burned a path over the exposed skin the neckline of her coat failed to conceal. Even though very little skin was visible, she felt naked. "I need to call you something besides 'Beautiful'." His voice was a sexy rumble and her gut clenched in response.

Soft warmth slid over her cheeks. He meant her name for the evening, not her real name. Resisting the urge to shake her head over her absentmindedness, she spoke.

"You may call me Miss Scarlet."

"Miss Scarlet." The false name dripped off his tongue like liquid honey heated in the sunshine. "A good southern name. It suits you."

Elle couldn't quite place his accent. Southern Mississippi? Louisiana maybe? Her hands landed on the tie of her coat and she gripped them, desperate to regain her composure.

He dropped her invitation into a basket on a small table near the door. "What position do you play?"

She blinked, totally lost. "Excuse me?"

He grinned and the gesture gave him a boyish appeal that would be irresistible to most women, including her. She swallowed hard. This man grew more dangerous by the minute.

He shrugged. "Sorry, it was a baseball reference. Are you a top or a bottom, Miss Scarlet?"

Irritated and sure he was mocking her, she crossed her arms over her chest. "I don't see how that is any of your—"

He waved a big hand to indicate three tidy piles of silk ribbons on the table. "I need to know which ribbon to give you."

"Oh." She felt more than a little foolish now. Surely he wasn't deliberately trying to confuse her, he was only doing his job. It wasn't his fault that she was on edge. "Bottom, please."

He reached for a slim, purple ribbon. "If you'll turn around, I'll give you a hand with this."

Flustered but not willing to show it, Elle turned away as he moved closer. The ribbon passed before her eyes and he placed it against her throat. Her thighs clenched and her nipples tightened painfully when his warm fingers slid over her skin.

"I hope you find what you desire beyond this door, Miss Scarlet." His breath was warm against her throat and her knees threatened to buckle. In a blatant caress, he slid his finger beneath the ribbon sending a shaft of heat down her spine. He gave the silk a gentle tug before releasing her.

Stunned by the strength of her reaction to this man, she started to move away when he caught her elbow.

"This way, please."

Flustered, she realized she'd been so startled she'd moved toward the parking lot and not the door. He guided her toward the entry then released her.

"Thank you. I hope you find what you're looking for, too." She winced when she heard her voice come out slightly higher than normal.

He smiled and leaned against the doorframe. Crossing his arms over his impressive chest, his bold gaze moved over her body. "I think I already have."

The heated look in his eyes set her stomach to fluttering and her nerves went into high alert. She turned to hurry away and ran into another tuxedo-clad man. Cheeks burning, she mumbled an apology and darted around the man, grateful to make her escape.

Just what was it about the doorman that made her so edgy, so...needy?

* * * * *

Blue's gaze followed the sassy Miss Scarlet's progress toward the coat check.

Now that was his kind of woman. He'd eat his pirogue for one night of pleasure between those thighs.

He ran his hand over his jaw. He couldn't remember the last time he'd felt such an immediate, white-hot sexual attraction to a woman. One glance from those emerald eyes and she'd rocked his world.

Though her silk mask had obscured her features and her coat concealed most of her body, he'd fuck her for the hair alone. Those beautiful sable locks created a cascade of long, riotous waves that would entice a man to tangle his fingers in the silken mass while her sassy mouth sucked his cock. He rocked on his heels. She looked like a woman who'd know how to suck a cock, too. This one wouldn't be timid, oh no. He'd bet his house she'd jump in with both feet and swallow him with pleasure.

The powerful image created such a rush of heat to his groin that his breath caught when his buttons prodded his hardened flesh. He shifted his stance in an effort to relieve the pressure.

It didn't help.

Miss Scarlet, oblivious to his heated thoughts, had reached the coat check. His mouth went dry when she slid the purple suede from her shoulders. She was even more beautiful than he'd imagined. His gaze skimmed her curvaceous figure. Judging from the other ladies he'd seen so far, she was a modest dresser, which intrigued him all the more.

Her black long-sleeved blouse was sheer, and the bodice was accented with dark purple beads. A black leather corset bra that laced up the front and left her lower belly bare confined her ample breasts. A simple black leather skirt covered her ample backside and ended just above her knees.

He was pleased to see that particular part of her anatomy was more than enough to fill a hungry man's hands. Her world-class legs were encased in black silk stockings and her feet were shod in a lethal-looking pair of high heels. The shoes alone were enough to enflame any man's baser instincts but it was no wonder she'd stumbled. While they were undeniably sexy, they looked painful to him.

Blue licked his lips. Just looking at her made him hunger to touch her, take her beneath him and spank that rounded backside until it warmed and turned rosy. He could well imagine those beautiful legs, with the heels and stockings in place, thrown over his shoulders as he ate her sweet pussy. Better yet, wrapped around his waist as he slowly fucked her into release, her big breasts in his hands and her long hair tangled over his pillow.

Oh yeah...

Blue smiled. He'd found exactly what he'd been looking for.

Chapter Three

Elle slid into a vacant seat at the end of the bar. Situated on the terrace, the bar commanded both an excellent view of the gardens and the crowded ballroom. She sighed when she slid one of her shoes off to dangle on the end of her toe. More importantly it offered a welcome place to rest her weary feet. She loved good shoes but she didn't understand why the really sexy ones always had to be such torture to wear. Surely the shoe designers could understand the need for a little extra padding in the soles?

After ordering her drink, she let her gaze drift over the crowd. Everywhere she looked there was exposed flesh and every shade of purple imaginable. Masks, thongs, pants, one adventurous guest even wore a purple leather straightjacket. Over-the-top was what came to mind when she thought of one of Ty's events.

She'd already made several rounds of the party and had recognized a few people from previous events. She'd made small talk and had received a flattering number of propositions though none interested her so far. One man easily could have been her grandfather's age. All it had taken was one swift glance at his sagging balls and she'd beaten a hasty retreat. Another man had been a distinct possibility until she'd seen his cock and balls had multiple piercings. She shuddered. Genital piercing did nothing for her and she certainly didn't want to have sex with a man who had more metal on his cock than was contained in most cars today.

She picked up the drink the bartender had placed at her elbow. Maybe she was being too picky?

An image of that pierced cock flashed before her eyes and she set her glass down. No, she wasn't being too particular, she had certain standards a potential lover needed to meet. One of them was no genital piercing and another was to be too young for an AARP card. She sighed and picked up her drink again. She'd seen a few friends, shaken some hands but so far she'd failed to accomplish the one thing she'd desired — finding a man to spank her and make her come and come hard at that.

Elle was more than a little disappointed and beginning to feel desperate for sexual release. She'd deliberately refrained from masturbating for the past few weeks just to build up the tension for tonight. She caught sight of a man with multiple purple ribbons tied around his cock and nothing else. It was starting to look like she'd wasted good lip gloss.

"I spy Miss Scarlet." A familiar voice sounded in her ear and her heart leapt.

"Master Tyson." She turned and smiled wide as the slim, handsome black man slipped into the seat next to her. "How are you, my friend?"

"I'm fabulous." He dropped a leather notepad on the bar before he kissed her on the cheek. "You look beautiful this evening."

"Thank you." Her gaze skimmed his burgundy silk pajama-looking outfit. "I must say you're looking pretty hot yourself."

He preened. "This is my latest acquisition from the fall shows in Paris." He waved at someone across the room. "Are you having a good time, Elle?"

"So far, so good." She sipped her drink. "It looks like you have an excellent turnout this evening."

He grinned and his slim chest swelled. "Everyone vies for an invite to one of my decadence parties. They *are* the talk of the underground." His brow arched and he gave her a coy look. "The question of the evening is, have you seen anyone interesting yet? With the way you look this evening the men should be panting for you."

She shrugged. "I made two circuits of the house and nothing has sparked my interest yet."

"Don't you worry." He patted her hand. "I've already found the perfect man for you. Peter has a houseguest who has been staying here for the past few weeks. This man is hot, he's got an accent you will not believe and I'm pretty sure he will fuck like a machine." Ty leaned over and whispered, "I'm sure he's packed like a racehorse.

"Girl..." Elle laughed as he waved one slim hand over his heated face. "If I knew he swung both ways I'd have bagged him already."

"I'll bet you would have." She shook her head. Tyson's sexual escapades were welcome fodder for many a dinner party.

"Don't you worry, Elle, I'll go find him and send him over here to sweep you off those heels and fuck you into oblivion." He squeezed her hand.

Her stomach flopped. "Ty, what did you tell him about me?"

He slid off the seat and gave her an innocent look she did not buy for one second. "Nothing except that I have a really hot friend who needs a little taming, a lot of licking and maybe a spanking or two."

Elle couldn't help but laugh as Ty sashayed off into the crowd. She picked up her empty glass then indicated to the bartender she'd like another.

She and Ty had met on the local club scene. He'd been the one to introduce her to the close-knit bondage community in Columbus. He'd encouraged her to explore the darker, more sensual side of her nature and he'd done everything to aid her in her quest. He'd been a good friend, trustworthy and he had the sexual morals of an alley cat in heat. What more could she want in a friend?

She grinned. If Ty had picked out a man for her then he must really be something. Hopefully he would be interesting enough to take her mind off that hot doorman who'd thrown her for such a loop. She sipped her fresh drink. It wasn't that she had anything against doormen, she really didn't. In her dating career she'd dated bartenders, a carpenter, as well as a neurosurgeon and the CEO of an insurance company. Their job or the size of their paycheck didn't matter to her as much as their personality and their ability to wield a paddle.

Very simply put, this evening she was determined her final Sub/Dom scene in Columbus be memorable, and that didn't include having chandelier sex with Ty's hired help. It was also very possible that if she took him up on the invitation she'd seen in his eyes that she'd run into him again sometime in the future. She planned to return to Ohio to visit her friends at least several times a year and that would include attending some of Ty's parties. The last thing she'd want would be to come face to face with the doorman again after having wild sex. One of her requirements for the evening was that she'd never have to see her partner in the future. It was just easier that way. In her opinion, serious relationships were highly overrated.

"There you are, Miss Scarlet."

Elle tensed as the warm velvet voice of the doorman stroked her ears. She closed her eyes for a brief moment in an effort to steady herself before facing him. She was feeling a little too weak, too needy to have to fight her attraction to him. He was disturbing enough as it was and she'd hoped to avoid him for the rest of the evening. She opened her eyes and turned just as he slid onto the padded stool next to hers.

She gave him a cool, pointed look then turned away. "I'm waiting for someone."

He chuckled and her toes curled in response. "What a coincidence, so am I." He rested his brawny arms on the edge of the bar. "We can keep each other company while we wait." He nodded toward the bartender then requested a beer.

More than a little on edge, Elle's gaze moved over the crowd, frantic to find Ty. Thanks to the terrace rail against her back, the bar on her right and the arrangement of potted palms on the left, she was trapped in a corner by this man's big body.

The only way out would be an undignified scramble over the railing or she'd have to shimmy past her tormentor. She glanced over the rail and noted the rosebushes below.

Shimmy it is.

She picked up her drink and made to slide off her stool.

"Running away, Miss Scarlet?"

The mocking tone in his voice brought her to a screeching halt. Was she running away?

Yes.

Irritated, she bit the inside of her lip. Just what was she running from anyway? Yeah, he was good looking but he was still only a man...a devastatingly sexy man but a man nonetheless. She could handle him with her hands tied behind her back—

In your dreams...

Stifling a groan she placed her drink on the bar then forced her gaze to meet his. "And what do you think I'm running from, Mr. Doorman?"

His mouth quirked. "Blue, you can call me Blue." He picked up his beer and leaned toward her. They were so close that his knees brushed against hers. Her skin felt electrified where he touched her.

"I don't know, Miss Scarlet." His drawl was sexy, sensual. "You tell me what it is about me that has you so spooked."

Elle feigned a laugh and hoped it sounded more natural than it felt. "You do not have me spooked," she lied. She crossed her arms over her chest to hide her erect nipples then leaned back in her chair to give him a superior look. "There is nothing about you that interests me in the least."

"Mais, yeah?" His heated gaze skimmed over her curves. "Your mouth says one thing yet your body says another. Which is the liar?"

"I—"

"Not that it matters. I want you, you want me, what more is there to be said? You're a submissive in search of a master, I'm an experienced master in search of a biddable submissive." He raised his beer in a mocking salute. "We're a match made in Central Ohio."

He was a Master?

"Not so fast, my friend." Elle picked up her drink. "Just because you're a Dom and I'm a Sub doesn't mean we're sexually compatible. There are a lot of things to consider before leaping into a mutually pleasurable venture such as this."

Just because he was a master and she was wildly attracted to him didn't mean she was ready to jump into bed with him. She wanted him; she would admit that to herself at least, but she wasn't about to admit it to him. Her relationship with Ken had taught her the danger in letting a man know she desired him as he would use the knowledge against her. Her former master had taunted her, using her rampant sexuality against her almost to the point of torture.

His pet nickname for her had been "whore".

Her lips firmed. She was determined to never put herself into an emotionally vulnerable position again and that included letting this man know how much she desired him.

Blue took another swig of his beer then set it on the bar. "Under normal circumstances I'd say you were right but this tells me that we are very sexually compatible."

Before she could move, his big hands landed on her knees, his palms seared her skin through the delicate stockings. Her breath caught as he skimmed his hands upward. Catching the hem of her skirt, he pulled her toward him until her knees were secured between his splayed legs. His thumbs dug into her inner thighs and forced them apart.

Her breath caught and their gazes clashed. Need glittered in the liquid depths of his eyes and she felt the deep pull of arousal in her lower belly. She fought the need to whimper when he slid his hand up her thighs to cover the damp material of her thong panties. His touch was as shocking as it was arousing.

"This tells me you want me." His voice was low, his accent grew more pronounced. "Your body tells me what your mouth denies."

A rush of need moved through Elle, so powerful she shook with the force of it. Her breathing deepened and she grabbed his wrist, not quite sure if she wanted to push him away or hold him in place. His fingers tightened and cupped her mound in an intimate caress. She couldn't prevent the soft moan that escaped her and her thighs tightened on their hands.

A knowing look came into his eyes and her stomach plummeted into her Manolo Blahnik shoes. She felt weak with arousal yet empowered at the same time. She knew instinctively that if she asked Blue to remove his hand he would. But was that what she really wanted?

Not on her life…

Taking her silence as acquiescence, he pulled her closer until she was just shy of sitting in his lap. Lifting her left leg, he draped it over his thigh to allow better access.

"You were born to submit to me." His voice was thick, heavy with need. "You were created to feel this heat, this fire that now burns inside of you." He now had both of his hands under her skirt, his fingers curled around the thin straps of her panties. "It would be a sin to deny yourself the pleasure you were born to receive." With a sharp tug the straps snapped under the pressure.

Elle moaned when he coaxed her hips upward to remove the ruined garment. Grateful for the shield provided by his big body, Elle's eyes widened as he held up her decimated panties. He lifted them to his nose to inhale her essence before he tucked the silken scrap into his pocket.

"You are any master's dream." His hand returned to her thigh and instinctively she parted her legs, stifling a moan when he cupped her dampened folds. He leaned forward to whisper in her ear, "I will make you mine, Miss Scarlet."

Elle was eager to straddle him by the time one thick finger breached her folds. She bit her lip when he stroked her needy flesh. His touch was expert, both gentle and searching yet firm and straight to the point. She'd been right about him. Here was a man who knew his way around a woman's body.

His lips brushed her earlobe. "I feel your need."

Her hands clung to his broad shoulders and she pressed closer, desperate to feel him against her. "Yes."

"Do you want me, Miss Scarlet?"

Her head urged her to scream a denial but she knew she'd only look the fool considering the evidence of her arousal dampened his hands. "Yes," she breathed.

"You will accept me as your master?" He nipped at her jaw and she shuddered, desire riding hard and low in her belly.

"Yes."

"And you will take no other man so long as I require it?"

She balked. This was a one-night deal, no more, no less. Surely that was what he was referring to? That she take no other man here at the party—

All rational thought was blown from her mind when his finger zeroed in on her clit. He gave the hard nub a firm stroke. Her grip tightened on his shoulders and she pressed against him.

"Yes," she gulped.

"Good." He bit her neck and that simple touch sent chills of need through her body. "I want to taste your heat, your fire."

His mouth grazed her neck and she shuddered. His fingers continued their easy movements and with each stroke her need spiraled higher. She was so close...so hot...

"Please." Her voice was low, begging. "I need to—"

Without warning Blue pulled away. He lifted her back onto her stool and Elle's head swam with arousal and confusion. She had to blink the sensual haze from her vision. Her need for release was so strong that her body shook with the force. Why did he stop touching her? Surely he had to know that even the lightest touch would bring her to completion.

"Not so fast, my little submissive." He slid off his stool and disengaged her fingers from his shoulders. "You'll have to earn your release by first pleasing your master."

Elle bit her lip to stifle the moan that threatened. The bastard. While she'd forgotten the game and why they were there in the first place, it was obvious he had not. From the moment he'd touched her she'd forgotten everything, including the reasons she didn't want to enter into a sexual relationship with this man. She pushed those thoughts away and stared up into his handsome face, stunned to her core at the level of her response to him.

How often did one find such pure, unadulterated heat between two people? In her experience it was rare, very rare.

Blue reached for her, running his fingers along the line of her jaw. "I can see your mind working and I will ask you once again, will you submit to me, Miss Scarlet?" He held his hand out toward her.

With her heart in her throat, she stared down at his big hand. Judging from the heat they'd generated she'd be a fool to walk away from him, from this possible earth-shattering experience. Then again, she had the distinct feeling this man could be dangerous for her. He wouldn't be quite as easy to manage as she'd first thought either. Then again, this was only a one-night stand, wasn't it?

Mustering her courage, she slipped her hand into his.

He raised her hand to his mouth and kissed her knuckles. "You won't regret your decision." Her stomach tightened when he winked at her. "And I'm not letting you back out, either."

Mute, Elle allowed Blue to help her off the stool. Why did she feel as if she'd just jumped from an airplane and left both her stomach and rational mind behind?

Strangely warmed and reassured on a level she'd didn't want to explore, she followed the tall man toward the steps leading to the upstairs. When she mounted the first riser she wondered what sensual pleasures awaited her above.

Chapter Four

Scarlet was as nervous as a wet cat.

Blue poured himself a small glass of scotch, all the while watching his new submissive out of the corner of his eye. She stood near the windows overlooking the backyard. Her body language proclaimed her uneasiness with the situation and how he'd turned the tables on her. Forcing her to admit to her attraction had been a necessary step, though it had put another layer of paint on the wall that stood between them. Her shoulders were stiff and her back was ramrod straight. Her slim arms were crossed over her ample breasts and she gnawed on her bottom lip with even white teeth.

In short, she was perfection.

"Can I get you a drink?" he spoke.

She turned toward him, her emerald eyes were shadowed behind the mask. "No, thank you."

She'd retreated behind a polite social façade most people employed when dealing with strangers even though she knew in a few short hours they'd be much more than mere strangers. They'd be lovers and consequently the starch would be removed from her spine.

His blood heating at the provocative thought, Blue picked up his drink and walked toward an easy chair.

"Miss Scarlet, you may join me." He picked up a crimson silk pillow from the couch and dropped it beside his chair. He sat down then waved toward the cushion to indicate she should sit at his feet.

For a few seconds she remained where she was, indecision written across her lovely face. What she was thinking he didn't know but he could imagine her mind whirling like a hamster on a wheel. He held his breath and wondered if she'd take him up on his offer or make a mad dash for the door.

He released his breath when she started toward him. Scarlet had the easy walk of a woman who was comfortable with her body and her sexuality. Taking this beauty beneath him would be all pleasure, no pain...unless she requested it, of course.

He cleared his throat. "How long have you been playing the scene?"

"Five years." She sank to her knees on the cushion, her face only inches from his left knee.

He took a sip of the scotch, enjoying the smooth burn of the liquid. Peter certainly provided the best for his guests. "What is it about the game that you enjoy the most?"

She shrugged and her gaze danced away, clearly uncomfortable with the question. "How long have you been playing?" she countered.

His brow rose. If she was to accept him as her master, he'd need to begin her training immediately. He put down his drink.

"Scarlet, if you wish to play the game with me, you must understand the rules. The first and most important one is that when I ask you a question, I do expect an immediate answer." He ran his finger over the smooth line of her jaw, enjoying the soft texture of her skin. "I believe I asked you what aspect of the game you enjoy the most."

Her eyes flashed fire and her lips tightened. She wanted to object, he could feel her resistance to being forced to answer his questions. Scarlet may have been playing the game for several years but she still retained a stubborn streak. He would take great pleasure in correcting the flaws in her training and teaching her the error of her ways.

Something shifted in her eyes and her gaze slithered down to where her hands rested in her lap. Her unease was almost palpable. Trust was an integral component of the game. If Scarlet didn't trust him to keep her safe, they weren't going any farther than the sitting room of his suite.

"I suppose it's the freedom to explore the boundaries of my sexuality." Her voice was soft. "All decisions are removed from me and I am forced to accept the pleasure that my body and Master requires of me."

Blue felt a rush of triumph. Her revelation was a small victory but an important one. Trust was a precarious two-way street. If he showed her that he trusted her, chances were she would relax and open up to him even more.

"That's an excellent answer." Blue captured a lock of her silky hair between his fingers. "Bondage play is about pleasure and sexual discipline. You will be casting your inhibitions aside and moving into a realm where you can explore your sexuality and realize your limitations." He drew the soft strands of her hair over her cheek and along the lower edge of her mask. "Would you like to keep this on?" He flicked the silken strands over her top lip. "The choice is yours, Scarlet."

She raised her head and her eyes were wide beneath the mask. Wordless, she nodded. "For now." Her voice was husky.

"From the moment I met you I could barely take my eyes from your mouth." He drew her hair along the plump curve of her lower lip. "I couldn't help but imagine how my cock would look between those beautiful lips of yours." He noted how her breathing had deepened.

He released her hair. "How much would you enjoy sucking your Master's cock, Scarlet?"

She swallowed audibly. "I think I would like that very much."

"Master."

"Master."

"You may remove my boots." Blue sat back then picked up his drink.

Scarlet bent her head and positioned a knee on either side of his left foot. With his assistance she raised his foot and removed first one boot then the other with a minimum of fuss.

When she was done, she sat back on her heels, her palms flat against her thighs and her head down ever so slightly.

Very nice.

Just to make the situation a little easier on her, he rose from the chair to unbutton his jeans. Considering they were as tight as sin and his cock was already hard, he didn't think he'd last very long if he asked her to do it. Just the thought of those slim fingers on his flesh threatened to send him over the edge. The last thing he wanted was to lose control like some untried schoolboy. He pushed down his pants and boxers then he sat again.

"You may now remove them," he said.

She rose onto her knees and eased the tight denim down until she'd managed to remove them entirely. As she worked he didn't miss the quick glances she gave his erect cock. Her lips glistened from the caress of her tongue, and when she settled herself on the cushion her breathing was erratic. She wasn't nearly as unaffected as she'd like him to believe. His blood heated. He couldn't wait to taste her, touch her, but first he wanted her mouth on his flesh, his cock in her mouth.

"You will now lick me, all over."

His eager submissive moved the cushion until she was perched between his thighs. Bending her head, she first nuzzled his cock then his balls. His breathing grew harsh when she began licking him with soft, little cat licks before switching to long, drugging strokes.

A low groan of pleasure escaped him as she sucked one ball into her mouth and gave it a gentle tug. Someone had taught her well. Scarlet moved to the other and gave it the same gut-clenching treatment until he forced her to slow by tangling his fingers in her silky hair.

"Now, my cock. Take it into your mouth."

She made a throaty sound of acquiescence. Releasing him, she turned her attentions to his straining cock. She opened her mouth and covered the broad head to tease the cleft with the tip of her tongue. Her slim hand encircled the thick shaft and gave it a tender squeeze that almost sent him leaping out of the chair. He gave a loud groan when her thumb caressed the sensitive underside of the head.

She took him deeper into her mouth, one sensitive inch at a time. The wet slide of her tongue coupled with the pressure of her hand around his shaft threatened to send him over the edge. His hands fisted in her hair as she began to move over him, her mouth and fist moving in unison to stroke and tease every straining inch.

All too soon he began slowly pushing in and out, fucking her lovely mouth. His breathing grew labored as his hips pounded against the chair. His movements grew frantic as his release neared. Scarlet seemed to realize he was close as she quickened her pace ever so slightly. Cupping his balls, she gave them a gentle squeeze.

It was just enough to finish him off.

A slow tingle began in the back of his calves then raced up his legs. His vision faded to a reddish haze, his blood thundered in his veins. The rush of release was so intense, Blue felt his eyes roll back into his head. Fire coalesced at the base of his spine before exploding out of his cock in teeth-jarring waves.

Scarlet didn't miss a beat. She sucked at his flesh, swallowing his release without hesitation. Now limp, he sagged in the chair, his eyes mere slits as his submissive licked him clean. When she was done, she licked her lips, now devoid of lipstick, then sat back with her eyes down. She had a slight smile.

The moment he'd seen her he'd known Scarlet would be a delight, but he had no idea the depths of her talents.

She would be a pleasure to train.

* * * * *

Every nerve was on edge by the time Blue took her hand. Elle was torn between the desire to jump out of her skin and run screaming from the room or drop to her knees and beg him to give her release. Instead she remained silent and placed her hand in his. He led her into the bedroom. Her gaze moved around the room and her breath left in a slow huff when she realized it was only a plain bedroom complete with a four-poster bed, dresser and armoire.

No toys…

No leather…

No swings hanging from the ceiling…

No spanking benches…

Nothing was out of the ordinary.

Blue seemed to sense her confusion and he squeezed her hand. "Patience, Scarlet."

A soft flush moved over her cheeks and he released her. Had she been so transparent?

"The bathroom is straight ahead." He walked toward the armoire as he spoke. "Please make yourself at home."

"Thank you." Grateful for a moment of much-needed privacy, Elle scooted into the bathroom. After shutting the door she sagged against it, grateful for the solid support. Her knees were shaking so badly she was afraid she'd fall down.

The taste of his luscious cock still resonated in her mouth. She licked her lips, enjoying his unique flavor. She'd always taken great pleasure in giving head to her man. While ultimately she craved the role of the submissive, she couldn't deny the rush that being in control for those few minutes afforded her. There was nothing like having a big, strong man melt like wax in the sun the moment her mouth touched his cock. It was better than buying new shoes.

Feeling steadier, she pushed away from the door and flicked on the lights. After making quick use of the facilities, she stepped up to the mirror to check her appearance.

Her hair was a silky tangle thanks to Blue's fingers, while behind the mask her eyes held a feverish glitter of need. Her lips were bare of lipstick, which now decorated his cock, no doubt. She pressed her thighs together, enjoying the spark of arousal that accompanied the movement. It would take so little to bring her off. She cupped her breasts and gave them a slow squeeze before allowing one hand to stray to her mound. Just a few quick strokes—

"Miss Scarlet, you'd better not be touching yourself."

Blue's lazy voice right outside the bathroom door caused her to jump. Her hand brushed the soap dish and sent it into the sink with a noisy clatter.

"N-n-no, I'm not." She grabbed the dish along with the decorative soaps and replaced it on the sink.

"Good." He gave a soft chuckle. "I'd hate to have to punish you so soon."

Elle swallowed hard. Somehow she doubted he really felt that way, as she knew she didn't. A little punishment sounded just fine to her. Turning on the water, she washed her hands then applied a generous amount of lotion, anything to give herself a few moments to regain her balance. Once she felt more in control, she opened the door.

Blue stood near the bed, his face impassive and his hands hanging at his sides. While she was gone, he'd lit a few candles as well as a small fire in the fireplace. The golden flames gave the room a soft, inviting glow.

Behind him the armoire doors were open and her throat tightened when she saw the secrets that were revealed. From rows of hooks hung all sorts of delectable toys. Floggers, whips, chains and various lengths of rope were neatly arranged. A shelf at the top held a selection of silk scarves, feathers and all sorts of other intriguing items, some of which she'd never seen before. She licked her lips and her vagina became awash with arousal as she imagined Blue's talented hands using some of those new toys on her body.

"Scarlet, look at me."

She blinked, her gaze meeting his. "Yes, Master?"

"Come to me."

On wobbly knees, she approached him until she stood several inches away. Heat radiated from his big body and his masculine scent, warm male mixed with his release, caused her breasts to grow heavy. Her nipples ached.

"How may I serve you, Master?" she dipped her head slightly.

"When you were alone in the bathroom, did you touch yourself?"

Trepidation mixed with excitement in her gut. "A little, but only through my clothing."

"Master."

"Master," she parroted.

"And did you find release?"

"No, Master."

His hand cupped her chin and he forced her head back until their gazes met. "Bien. Do you know what would've happened if you'd done so?"

She swallowed again, her tongue felt thick and uncoordinated. Not trusting herself to speak, she shook her head.

"I'd have to severely punish you." His thumb took up a lazy stroke along the edge of her lower lip. "As your master it is up to me to determine when you will climax. It is my decision and mine alone. You are my vessel, my servant and it is my responsibility to see to your needs. Do you understand this?"

"Yes, Master." Her voice was barely above a whisper. By now her legs were shaking so hard she could barely stand and her body was awash with excitement.

"If I wish to touch you, I may do so without asking you." He released her chin to cup her one breast. A rush of excitement flooded her body. "I have dominion over you, don't I, Scarlet?"

"Yes, Master."

"But this doesn't mean you are without control." His thumb traced a tight circle around one nipple sending her nerves into overdrive. "You do have a measure of control and I'm going to give it to you." He gave the hardened bud a tweak. "If there is anything I do that makes you uncomfortable or causes you discomfort, all you have to do is say the word 'magenta' and I will stop. Do you understand?"

"Yes, Master."

"What is your safe word?"

"Magenta, Master."

His handsome face was transformed by a slow, wicked smile. "Good girl. Now that we have the details taken care of, shall we get down to having some fun?"

His head dipped toward her and her heart almost stopped when their lips met. His taste, a mixture of scotch and aroused male, set her heart to fluttering. Her mouth opened with a soft moan and she welcomed him inside. His tongue was soft yet insistent as he kissed her senseless. Unable to help herself, she moaned and leaned into his broad chest. Wrapping her arms around him, she clung to his broad frame for support. One hand tangled in her hair and he angled her head for a deeper, more aggressive kiss.

His other hand landed on her butt and he gave one cheek a firm squeeze that sent her squirming. Never had she been quite so aware of her body as she was in that moment. Her softness pressed against his hard strength, his muscular arms around her, his hands and mouth commanding her every sensation, her every move.

Elle was shaking when he broke the kiss. He eased away from her. When she was steady on her feet, he released her.

"We need to start with this." Blue retrieved a green silk scarf from the bed. "I find that limiting one's senses serves to magnify and enhance the experience."

Elle licked her swollen lips; excitement had rendered her mute. She turned and felt Blue loosen the ties of her half-mask.

She started to object until she felt the slide of cool silk over her eyes.

"Since you're wearing this blindfold, we can remove your mask for now. If you feel the need later, you may put it back on."

Pacified, Elle relaxed as he secured the blindfold. With her sight gone, almost immediately her other senses kicked into overdrive. The sound of his footsteps across the carpet was audible while the snapping of the sap in the firewood sounded as loud as a gunshot. Her breathing was harsh and her body ached with unfulfilled need. She touched the edge of the blindfold. She longed to scream at the increased tension it had introduced.

"Remove your blouse, Scarlet."

"Yes, Master."

With trembling fingers she unbuttoned the garment, all the time very aware of the soft currents of air that caressed her exposed skin. She slid off the shirt then felt Blue take it her hand. Even thought the shirt had been sheer, she felt chilled without its dubious protection.

"You're very beautiful." His husky voice sounded near her right ear.

She started when his hand touched her shoulder. He stroked one arm then the other, once, twice. He stopped; his big hands captured her wrists and lifted them. She felt the soft caress of velvet around her wrists and her breathing almost stopped.

He was tying her wrists together.

"You're so beautiful that I fear I need to restrain you while I contemplate what exactly I want to do with you." He bound her hands then gave them a gentle tug to test the knots. "What I want to do *to* you."

Her pussy clenched as a flood of heat washed over it. She thought for a moment she might come right then and there. She gulped for air and struggled to regain control of her senses.

43

"Come, Scarlet."

Blue took her bound wrists and walked with her until she felt the bed against the back of her knees. He lowered her to sit on the edge then guided her into the middle of the bed. Without a word he raised her hands over her head and secured them to the headboard. She heard a metallic snick and she gave her arms an experimental jiggle. She was well and truly bound.

"Just beautiful," he whispered.

His hands seemed to be everywhere at once. He stroked her arms, over the exposed flesh of the tops of her breasts, along the waistband of her skirt and across her soft belly, down her sides to her hips, her thighs, calves then her ankles.

"I don't think I'll bind your legs this time." His voice sounded dreamy as if he was speaking more to himself than to her. His accent was more pronounced now.

Torn between excitement and disappointment, Elle gave a soft moan.

"You think to object, Scarlet?" His hand slipped up her thigh then stopped, mere inches from the tops of her thigh-high stockings.

"N-n-no," she panted.

"Master."

"No, Master."

He chuckled. "I thought not." His hand resumed its leisurely journey along her thigh. "I'd hate to have to punish you already."

Elle bit her lip as he urged her to lift her hips. He pushed up her skirt around her waist leaving her lower body exposed to his touch, his gaze.

"You have a beautiful cunt." His hand covered her. "I can see why you'd wax it the way you do." He petted the soft strip of dark hair on her mound and she bit back a sob. "It seems a shame to cover it up with clothing."

She choked back a laugh. "Well, it isn't very convenient to wander in public with no pants on."

"Mmm." He tangled his fingers in the curls and then gave a gentle tug, wrenching a moan from her. "If you were mine I'd keep you naked and available to me at all times of the day or night."

She felt the brush of his mouth just above her damp pussy.

"You'd awaken in the morning and take your bath then prepare yourself for me." Broad fingers parted her damp flesh and she held her breath, longing for that first touch of her clit. "You'd be at my beck and call, awaiting our mutual pleasure."

She couldn't contain the moan when his finger stroked just inside her dampness. "You're very wet for me. How aroused are you, Scarlet?"

She was panting now. "Very, very aroused."

"I see." He pulled away and she had to bite her tongue to curb her strenuous objections. "I want you to restrain yourself. You may not find your release until I tell you to do so. Do you hear me, Scarlet?"

She gulped, her heart thundered in her ears. "Yes, Master."

"Good."

He parted her thighs and she felt him settle between them. He lifted her legs over his shoulders before his fingers plundered her aroused flesh. Spreading her open, she almost went over the edge at the first stroke of his tongue. She bit her lip hard and with each swipe of his tongue the tension increased until she was panting and straining against his mouth. She pulled at her bonds, her body bowing toward him. Her head dug into the pillow as his wicked tongue possessed her. His fingers breached her damp channel, filling and stretching her until she cried out. Her hips jerked to meet each thrust as he slowly finger-fucked her.

"Scarlet—"

Elle paid no heed to the note of warning in his voice as with one final stroke she spun out of control. With a scream, her body snatched the release it so desperately craved. Spasm after spasm of orgasm took control of her senses and sent waves of need crashing over her nervous system. Light sparked against the confines of her blindfold as she went into overdrive, her mind short-circuited with pleasure.

A few moments later reality returned and she realized she lay on the bed, alone.

Alone?

She raised her head and wanted to curse her blindfold. Since she was still bound, it wasn't as if she could just remove it.

"Blue?" Her voice was faint, shaky.

"Master," he prompted.

"Master?"

"Yes, Scarlet?"

"Where are you?"

"Standing by the bed." She felt the bed move when he sat down. His hip brushed hers. "I'm very disappointed in you, Scarlet."

Disappointed? How could anyone be disappointed in a world-class orgasm like she'd just had?

She cleared her throat. "Why did I disappoint you, Master?"

"You came, didn't you?"

Her breathing hitched. "Yes, Master."

"And I didn't give you permission to take your release, did I?"

"No—"

"So you've disobeyed me."

"But I couldn't help myself—"

"Restraint, Scarlet. You must practice restraint. When I'd pushed you to the point of release you should've used your safe word to ask me to stop. If you had done so then we wouldn't find ourselves in the predicament that we're in now."

Her heart almost stopped. "W-w-which is?"

"You've disobeyed your master, Scarlet, and now I'll have to punish you."

Chapter Five

She was exquisite.

Blue's gaze drank in the arousing sight of his bound submissive waiting for his return. Her skin was flushed from her explosive release just minutes ago and a fine sheen of sweat gilded her toned limbs. Her dark hair was tangled across his pillows and her bewitching eyes were still shrouded by her blindfold. Still wearing her bra, stockings and heels, her skirt was scrunched up around her waist. He wanted to unwrap her like a Christmas present.

Anticipation was a strong ingredient of the game. Letting a sub stew over a potential flogging only served to heighten their senses and ultimately their response to their punishment. After he'd announced his intention to discipline her, he'd left the room for a few minutes to give her time to contemplate his next move. Judging from the sheen of sweat on her upper lip, his absence had the desired effect.

Without acknowledging her, Blue headed for the armoire stuffed with toys. Just what should he use on his disobedient woman? His gaze flicked over the selection of floggers, paddles and short whips. A flogger just might do the trick. He selected a soft rope flogger with a dark purple handle and purple and white cotton strands. He smacked the rope strands against his palm with just enough speed to elicit a slight sting. With the right amount of pressure, this little toy was guaranteed to send his Scarlet over the edge, again and again.

He selected a set of ankle cuffs and leather restraint straps. This time his lovely submissive would be fully bound. Anticipation hummed in his veins. With his goodies in hand, he turned toward the bed.

She lay in the same position but her head was turned toward him, alerting him to the fact she was aware of his presence. He placed his toys on the bedside stand then sat beside her.

"Have you missed me, Scarlet?"

She licked her lips and he enjoyed the sight of her soft, pink tongue. He wanted to feel it on his skin and soon. She had a very talented mouth and later he'd put those talents to work on him again.

"Yes, Master." Her voice was high, faint.

"Good." He touched her thigh, trailing his hand up to the top of her stockings then back again. She had magnificent legs though they'd look even better wrapped around his waist. "You know what will happen now, don't you?"

Her breathing grew labored and her nod was jerky.

"And you remember your safe word?"

She nodded again.

"Say it."

"Magenta."

"Good girl. Now turn over."

He helped her roll onto her belly and in the process he removed her skirt. She made a mouthwatering sight with her bare ass revealed. He couldn't wait to see it turn pink from the flogger and his own hand.

"You realize I'll have to bind your feet, don't you, Scarlet?" He ran his hands along her legs to her ankles. "It is for your own good."

"Yes, Master."

"Such an obedient servant. You've learned quickly." He made fast work of restraining her legs by sliding the velvet cuffs around each ankle then attaching their leather straps to the O-rings on the footboard. With Scarlet spread-eagled, face down on the bed, he could see the moisture between her sweet thighs. His blood stirred and his cock hardened.

He laid his hand on her lower back. Muscles flexed beneath his palm.

"Are you ready to pay the price of disobedience, my slave?"

Her face was buried in the pillows and she nodded.

Nodding was not good enough. He'd already reprimanded her once about not answering him verbally. This time he would have to step up her punishment.

With his palm flat, he smacked her on one butt cheek, enjoying both her startled squeal and the firm resiliency of her flesh. She would be a pleasure to take from behind. That butt of hers was the perfect size to cradle his cock.

"You will speak when spoken to," he said.

"Yes, Master," she gasped.

Blue picked up the flogger and trailed the ends over one curve of her butt cheek. "Much better." He didn't miss how she tensed in anticipation of the first blow. This wouldn't do at all.

He reached between her thighs and cupped her pussy before sliding one long finger deep inside. Her hips bucked, though whether to dislodge him or take him deeper he wasn't sure. He added a second finger, eliciting a moan from Scarlet.

"You like that don't you, my slave?"

"Y-y-yes, Master."

He withdrew his fingers then thrust them inside, harder and deeper this time. She squirmed and pushed her hips back into his hand in a silent plea for more.

"You will learn to submit to me, Scarlet." He began to slowly finger-fuck her. "You will learn who is the master in our relationship and you will think twice before disobeying me in the future."

"Yessss." The single word came out as a long, drawn-out moan.

He removed his hand from her sweet pussy.

Her head popped out of the pillows. "I want—"

He brought the flogger down with a flick of his wrist. The long, thin tendrils snaked across her buttocks. Her back arched and she gave a startled yelp.

"I think you forget yourself, Scarlet. You are not in charge here." He brought the flogger down again, careful not to strike the same place he'd just hit. "Who is in charge here?"

"You are, Master." She was panting.

He struck the plump curve of her buttock with the flat of his hand.

"And who am I?" he challenged.

"Blue! You're the Master, Blue."

He brought the flogger down one more time then dropped it on the bed. Her buttocks were just beginning to turn a pleasing shade of pink.

"That's correct, Scarlet. I am your master and I will determine what you need." He picked up a bottle of almond oil from the bedside table. "Your pleasure and pain are solely in my hands." He poured a generous amount of oil onto her back. "Never forget that."

He began rubbing the sweet-scented oil into her skin. As he worked he noted how her body relaxed into her bonds until she was limp, boneless. By the time he moved between her thighs her entire body gleamed with oil. She was any Master's dream, trussed and prepared as she was.

"I enjoy seeing you like this." He smoothed more oil into the sensitive crease where her buttock met her thigh. "Open, vulnerable to my touch." He slid his hand between her thighs, his oily fingers lubricating her slick flesh. "I can see and touch you as I wish." His fingers darted into her sweet pussy. "You are totally available to me. You can't even close your thighs against my invasion." Her breathing grew ragged.

With his other hand he picked up the flogger. "Your skin marks up beautifully. If only you could see your hot little ass right now." He trailed the tips of the flogger over one plump cheek. "Now I'm going to turn it a lovely shade of pink."

The flogger came down across her butt and she moaned, her buttocks arching upward.

He held the flogger just inches over her body. "Do you want to use your safe word?"

"No, Master." Her voice was strained.

"Good. I want you awash with your juices before I will permit you to come. You will learn your lesson, slave, as you will relish my mastery over you."

Satisfied she was enjoying her reprimand as much as he, Blue brought the flogger down across her upper thighs. Again and again he flogged her, his cock growing tighter with each blow. Her shoulders, buttocks and thighs received his attention until he lost count of the blows. Her skin was now a rosy pink and she was begging for release.

"What did you say, slave?" he panted.

"I need to come," she moaned. "Please, I'm begging you…"

"Indeed." Blue reached back and released her ankle restraints from the bed. "On your knees, slave."

She moved with flattering haste to perch on her knees with her chest still flat to the bed. Her curvy ass was up in the air and her legs were spread leaving her beautiful cunt open and displayed for him. He ran his hands over the curve of her buttocks and her hips gave a shimmy. She smelled of female arousal mixed with a scent uniquely her own. Judging from her engorged clit and her slick, red flesh, she was ready to come at the slightest touch.

Now she was ready.

Blue rose to shed the rest of his clothing. Coming between her thighs, he gripped her hips and entered her with one smooth thrust until his cock was buried in her pussy. She moaned and pushed back against him, taking him even deeper. Keeping a firm grip on her hips, he began to thrust.

Nothing he'd ever imagined could prepare him for the reality of fucking Scarlet. She fit him perfectly, her beautiful, sweet cunt tight and hot around his cock. Their legs tangled, his hips hammered at her, every motion adding to the level of arousal building inside him. With each thrust she made low, throaty moans. Her hips slammed backward into him, her body shaking with her need for release, and he realized that while she enjoyed his possession, he wasn't touching her where she was desperate to be touched.

"You may come now, Scarlet."

He reached around her hips to zero in on her clit. With a single stroke, her body jerked as if electrified and she tightened around him in release. He gritted his teeth against the sensations that raced up his cock as her pussy milked him, determined not to come quite yet.

Finally she sagged beneath him. Before she could catch her breath, he reached over and released her bound hands from the bed. He pulled out and neatly flipped her onto her back.

"What are you doing?" she gasped.

"You will know who your master is, Scarlet." He pushed her thighs wide and positioned himself between them. "You will know who is fucking you." He tore the blindfold off her face.

His fingers sank into her hips as he entered her with a hoarse cry. He was so far gone now, he couldn't stop if the devil himself rode into the room. His hips slammed into hers, his cock thrusting long and deep into her sweet cunt. Her emerald eyes had gone foggy with need and she cried out again and again as her body took its pleasure but still he didn't stop. He was a man possessed by her sweetness, her tight little body and sassy mouth.

He was determined to possess her as no other man ever had.

His consciousness faded to the woman in the bed beneath him. Nothing else existed but his engorged cock and her slick, welcoming pussy. He rose and gripped her ankles, bringing them up to rest on his shoulders. This new position left her totally open and exposed to him.

His awareness dimmed, narrowing to the increasing pressure in his lower gut. Her soft cries mingled with his moans as his release beckoned. His mind went hazy and his body took over. When her tight muscles moved around him in yet another release, he let go. He came with a roar, his release shooting hard from his cock and he felt as if he would never stop. On and on it went until he was sweating and shaking, swaying on his knees. For the first time in his life he wondered if he was going to pass out from the unbearable ecstasy of release.

It would seem that the Master had met his match in Miss Scarlet.

* * * * *

Elle lay in the darkness beside Blue, her mind whirling. Sound asleep, his arm was heavy across her belly but she didn't mind the weight at all. She rubbed her fingers over the prickly hair on his arm. There was only one word to describe their experience.

Wow.

She shifted around until she could look at the man who'd brought her more pleasure in a few hours than all the other men combined. His hair had come undone and the thick, wavy locks obscured most of his face. Her fingers itched to brush the hair out of the way just so she could look at him.

Double wow.

Her stomach clenched. She couldn't put her finger on what made Blue different from the others. It wasn't just the multiple orgasms, though that was certainly appreciated. She bit her lower lip as a panicky feeling swamped her.

This can't be happening…

She turned away. He was no different than her previous masters and that was that. She was leaving for New Orleans in a few days and she couldn't allow herself to think otherwise. An emotional entanglement was something she could ill afford.

She swallowed hard, trying to push the panicked feeling down into her gut. She didn't want to become involved with anyone right now, not here in Columbus nor down in New Orleans. She had a fabulous new job to concentrate on and that's exactly what she planned on doing. In her experience with men, she'd learned they always expected to come first. While it was okay for them to put their careers before their women, it wasn't okay for her to do the same.

She rubbed a hand over her eyes.

There was no doubt that her relationship with Ken had ended badly. He'd constantly ignored her desires, thinking that because she'd allowed him to master her sexually that she was a nonentity in other areas of his life. She'd been looking for an equal partnership and instead she'd ended up with a man who'd used her sexuality and need to be dominated against her. Just because she'd wanted to be submissive sexually, that did not make her a Barbie doll with all boobs and no brains. Just because Blue knew how to touch her darkest desires did not mean she wanted to keep him in her life and in her heart.

Chapter Six

Elle awoke to the feel of a hand stroking the upper part of her breast. She opened her eyes, blinking several times to remove the sleep from her vision. Blue lay beside her, his head propped on one hand and the other was petting her as if she was a cat. It was all she could do to not start purring.

"Hello, Scarlet." His voice was rough as if he'd just awoken only a few minutes before her.

"Hi." A soft flush moved across her skin as the memories of only a few hours ago assailed her.

"Sorry I forgot to untie you before we took our nap." He removed the velvet ties from her wrists, taking care to kiss each one before he let her go.

"I wasn't uncomfortable at all." Elle stretched, her body sliding against his. She felt lazy, replete from their earlier excesses. She rotated her shoulders, arching her back to remove all the kinks from her spine.

"I'm glad." His avid gaze focused over her breasts, which threatened to spill from her bra. "Are you up for some more fun and games?"

She fought a yawn, torn between talking and going back to sleep. "Just what did you have in mind?"

"Peter has a playroom down the hall and it's stocked with quite a few gadgets designed to interest a little submissive such as yourself." His fingers stroked across her exposed breasts. "Racks, swings, slings, a Catherine wheel, bondage chair and more restraints than a little girl like you can handle."

A spark of excitement blossomed in her belly and a soft, throaty laugh escaped her. "You'd be surprised at what I can handle," she purred.

He laughed and nuzzled her throat sending chills of arousal over her skin. "No, I've already partaken of your considerable talents." His hand covered her pussy. "Are you up for some play?"

Elle placed her hand over his. "What are we waiting for?"

Like excited children, they raced out of the bed. Elle almost tripped when she realized she still wore the ankle restraints Blue had put on earlier. With haste she ripped them off then was forced to get on her hands and knees to find her skirt that had ended up under the bed.

"That is a sight," Blue spoke behind her.

She gave her bare backside a wiggle. "Not on your life, Master. I want to play first." She located her skirt then scrambled to her feet. "No touching my ass until you have it strapped to something."

He made a grab for her skirt. "Promise?"

She laughed and together they wrestled her into the leather garment. Her bra was perfectly concealing so she opted to forgo her blouse. When she was ready he took her hand and together they exited the suite.

Elle had no idea what time it was. Vaguely she could hear sounds from the party going on one floor below, so it wasn't too terribly late. It seemed like days since they'd met but in reality it had only been a few hours.

Blue led her down the hallway to a closed door. He removed a key from his pocket and unlocked the door. Opening it wide, he stood back and ushered her in first. It was dark until he hit the lights and Elle's eyes went wide at the scene that greeted her. It looked like a chamber of sexual horrors that would delight the Marquis de Sade.

The floors, walls and ceiling were covered in fake stone giving it the appearance of a gothic-style dungeon. Faux candle chandeliers hung overhead and leering gargoyles were perched in the corners and on shelves along the wall. Centered on the far wall was a Katherine wheel, a round wheel with leather restraints that enabled the Master to strap his willing slave into the contraption and be turned every which way including on their head.

Elle wrinkled her nose. Being on her head wasn't her cup of tea.

Next was a row of cages of varying sizes. Several were dog style in which the slave would have to crouch in order to fit comfortably. One cage was tall enough that she would be able to stand upright. At Blue's questioning glance, she shook her head and moved on.

Next was a spanking bench. It resembled a sawhorse with braces on the legs for extra stability. The center bar was heavily padded and there were two additional bars added, one on each side, to rest one's bent knees upon.

"This is a definite possibility." She drew her hand over the soft, supple leather as she moved on.

A horizontal rack was arranged on the far wall and it could merit a test run. Roughly the size of a twin bed, instead of a mattress it boasted a series of ropes that were entwined to create a webbed surface to which she could be bound. Interesting but nothing unusual that couldn't be accomplished in the privacy of Blue's suite.

Along the wall was a series of pegs from which hung a wide variety of restraint devices. Chains, leather belts, hoods, blindfolds and various sets of paddles, whips and other party favors occupied the hooks. Elle trailed her fingers over a purple suede flogger.

"This might be interesting," she said

"Indeed." Blue picked up the item and hit it against his arm. "I have to agree with you."

In the far corner of the dungeon, Elle found the one item that made her little heart flutter and her vagina flood with heat.

A swing.

Suspended from the ceiling was a thick chain with a chrome horizontal crosspiece. From the X hung four chains and in the center was a leather sling. Elle licked her lips as her gaze slid over the supple leather device. She'd never tried out a swing but she'd heard they were the ultimate submissive experience, especially if a blindfold was used. Loss of spatial reference was a particularly powerful experience in the B&D world and she couldn't wait to experience it for herself.

"You like this, don't you, Scarlet?" Blue's hands landed on her shoulders and he gave her a quick squeeze.

She licked her lips. "Yes, Master. Very much."

"So you'd like to play in the swing?"

"Yes, Master."

"The swing it is then." Blue kissed her shoulder then moved away. "You may remove your clothing while I gather a few toys."

She made quick work of removing her clothing, her fingers thick and uncoordinated in her haste. She'd stepped out of one shoe when Blue's voice sounded from somewhere behind her.

"You'll keep the shoes and stockings on, Scarlet. I like them."

Elle smiled and put the shoe back on. If he liked them she'd wear them all the time. She had all different colors —

He's not yours to keep.

Her shoulders slumped. In a few hours she'd be out of his life forever. New Orleans was calling and she couldn't turn back now, not when she was on the precipice of realizing a lifelong dream.

"You look serious, Scarlet." Blue stood close behind her and she could feel the warmth of his big body. "Have you changed your mind?"

Elle turned and forced a bright smile. "Not on your life, Master."

"Good." He held up a black silk blindfold and her vagina heated. "We'll start with this."

He tied the silk scarf over her eyes. Once again her senses kicked into overdrive and her skin felt warmer and more sensitive. Her nipples hardened. He took her arm and led her toward the swing.

"You're very beautiful, Scarlet." His fingers latched onto her wrist and she felt the smooth slide of leather against her skin. It felt like a cuff restraint. "I'll bet hundreds of men have told you this."

"Not hardly," she chuckled. "I'm afraid I really don't get out as much as you seem to think I do."

"Are the men you associate with blind?" He placed another restraint on her opposite wrist.

"I don't think so. They just see me as me. Nothing special." Elle felt the brush of leather against her buttocks as he guided her closer to the swing.

"Then they are fools."

Blue raised her arms and she heard the slide of metal as he attached her left arm to a chain before he secured the right. With her arms suspended from the cuffs and chains, he helped her up into the sling. The leather was cool and erotic against her back and buttocks. As he worked to restrain her ankles, the swing swayed with his movements.

This was going to be too much fun.

When she was fully restrained, Blue's hands slid up her thighs stopping just before reaching her pussy. He gave a low whistle.

"Miss Scarlet, you are a sight, that's for sure." He gave the swing a gentle push. "Are you comfortable?"

Elle wriggled her arms and legs. It was surprisingly comfortable. The sling held her body weight while her arms and legs were afforded some room to move, just not too much. A delicious thrill of fear and excitement swamped her. She was well and truly bound, unable to escape whatever devious fates Blue had in store for her.

"Yes, Master."

"One feature this swing has that most others don't is a motor. Peter had a motor installed in the ceiling so that it can be raised and lowered at will." He chuckled. "This will come in handy, later."

She shivered at the dark promise in his words and the swing began to move back and forth.

"Miss Scarlet, you're all dressed up and now it's up to me to figure out what to do with you." He gave her pussy a quick pet before the swing forced her away. "What do you want from me, Miss Scarlet?"

Elle ground her teeth together. She was so hot and bothered now all she could think about was a quick orgasm. She didn't know how much longer she'd be able to wait.

"Make me come, Master." Her voice was soft, breathless.

"Already? You're very responsive to me, Scarlet."

Elle squirmed against the leather when she felt Blue catch the swing and slow its movement. Ken had used her rampant sexuality against her time and time again. Would Blue do the same?

"I really enjoy that facet of your nature," he said.

A soft whirring noise sounded and the swing began to move, though whether it moved up or down, Elle had no idea. The unexpected touch of his tongue against her clit caused her to scream. Her back arched as his mouth closed over her wet sex, his tongue sweeping deep into her folds to search out her dark secrets. She gasped and moaned, her body jerking uncontrollably against his mouth. The swing swayed with her movements but he kept with her by gripping her thighs, not breaking that magical touch.

Elle wrapped her hands around the chains that bound her arms, desperate for something to cling to. His mouth closed on her clit and her body went into orbit. Behind the blindfold the darkness was complete with the exception of the bolts of fire that bloomed before her eyes. She lost all sense of direction as his mouth plundered her exposed sex. His fingers stroked her soaked vagina while his tongue continued its dark dance. With a scream she came against his mouth, the chains bit into her palms and she took her exquisite release.

The soft whirring sound roused her enough to open her eyes. Not that it helped, the blindfold was still in place. In that moment Elle was very aware of two things—she was still very much at his mercy and two, he hadn't fucked her yet.

Despite her powerful release, her vagina clenched at the thought of his cock entering her.

"Now, Scarlet, you may pleasure me."

The swing swayed and she felt the brush of his masculine thigh against her side. Something hard prodded her in the chin.

"Open for me."

She opened her mouth and felt the brush of his cock against her lips. She inhaled the rich, masculine scent of his body mixed with her arousal. Her tongue darted out and she lapped at the head of his cock then took him inside. He bit off a groan as her tongue sought out the sensitive underside. Without the benefit of her hands, she was limited in what she could accomplish but she would try her best.

Like he was a lollipop and she a starving woman, she sucked his luscious cock. Creating a gentle suction with her cheeks, she worked her mouth over his length before flicking her tongue over the sensitive head. Over and over she worked him until she felt his thighs tremble against her sides. He was close to release.

"Stop."

Surprised, Elle allowed him to slip from her mouth before it even registered that he'd pulled away. The swing spun and the soft whirring noise sounded again.

"I'm going to fuck you, Miss Scarlet." His voice was guttural, his southern accent thick. "Speak now if you have any objections."

"I—"

His cock slid deep inside her cunt, stretching and filling her deeper than ever before. He rocked back and forth, the swing giving her a weightlessness that enabled her to meet each thrust with no effort on her part at all. His hips pounded at hers and she lost all sense of self. Beneath her, the swing moved and swayed, a welcome partner in their sexual act.

"Please." Her moan was low.

"Greedy little slave," he panted. "Don't worry, you will get what you deserve and more. Much more."

The pace increased and reality faded to a soft, red haze. Their breathing was loud and ragged as the storm raged over her senses. His balls made a soft, slapping sound against her buttocks as the precipice beckoned to her.

"You may come now, Scarlet."

The motion of the swing grew rougher when he thrust harder, faster. His fingers slipped between their bodies and zeroed in on her clit. He gave it a firm, assured rub then a quick pinch, just enough to send her off the edge. Her world shattered and she soared into the cosmos.

Chapter Seven

Blue buried his nose in Scarlet's mass of dark hair and inhaled her spicy fragrance. After their explosive games in the dungeon, they'd returned to his suite and climbed into bed for a nap. She'd fallen asleep immediately while he was still wide-awake.

The party below stairs had died and the house was quiet. Only a few candles remained burning in their bedroom, and the fresh night air drifted in through the open windows. He tangled his fingers in Scarlet's silken locks. He couldn't remember ever feeling quite this content, this peaceful.

Beside him his eager submissive still slept. Her breathing was even and it had been a while since she'd moved. Holding his breath, he pulled away the bedsheet until his lover was revealed.

Scarlet lay on her stomach as bare as the day she'd entered this world. He'd told her to remove her stockings and heels after they'd stumbled back to his bedroom, exhausted and sated from their sensual excess. Her delightful backside was pert and still retained a hint of blush from the flogger. Blue longed to sink his teeth into a plump curve.

She made a soft sound in her sleep that sounded like a cross between a snore and the purr of a kitten. Candlelight kissed the exposed curves of her back, buttocks and thighs, like a lover. She was the most beautiful woman he'd ever seen, and considering the women with which he'd consorted, that was saying something. In his youth he'd collected women the way some men collected sports memorabilia. He skimmed his hand along the inside of her thigh, his touch light and undemanding. Her breathing hitched.

Blue pulled back and allowed her to settle down. Once he was sure she was still asleep, he rose onto his knees to lower his mouth to her spine. He trailed soft kisses down her back then along the curve of her butt cheek. Seeing her here, naked and vulnerable, was a powerful turn-on. His cock, already hardening, leapt forth. Blue was amazed at his stamina. He'd always been a highly sexed man but with his delectable Scarlet, he'd become a sexual Olympian.

He adored her ass. His teeth grazed the plump curve. She was the perfect size and shape, just right to cushion his body when he took her from behind, which would be any minute now.

He slid his hand between her thighs and parted her cunt. Zeroing in on her clit, he stroked the tender bud. She made a soft sound and her hips shifted in a restless movement. He leaned forward and nipped at her buttock as his fingers plundered her hidden treasures.

"You're already wet for me, my slave."

He caressed the bundle of nerves and she began to awaken. Her hips shifted and she moaned, still more than half asleep. He settled into a slow caress and her hips began to move in response to his touch. Soft throaty sounds came from the pillows where she'd buried her head. His fingers continued their assault and her sighs grew deeper, more impassioned. With his other hand, he entered her vagina, relishing the feel of her muscles clamping down on his fingers. He wanted to make her wild and he would accept nothing less.

"Blue?" Her voice was both aroused and sleepy.

"Scarlet?"

He removed his hand then stretched out over her. Nudging her thighs wide, he entered her from behind. His teeth came together with a sharp click as the perfection of their joining washed over him.

"Oh, heaven," Scarlet purred.

Not quite yet…

Blue reached for the bed stand and opened the top drawer. Pulling out a pair of standard police issue handcuffs, he dropped the keys on the table before placing one cuff around her right wrist.

"Now this is my idea of heaven." He placed the other end around his right wrist and locked them together. "Never forget that you're mine, Miss Scarlet."

"Yours." Her voice was faint. She arched her back, taking him deeper.

He balanced his upper body on his elbows, their fingers entwined. His hips maintained a slow pace while his mouth tasted the curve of her shoulder. With her perfect backside cushioning his body, Blue would be content to spend the rest of the day in just this position.

But Scarlet would have none of it. Beneath him she gave an impatient wiggle, urging him to pick up the pace. He ignored her. Giving her a sharp slap on the buttocks that startled her into submission, he fought the urge to drive himself mindlessly into her tight little body until he reached release. His teeth grazed the tempting curve of her neck. He would be content to fuck her all day and all night. Even though he'd already taken her several times in the past few hours, he was in no hurry to finish the ride, but his slave wasn't quite so patient.

She shifted her buttocks, taking him deeper. As he fucked her, the rhythmic clenching of her cunt around his cock was slowly fraying his restraint. She made soft, sexy sounds of pleasure and her nails scraped across the sheets. Their clasped hands tightened as together they ascended the peak.

"Master, please... I—"

"You may come, Scarlet," he gasped.

Beneath him he felt her tense then shatter. Hearing her cries of release was enough to send him over the edge. His hips pounded against her buttocks. A slow tingle blossomed in his lower gut then spread out to encompass his body. Arching his back, his head came up as he growled out his completion.

Trembling, he collapsed over her, his heart thundering. He had no desire to move from this position ever again but he had to be crushing her. Reluctantly he withdrew from her body and moved to the side to spoon with her.

"That was very…satisfying," she purred.

He grinned at her tone of pride. She'd managed to drive him over the edge with very little effort on her part.

Blue yawned. "Oh yeah. If you give me a few minutes we'll see about that."

She chuckled. "Okay, stud…"

He allowed his eyes to slide shut. His arms were wrapped around Scarlet, their wrists still handcuffed together. As he drifted off to sleep it suddenly occurred to him that he didn't even know her real name. He would need to remedy that the moment he woke up.

* * * * *

Elle fingered the miniscule handcuff keys. Their soft clink marked the passing seconds, her last with Blue. He lay heavy against her back, his soft snores in her ear oddly reassuring. Their arms were side by side, their fingers still entwined as the cuffs kept them locked together.

Somehow he'd managed to steal his way into her heart.

She closed her eyes as a shaft of pain shot through the troublesome organ. It didn't matter how she felt about him, she was leaving for New Orleans very shortly.

Maybe you could visit him when you come back for the holidays…

No, that wasn't the answer. She ran her thumb over his forefinger. Blue wasn't hers to keep. She didn't want an emotional relationship with him, with anyone. Emotions were too tricky, too messy. She would never be able to offer him anything more than this, mindless amazing sex several times a year.

Elle opened her eyes. Outside the sky was growing brighter with each passing minute. A new day was here and these were her last moments with this amazing man. It was too painful to contemplate, seeing him, being with him, yet knowing he wasn't hers. Blue needed to find one woman—that perfect submissive—and keep her at his beck and call. While it was a fun dream, it wasn't for her. The chance of a lifetime awaited her a thousand miles away and his life was here in Columbus.

Blue stirred, his other hand shifted from her hip to her breast. Her breath caught as he cupped the mound. His thumb gave her nipple a lazy brush sending a bolt of heat straight to her groin.

With that simple touch her body responded in record time. Even now, sore from their sexual exploits, she wanted him again. Their last bout of excess had been more than sex, more than just a bondage mindfuck, it had been making love and they'd both known it. She'd bet her favorite shoes that he'd felt it as much as she did.

Which meant she needed to get away before she left something important behind, like her heart.

She slipped the key into the lock and released her cuff with a metallic snick. Holding her breath, she took the hand that was on her breast and removed it. Almost immediately she mourned for the warmth of his palm. Gathering her courage, she rolled away from him, her movements cautious, as she didn't want to risk waking him.

After gathering her clothing and shoes, she slipped into the bathroom and made quick work of getting dressed. Just as she was about to walk out of the bathroom, she caught sight of herself in the mirror.

She looked...afraid. Her eyes were dilated and marred with shadows. Her skin was pale, much more so than usual.

You're making a mistake...

Her lips firmed. No, she wasn't. She was through making concessions for the men in her life. Her pursuit of love had always ended disastrously and she wasn't about to make that mistake again no matter how good he was in bed.

Shoes in hand, she exited the bathroom. Blue lay where she'd left him. Her gaze made one final sweep of the room to ensure that she wasn't leaving anything behind. On the floor something black caught her eye.

It was her mask.

She picked up the scrap of silk with a trembling hand. There were a lot of memories tied up with this dime-store trinket. Her gaze moved over her lover. The sheet had shifted and now barely covered his slim hips. His skin was tawny against the pale sheets, his dark hair had obscured most of his face. Only his strong jaw was clearly visible.

She bit her lip, torn between wanting to climb into bed and run out of the room as fast as she could. She knew in that moment that if she allowed herself to return to bed, she'd never leave this man. She'd never realize her lifelong dream and she'd leave herself vulnerable to a broken heart.

Her eyes stung when she dropped the mask on the bed and turned away. She had no time or patience for emotions. It was time to put away foolish dreams and get on with the business of life.

Elle exited the room, her stocking-clad feet made no sound on the plush carpeting. With her shoes clutched in her hands, she ran down the wide steps and through the empty hallway toward the front door. As she approached, a tuxedo-clad man stepped forward and opened the door, hastening her escape outside.

If she was making the right decision, why did she feel like Cinderella after the ball?

Chapter Eight

Elle walked down Bourbon Street, the winter breeze cool and damp against her cheeks. She'd been in New Orleans for four months and she'd fallen in love with the city the moment she'd arrived. It was a living, breathing entity. The city had a personality, an energy, a taste in the air that was particular to this area. While she missed her friends and family in Ohio, she knew she'd never want to live anywhere else. She'd come home.

She plunged her chilled hands into the pockets of her purple suede coat, frowning when she felt something in the pocket. She pulled out a slim purple ribbon. For a moment she stared at it blankly then her heart fell.

Blue.

She rubbed the silk between two fingers. She missed him.

You're a fool to pine for a man you've met only once…

Elle pushed the intrusive thought away. She realized it was irrational to fancy herself in love with Blue. She barely knew him, but try telling that to her heart. She sighed. The funny thing was that Blue was the man Ty had picked out for her. Her heart gave a sharp twinge.

He'd been the right man for her all right.

She tucked the ribbon back into her pocket. She missed his smile, his teasing laugh and his low voice with that sexy accent that grew heavier when he'd become aroused. She longed for the feel of his skin against hers, the taste of his cock and the look in his eyes when he desired her.

What was he doing now? Had he found another woman to act as his sexual slave?

Her stomach gave a queer little jerk and she forced herself to continue her slow walk. Even though it was unseasonably cool, Bourbon Street was crowded with tourists. She wove her way through the throng, very aware of the petty thieves that longed to liberate her cash and credit cards from her pockets.

The thought of Blue with another woman was disturbing —

What does it matter? You've made your decision…

She sidestepped two giggling teenagers who were more interested in each other than watching where they were going. She loved her job at Belle Femme. It was everything she'd imagined it would be — challenging, fast-paced and ever-changing. Every day she walked into her plush office she knew she'd have to think on her feet and make decisions that would affect million of dollars in sales and the future of the company. It was the job she'd dreamed of her entire life.

But why did she feel hollow?

Because of him…

She shoved the thought away. It wasn't Blue's fault she was lonely. She'd made some friends at work but she hadn't had a chance to explore the underground B&D world in New Orleans. Maybe she should make that more of a priority?

She shook her head. Unfortunately for her sex life, she didn't feel like making that leap. She wasn't ready to take another lover, though the bondage scene didn't always have to include sex. She sighed. No, she just wasn't in the right frame of mind. It looked like it would be yet another exciting Saturday night with her electronic best friend —

An elbow slammed into her ribs and almost knocked her off her feet. She stumbled and reached out for a plate glass window to catch her balance. Turning, she glared after the retreating figure that had run into her.

"Well, really — " she muttered.

Turning, she caught sight of the window display. Her eyes widened as memories assailed her.

It was a leather swing like the one she and Blue had used. Below the swing was a length of red velvet that sported a variety of toys.

Floggers, whips, and handcuffs…oh my!

Elle stepped back to read the name of the store.

The Dominion, Fetish-wear & Bondage Accessories

She grinned. If there was ever a sign as to what she should do or where she should be, this was it. Elle headed for the front door.

* * * * *

The ever-present crowds parted as Blue walked along Bourbon Street. He was headed for the leather store to pick up his bomber jacket. Last week he'd caught the sleeve on a nail while working on one of his boats.

Ahead, the crowds parted and he caught a glimpse of dark, sable hair and his gut clenched. He couldn't get her out of his mind. After waking up in bed alone, with only her mask for company, Blue had wasted no time in tracking down Tyson. Unfortunately for him the party planner was a very loyal friend to the mysterious Ms. Scarlet. He would give no other information than the fact her name was Elle and she didn't live around Central Ohio.

Damn.

Blue had asked everyone he'd known at the party but no one would offer up any information he could use. The B&D crowd was very closemouthed about their activities and understandably so. He'd thought about hiring a private detective but seeing he didn't even have a full name let alone a city of residence, he'd decided it would be a waste of money.

But that didn't mean he'd given up yet. He'd convinced Peter to host another party on New Year's Eve and Pete had hired Tyson to arrange the event with the caveat that he was to use the same guest list as for his August party.

Bingo.

Chances were the mysterious Elle would be there again and Blue would be there to greet her. This time he wasn't about to let her get away. Instead he'd chain her to his side and throw away the keys. She was the woman for him and he'd known it within minutes of meeting her. The last time they'd made love, it had been just that, making love, and he'd bet his pirogue that the act had scared her into running away from him. All he needed was five minutes with her and he'd know if they had a future, a real future together.

When he entered the store, bells sounded overhead and the pleasing scent of leather assailed him. There was nothing like the smell of fresh leather in the morning. Iggy, the store's owner, waved at him from behind the counter.

"Where y'at, Remy?" he called.

Blue grinned at the familiar greeting. "Quoi de neuf?"

"Not a ting, nig." Iggy held out his fist and Remy knocked his knuckles against his friend's. "Ya wan' your coat?"

"Is it ready?"

"Aye, 'tis. I be back."

Blue turned to check out a rack of new merchandise that included a new line of leather-lined handcuffs. Automatically his hand went to his jacket pocket and he squeezed the familiar lump inside. It was Scarlet's—Elle's, he mentally corrected—handcuffs and mask.

He was obsessed with her. He'd already done everything he could and now it was a waiting game. It was two weeks until New Year's Eve. Two weeks until he would see her again.

If she attends the party.

He turned away from the racks. He didn't want to think about that, as other than trailing Tyson for who knew how long, it was his only option. She had to attend the party, she just had to.

A flash of dark hair caught his attention and his heart almost stopped. A curvaceous figure in a purple coat vanished into the back room where Iggy stocked his custom leather clothing.

It can't be her...

Even as he thought it, his feet carried him toward the back of the store. There had to be thousands of black-haired women in New Orleans and surely some of them would have a purple coat...

There were several women in the back room and he quickly dismissed them when he saw they had the wrong hair color. He circled the crowded racks, his gaze searching out his prey. He stepped around a display of leather corsets before he saw her in the far corner near the masks and riding crops.

Elle.

With her dark hair loose about her shoulders and her hot little body clad in purple suede, he was transported back to the first time he saw her. The only difference was the stockings and heels were replaced with jeans and black running shoes.

She was rummaging through a rack of leather bras, her perfect teeth nibbled on her lower lip as she contemplated the selection. Blue removed the handcuffs from his pocket. Dangling them from one finger, he approached.

"Are you looking for something, Miss Scarlet?" he drawled.

She jumped as if he'd poked her with a live wire. She spun toward him, her eyes widening when she realized who it was. Surprised twisted her features and her teeth released her lower lip with a soft pop.

"Blue," she stammered. "What are you doing here?"

"I could ask you the same thing." Standing this close he could detect her perfume.

"I live here now."

His brow arched. "In New Orleans?"

She nodded.

"That's interesting as I live southwest of here." He slipped the cold steel bracelet around her wrist and closed it with a snick.

She cocked her head, a soft little smile played across her mouth. "You do?"

"I do." He fastened the other bracelet on his wrist and closed it. "We could be neighbors."

Her smile grew. "We could?"

He dipped his head toward hers. "Do you remember our agreement, Miss Scarlet?"

She swallowed audibly and her voice was several octaves higher. "Which one?"

"The one in which you accepted me as your master..." His lips brushed her cheek and her scent flowed over him.

"Yes."

"Master."

"Yes, Master." Her breath was warm on his skin.

"And you do remember our agreement that you'll take no other man without my permission?" His mouth sought out her earlobe.

"Y-y-yes, Master."

"Very good, Elle. Now, how do you feel about spending your weekend tied up at my house?"

Trademarks Acknowledgement

The author acknowledges the trademarked status and trademark owners of the following wordmarks mentioned in this work of fiction:

Barbie Doll: Mattel, Inc.

Benz (Mercedes-Benz): Daimler-Benz Aktiengesellschaft Corporation

Hummer: AM GENERAL CORPORATION

Lexus: Toyota Jidosha Kabushiki Kaisha Corporation Japan

1

Manolo Blahnik: Blahnik; Manolo INDIVIDUAL

About the author:

Dominique Adair is the pen name of award-winning novelist J.C. Wilder. Adair/Wilder (she chooses her name according to her mood—if she's feeling sassy and brazen, it's Adair; if she's feeling dark and dangerous, it's Wilder) lives just outside of Columbus, Ohio, where she skulks around town plotting her next book and contemplating where to hide the bodies (from her books of course—everyone knows that you can't really hide a body as they always pop up at the worst times).

Dominique welcomes mail from readers. You can write to her c/o Ellora's Cave Publishing at 1337 Commerce Drive, Suite 13, Stow OH 44224.

Also by Dominique Adair:

Last Kiss
Party Favors anthology
Tied With a Bow anthology
Xanthra Chronicles: Blood Law

Writing as J.C. Wilder

Ellora's Cavemen: Tales From the Temple II anthology
In Moonlight anthology
Things That Go Bump In the Night 2004 anthology

LOVE AND KINKS

By Madeleine Oh

Chapter One

"I don't understand why you're hesitating," Maggie said.

Jane Winston restrained an exasperated sigh. Of course Maggie didn't understand. Jane's best friend she might be, but happily married and great with her third child, Maggie was long past dating angst. Jane wasn't.

"You like him, don't you? Heck, you've been going out with him five weeks!"

Yes, she had, but afternoons on the river, dinners in stylish restaurants, even a couple of wildly passionate overnights in Alan's flat were not the same as the current proposition.

Maggie took the rectangle of shiny card from Jane's hand and eyed the curly, copperplate script. "Alan Branis requests the pleasure of Jane Winston's company for a weekend of fun and games. Mmm..." She tapped the corner of the card against her chin. "Definite style. Rather romantic really, but..." she paused, "I wonder what 'fun and games' means?"

"I don't think he's talking about Scrabble or Tiddlywinks!"

Maggie gave a wicked grin. "I should hope not—hell! Jane, he's asking you away for a sexy weekend. Better stock up on condoms!"

"He always takes care of..." Jane broke off. Maggie and she were darn close, but there were some things she did not need to share.

Maggie positively leered. "So you have done the deed! Good for you!" Jane's cheeks burned as Maggie grinned even wider. "Good was he?" Better than Jane's wildest dreams and her dreams had always been pretty wild. "Tell me, Jane," Maggie coaxed, "How was he?"

She'd have to drop a crumb to keep Maggie satisfied. No way was she telling her how Alan had held her hands down over her head, pinning her to the bed or how he'd used his mouth to give her a succession of climaxes that left her sweating, gasping and boneless. "He's a very good and considerate lover." Assuming keeping her hanging on the edge for what seemed like hours and making her beg for a climax could be called considerate. "Fantastic in fact." Cripes! She was blushing again.

"Why hesitate?" Because he'd promised to tie her down and make her completely helpless, and told her that... "By the sound of things, this Alan of yours is a man to grab with both hands."

Not just hands. Jane's face burned as she remembered taking his cock in her mouth and working her lips up and down. "I think you're right. I'll tell him I'm game."

"Good for you!" Maggie hugged her. "You really do need a nice man."

As Jane closed the door on Maggie, she wondered anew if making her spend an afternoon walking around London minus her panties came under Maggie's definition of "nice".

Not that Jane much bothered what Maggie thought. She wasn't the one who spent the afternoon aroused, until Alan finally gave her the climax of her life bent over the back of his sofa.

Jane was half-scared over what Alan's "fun and games" might include but she was darn sure, humdrum and dull would not be part of the agenda.

With the tea things tucked in the dishwasher, Jane picked up her phone and punched in Alan's number—he'd been on speed dial for the past four weeks—and got his damn voice mail. "It's me, Jane." Her heart raced as she spoke. "It's about your invitation. I'm completely free that weekend."

She clicked off her phone, hoping "free" wasn't a synonym for "easy". Or did she really? Since meeting Alan at the kinky boutique opening she'd covered for a magazine, her personal rules had changed. Just about anything went, and she didn't have one regret—except perhaps not getting enough of him.

He called back minutes later, the buzz of traffic in the background. "Jane."

Just the sound of his voice had her wet between the legs. What was it with this man? "Alan, I got your invitation."

"Yes, my dear. Didn't it arrive yesterday?"

It had. "I've been thinking about it."

"And?"

Deep breath here. "I'll come."

He chuckled. "I'll make sure you do, my love, repeatedly."

Her throat went dry. She didn't doubt him for one moment. "I'll need directions." Unless he planned on driving them both down to his cottage.

"No, Jane. I want you to take the train. I'll send you a ticket and a seat reservation. I'll meet you in Guildford." Fair enough, but... "Listen carefully, Jane. I'm not repeating this. When you get on that train at Waterloo, you're to be wearing just a skirt and a top and sandals. Nothing else. What are you going to wear?"

Deep, deep breath here. "Just a skirt and top, and sandals, no underwear."

"Good. I warn you Jane, sneak on a pair of knickers on the train and I will know. I'll check you for elastic marks when you arrive." Cripes, she didn't doubt it! "I'm glad you're so compliant. Now, listen to the rest. You're to bring nothing of your own. I have a spare toothbrush here and plan on keeping you naked all weekend." Goose bumps inched down her spine at that promise. "All you are to bring, other than your tickets and a little money in case of emergency, is the package I'll have delivered to you on Thursday. There will be a small zip bag in the box, pack everything in that and bring it with you. Don't leave it on the train or I'll make you describe the contents to the lost luggage office."

He damn well would too! "Don't worry, I'll not forget it."

"Didn't think you would, dear. Better not forget any of the items, even if you don't fancy the look of them. I know exactly what I'm sending."

And this was what Maggie called a "nice man"! "Alan, I said I'd come. I'll be there, toting the lot. Just don't leave me standing at the station!" Snippy but hell...

"Oh, Darling! That, I would never do. I'll be there. Hard and ready for you. Don't you dare miss that train."

She was now half-considering it.

Jane would either be the end of him or the answer to his dreams. And right now, everything leaned towards the latter. Assuming it wasn't all far, far, too wonderful to be true, Alan Branis believed he'd met his soul-mate.

But...

Wasn't there always that sneaking doubt? The insidious insecurity, the halting unease. Despite all his hopes and dreams, it had never worked out before. Maybe, with Jane...

He shook his head. Talk about hope springing eternal in the breast! He was pinning his hopes, not on Jane's admittedly luscious breasts but on her mind and heart. So far, she was close to perfect. But was she too perfect to be true?

His pickup line had been completely from the heart. He had admired and read her column religiously. Sometimes she covered current affairs, other times arcane subjects, always putting her slant and opinions to the fore. Not, he sensed, to impose her ideas, but more to incite discussion. He'd overheard more than one heated debate at work or in his club over "Jane Winston's new column".

She might have found her first job though connections—having an uncle who owned the company, and a father a Member of Parliament, couldn't hurt. But her current position was due to her brains, her skill and "I dare you" attitude in print. Strange that the Jane in the flesh was so different—quiet, almost to the point of shy—at least until he kissed her. Then it was like holding ignited fireworks in his arms. That demure, convent girl exterior concealed a wild, sensual woman.

And she was brilliant. Each time, he'd pushed her a little farther sexually. More than once, he'd been half-scared he'd gone a hairsbreadth too far, but every time she'd surprised him. He had this weekend all planned out. He wanted her panting, begging and sweating for the multiple climaxes he planned on giving her. Wanted her naked, on her knees, her dark eyes looking up at him as her luscious lips engulfed his cock. He hoped to hell he wasn't pushing too hard or too fast, but when he'd looked her in the eyes and told her he intended to tie her hand and foot so she was utterly helpless, she hadn't reacted in horror or slapped his face or stalked off in high dudgeon. She'd blushed a wondrous shade of warm pink, her breath catching as she bit her bottom lip, her eyes gleaming with interest and excitement.

Yes! Jane was the woman of his dreams. He wanted her naked, helpless and panting for his cock, and a weekend was not going to be enough. It was up to him to convince her he could give her what no other man could and that he was her best bet for the rest of her life.

A pretty tall order but Jane was worth the effort.

* * * * *

Alan took Thursday and Friday off—the City could do without him for forty-eight hours—and had fun picking out the toys and goodies, before sending them off by courier, giving her just enough time to worry a little, but not enough to get cold feet and back out.

That done, he made a stop by a small and very expensive caterer in Surrey to load his car with enough food to last them the weekend, packed the lot in his boot, along with a box of his favorite videos—all X-rated and most of them kinky, and a bag full of toys. John kept the cottage well equipped but Alan liked the feel of his own whips in his hand. And when the tresses connected to Jane's sweet, pale flesh...

Hell! He was hard just thinking about it.

By the time he joined the A3, he was singing to himself as his car headed southwards.

For three days, Jane ran from deadline to crisis and had little time—apart from every few minutes—to think about Alan and the looming weekend. But when the parcel arrived by courier on Thursday, the full reality of what she'd agreed to hit her hard between her heart and her mind. A glance at the articles packed in dark blue tissue paper and bubble wrap, sent Jane straight to the kitchen for a very generous G-and-T. Just in case one wasn't going to be enough, she brought the bottle and the tonic with her as she tipped out the contents of the box onto her coffee table.

The brief glimpse she'd had of the bright blue, suede-handled whip had been enough to send her to the gin bottle. This little stash might have her draining it.

What had she agreed to?

Okay, she could back out. Hadn't Alan told her that at every turn? Her mouth went dry as she stared at the sex toys on her coffee table, while trying to ignore the tube of lubricant that rolled on to the floor.

She grabbed the lubricant, not wanting to consider what that was intended for, and spread out the collection—velvet restraints. Four of them. He'd meant it about tying her hand and foot. Three—she counted them—butt plugs of varying sizes: baby, mamma and daddy bear. The two smaller ones looked bad enough but the big, purple one, she was tempted to lose. She could pretend it rolled under the sofa but remembered Alan's words about knowing exactly what he'd sent. He wasn't likely to forget the heavy-in-her-hand, red glass dildo either. The nipple clamps looked downright nasty, but the two bottles of massage oil sort of made up for them. Alan had wonderful hands—apart from the time he'd spanked her for delaying taking off her knickers. She wasn't making that mistake again. She'd leave them at home this weekend.

Was she totally, utterly and completely nuts?

Was she seriously considering a weekend with a man who planned on using all these—and most likely more—on her?

Was she really going through with this?

If she had any trace of self-preservation, she'd throw the lot in the bin and get the first train in the opposite direction from Guildford.

But to do so would deny herself the special thrills and pleasure only Alan Branis could give her.

Trying, quite unsuccessfully, to keep her eyes off the narrow, blue tresses of the flogger, Jane took a sip of her gin and thought long and hard about her incredible relationship with Alan. Had it only been five weeks? Five weeks and seven dates. The last two culminating with wild, uninhibited sex. Jane had had several lovers in her twenty-seven years, but all had left her mildly dissatisfied, even when the sex had been good. As each relationship ended, she'd been left wondering what was missing and asking herself if she lacked the spark. She'd pretty much decided the whole earth-moving, mind-shattering climax mythology was a creation of romantic novelists.

Then she met Alan.

From his very first, "Hello, I'm Alan Branis. You're Jane Winston, aren't you? I'm thrilled to meet you. I love reading your column." She'd been snared by his rich, deep voice and his bright, compelling eyes. And when they'd actually kissed in the taxi taking her home, she'd felt it right down to her cunt. By the time they pulled up in front of her flat in Hampstead, she'd been half-drunk on the scent of his body and the security of his arms. She'd almost cried with frustration when he declined her offer to come in for coffee—an offer she seldom made and never at first meeting—but he softened the letdown by asking her to meet him for lunch two days later.

And now, five weeks on, he talked of taking things "farther". Right! Judging by the little collection in front of her, he was planning on taking her places she'd never even dreamed of going.

More than anything in the world, she wanted to go there with him.

Chapter Two

Jane frowned at her computer screen. For all the work she'd done today, she might just have well stayed in bed. On the other hand…maybe not. Lying between her sheets brought back too many vivid memories of lying legs spread while Alan worshipped her cunt with his mouth. She was marginally better off at work. And she had cleaned out her email — if that could be called productive employment.

At one, she left for lunch. Maggie was spending the morning at the dentist with two of her offspring and had convinced Jane that lunch with "Auntie" would make their young lives complete. As it turned out, a cheese and ham family size at Uncle Paulo's Perfect Pizza was a hell of a lot better than lunch with friends who'd ask anticipatory questions about her coming weekend, and the presence of a seven and an eight-year-old suitably repressed Maggie's inquisitiveness. She limited herself to, "Have a lovely weekend, Jane!" as she bundled her offspring into a taxi for Paddington.

Jane waved them goodbye and took the tube back to Hampstead. She had to be completely nuts she decided as she stood under the shower and massaged lemon-scented shampoo in her hair. She was getting herself all done up for a man who insisted she travel down to see him sans underwear, and by his heated promise on the phone two nights ago, was going to tie her hand and foot and let her feel the touch of her very own bright blue flogger that now lay at the bottom of the tartan tote bag. She'd felt the silky tresses of the bright blue whip as she lifted it out of the box and hefted it. The tresses felt warm and soft sliding between her fingers, but she didn't miss the little knots on the tails. If he hit her hard…

She'd find out, wouldn't she? No doubt about it, she was utterly mad, halfway in love and aroused.

This was going to be some weekend.

She'd spent ages deciding what to wear on the train down. With no undies, a short skirt was out. So were skinny rib tops. She was not riding all the way to Guildford with twin peaks poking through. She settled on a short-sleeved, summer dress with a loose bodice and an almost-to-the-ankle, flared skirt. Lots of nice coverage, and the dark peacock blue was a color that suited her. Might as well look as good as she could before he had her strip naked.

Her throat tightened at that thought. This was going to one hell of an unforgettable weekend! And if she didn't get a move on she'd miss the damn train! Much as the thought of a spanking turned her on, she wasn't about to invite one.

Luck was on her side, she got a taxi right away. The crowd at Waterloo was no worse than expected for a Friday afternoon, and she found the first class reserved seat right away. She had to hand it to Alan, he didn't stint.

* * * * *

He didn't miss a trick either. As he greeted her with his heart-quickening smile he wrapped her in his arms and kissed her, his hands eased over her back where her bra would have been and then down to cup her bottom, feeling for would-be knickers.

"Brilliant," Alan whispered in her ear. "You really did it. You came down naked under that rather fetching dress."

"Of course! I didn't fancy starting the weekend with a spanking."

He took the tote bag from her. "You might still get one, if I find you've forgotten something."

"I haven't." It came out sounding smug but keeping her voice even with her heart racing and need stirring between her legs wasn't easy.

"Maybe I'll find another reason," he replied with a grin. "I rather fancy having you over my knee and spanking your lovely arse pink."

Damn good thing he'd parked close. She didn't think her knees would have made it much farther.

The bag disappeared into the boot. "We won't need those until we get there," he said as he slammed the lid down. He opened the door for her and fastened her seat belt, his hand lingering over her breasts as he reached over to click in the buckle.

She was alone in his sports car, surrounded by expensive leather upholstery and her anxieties. It made for a heady mix. Add to it, Alan, now unlocking the driver's door, easing his long legs towards the pedals, and resting his left hand on the gear lever as he shifted into neutral and she was halfway to getting drunk on his presence alone.

Alan had beautiful hands. Very male, long-fingered and large, with a tiny scar below one knuckle where, he told her, he'd nearly cut his finger off with a penknife trying to carve his name on his desk at school. Jane couldn't help smiling thinking of his tall, male presence once being a scabby-kneed schoolboy.

"You're smiling," he said as he turned the keys in the ignition. "Happy?"

She was. Utterly. Beside Alan she felt safe. Completely nutty really as she certainly didn't feel unsafe or incomplete on her own, but it was as if Alan added what she never thought was missing. She gave a sigh. She was getting sappy.

"Worried?" Alan asked as he paused at a roundabout.

"Not worried," she replied, and truth be told, she wasn't. No matter what Alan might do or not do to her, she wasn't worried. But... "I am a bit scared."

He took his hand off the steering wheel and stroked her knee, easing her legs apart, his hand warming her through the thin cotton. "That's good. A smidgen of fear ups the anticipation." He took his hand away as the lights changed and he steered through the traffic. "Don't worry, love. I give you my word. I'll never harm you, Jane, ever."

She was nutty enough, or besotted enough, to believe him. Resting her hand on his, the gentle vibrations of the engine added to her own peaked awareness. Jane glanced sideways at his profile—his strong nose and square chin, the dark eyes crinkled at the corners as he smiled her way.

"You look really happy," he said, his voice warm with pleasure, as if aware he'd contributed to that.

"I am."

"I hope you never regret coming with me," he said, opening his fingers so they meshed with hers.

"You promised I'd come several times," she reminded him.

"You will, but first you have to learn obedience, my lovely Jane. So far, you've impressed me. Let's see how much farther you're willing to go. Open your legs as wide as you can and lift that skirt of yours and show me your thighs. You can leave your pussy covered. For now."

Her blood pounded so hard in her ears, she was lucky she could still hear. This was nuts! What if they had an accident, or Alan got stopped for speeding? What if… She shivered right down to her toes and taking a deep breath, parted her knees and eased up the skirt of her dress.

He didn't say a word, but she felt his pleasure like a soft caress across her exposed flesh. Why did this thrill her so much? And how much more was he going to ask? The answer lay in the tartan bag now locked in the boot. Jane shut her eyes and thought of the hard round plugs and the long sweeping tresses of the flogger, and a slow, anticipatory shudder rippled through her.

"Take three, very deep breaths and relax."

Easy for Alan to say, much harder to do, but she made her shoulders go slack until her hands lay limp on her lap.

"Keep those eyes shut. It'll give you practice for when I blindfold you."

And he talked about relaxing! Cripes!

Oddly enough, she did relax. At least her body did. Her mind raced in wild circles of anxiety and anticipation, taking the odd pause to ask herself why she didn't tell him to stop so she could get out of the car. Since she couldn't come up with a good answer to that one, she lay there, eyes shut, heart racing and waited.

"Hold still, Jane."

Her seat eased backwards, until she was all but lying on her back, legs spread, and it wasn't chance that her skirt rode up even higher.

She lay there, wondering what came next. The CD player clicked on and the slow sultry sounds of Miles Davis filled the car.

"You might as well doze," Alan told her. "I'm going to work you hard when we get there."

Chapter Three

The car slowed as they turned off the main road, drove along a twisting lane for a good distance, then bumped over an unmade drive. Moments later after a sharp left turn, they stopped.

"Don't move until I give you permission."

Jane turned her head as Alan spoke, opened her eyes and caught his frown as he stepped out of the car and slammed the door.

Turning her head constituted moving, didn't it? Or had he meant not sit up?

Oh, shit!

She was cold and prickly between her shoulder blades by the time Alan returned. She remembered, just in time, not to turn her head. For good luck, she kept her eyes closed. Seemed he stood there an age. A cool breeze, from the open door, brushed across her bare thighs. She waited, listening to a blackbird singing in the distance and the sound of running water nearby.

The last had her wanting to pee and she couldn't even cross her legs.

"Jane, love, open your eyes and look at me."

He was smiling as he leaned in, resting a hand on her breast. She felt every fingertip though the thin cotton.

"You are learning. I am impressed. Apart from your one small transgression when we stopped, I believe you haven't moved." He kissed her as he reached over and unsnapped the seat belt. "Let's get into the house."

He picked her up, holding her tight against his chest, as he walked up the brick path to the open front door. She caught a glimpse of a little stream running beside the tile-hung cottage, a cluster of apple trees heavy with swelling fruit and a dark red, scented rose in full bloom around the door. He carried her into the entry hall and set her on her feet.

She looked around at an inglenook fireplace, empty now, but she pictured it piled high with blazing logs in winter. Today, the room was filled with garden scents and fresh air from the open windows on both sides.

"It's lovely," she said looking around at the Turkey red rug on the flagstone floor, the soft, leather furniture, and the fur-lined leather handcuffs and chain suspended from one of the dark oak beams. She couldn't take her eyes off the cuffs swinging gently in the breeze.

Alan tugged at her arm. "Don't worry about that. That's for atmosphere. How about a nice cup of tea?"

Might just help settle her nerves. It helped during the Blitz, didn't it? He led her into a large kitchen that opened onto the back garden and the stream beyond. "This is gorgeous!"

"Isn't it? Not mine, I'm afraid. Wish it were. It belongs to an old friend."

"He knows about the hook and chain in the sitting room?"

Alan grinned. "Jane, dear heart, he left it there for us. Would you prefer Earl Grey or Darjeeling?"

Dammit! Her mind was tangling over the possibilities of chains and handcuffs, and he expected her to think about tea! She took a deep breath. "Earl Grey, please."

He plugged in the kettle and measured out tea into the pot before hooking it over the kettle to warm. "Have a seat." He indicated a pair of rush-seated stools by the countertop. "Won't take long."

She perched on the stool, watching as he reached for cups and saucers in the cabinet, and fetched a tin of biscuits from one of the boxes on the countertop.

"You know, Jane," he said, as he crossed to the fridge for milk, "for your little disobedience in the car—turning to look at me when I told you not to move—I should take you in the other room, bend you over the back of the sofa, raise your skirts and give you a few good, hard slaps with my belt."

How could he! Jane reared back in shock, forgetting she was perched on a stool and would have fallen, but Alan's hand on her shoulder steadied her.

"I said I 'should'. Not that I will. I have every intention of letting you off this time. But you need to learn to obey without hesitation. Remember our conversation last weekend at the Black Swan?"

"I remember you saying I could say 'no' any time I wanted and we'd use a safeword. Suppose I said 'no' to getting the belt?"

She had him there—or had she? His luscious wide mouth twitched at the corners.

"Jane, my love, if you truly felt the punishment was undeserved, then yes, you should refuse. But tell me, did you, or did you not, disobey me when I told you not to move?"

"Not deliberately. I turned without thinking because I wondered what you were doing."

He put down the bottle of milk and rested both hands on her shoulders, moving close so her knees brushed his thighs. "I thought so, dear." His hands eased down to cup her breasts. She leaned forward to increase the pressure of his fingers against her flesh. "That's why I decided to let you off. You'll learn. I intend to be a thorough and attentive instructor."

"What if you have a recalcitrant student?"

"Then, my dear, you will feel my belt."

She was nuts. Utterly bonkers to sit here but he was turning her on with his talk of punishment. She trusted him, was halfway in love with him, but would she really let him hit her? He'd spanked her that once, but that was half in play and hadn't really hurt. A belt damn well would.

"What's the matter?"

"I'm wondering if I'm loony to even be here!"

He brushed his hand down the side of her face. "No, love, you're here because I can give you what you need."

"What do I need?"

He fastened his mouth on hers, opening her lips and kissing slowly, as if sipping her doubts away. Her already hard nipples went rigid and her cunt ached with wanting. With a little muffled sigh, she wrapped her arms around him and kissed back, delving into his mouth with her tongue and leaning in to press her body against his.

She'd answered her own question, but as if to underscore things, as he eased his mouth off hers, Alan whispered against her lips, "You need my sort of loving. You want to be overpowered."

It was a damn good thing she was sitting down.

"Milk and sugar, right, Jane?"

How, after a kiss like that, to say nothing of the preceding conversation, could he calmly ask her how she liked her tea? Deep breath time. "Yes, please."

"We're all set then." He picked up the tray. "Let's go sit at the table by the window, but first, take that dress off."

So, he'd meant it about keeping her naked! But she'd be lying to herself to pretend the prospect didn't turn her on. If it were possible to get more aroused... She stood up and pulled the dress over her head. "Where shall I put it?"

"Hang it up in the hall wardrobe by the front door. There are some pegs there."

Not just pegs! Jane stared as she opened the door. He'd been right—there were lots of pegs. Rows of them, holding the biggest collection of whips and floggers she'd seen outside a shop.

Talk about breaking out in a sweat. It was running down between her shoulder blades. And if she stood here goggling much longer, Alan would know exactly why! Damn him, he'd sent her here, knowing full well what his old pal kept in his hall wardrobe. She hung her dress on the same hook as a rather pretty pink and white flogger that looked as if it would hurt nastily, and went back into the kitchen to face Alan with as much equanimity as possible.

The butt plug sitting in the middle of a plate of shortbread obliterated any poise she might have mustered.

"Oh!" she managed, as she sat down on the chair Alan held for her. "Never realized it was intended as a table decoration!"

"Be careful, Jane," he replied as he eased in her chair. "You'll soon find out it's not for decoration." She bet!

"Are you trying to spin me around like a yoyo on a string?"

His grin answered that one. "You're objecting?"

"I'll let you know when I do."

"I trust you will, Jane, Have a piece of shortbread. It's made by the local Women's Institute."

The local Women's Institute hadn't provided the bright blue butt plug! Jane was tempted to grab it and toss it across the room to see if it bounced, but instead... "Thank you." She reached for the nearest piece. After all, the sugar might give her a bit of energy, and she suspected she'd need it.

"Scared?" Alan asked.

Since her mouth was full of shortbread, she nodded, chewing fast before replying. "To be honest, yes. First, I'm sitting here naked and wondering if the milkman comes late in these parts and second, third and fourth, the contents of that wardrobe wasn't intended to reassure was it?"

"Of course not," he agreed. "Anticipation is part of the fun, and a little bit of fear heightens your excitement."

"I'm not sure about that."

"I am."

"Right! So you go around beating women, tying them up and shoving plastic things up their arseholes." Crude, yes, but...

"Jane!"

She scowled at him. "Raising your voice is the first step I suppose!"

"No, dear, that was to get your attention. I don't beat women, never have and never will. What I'm offering is sensual torture. I can make you come just with the tresses of the flogger you brought with you. I can bring you to an incredible climax after tying you hand and foot to the bed. You're aroused just by listening to me. Won't you let me show you what I can give you?"

"What if your idea of 'fun' isn't mine?"

"Stop me. Use that safeword. Nothing will happen that you don't agree to. Trust me, Jane. We've known each other several weeks. Have I ever pushed you for more than you wanted?"

"We've never done anything really kinky."

"No?" His mouth twitched at the corners. "What about going into the pub without knickers? Or the time you took off your bra and tossed it in the river."

Blood surged to her face, remembering. Had she been drunk both times? Drunk on Alan. "I got carried away."

"You certainly did, my sweet, and it's going to happen again. I want you whimpering in my arms and begging me to let you come."

"I've never had a problem coming with you." Wrong thing to say. Smug was the only word for the expression on his face. Watching her, as if waiting...for what? Hell if she knew.

"Want another cup?" Alan angled his head towards her rapidly cooling tea. "I could warm it up for you."

Must be something about sitting naked that shoved innuendoes into the most innocent remarks—always assuming anything Alan did was innocent. Jane smiled, willing her face to appear calm. "Half a cup, please."

She had to give it to him—he made a good cup of tea. Not that she tasted much with her dry mouth, but it was warm and wet, and sipping it slowly put off the inevitable next step—going upstairs.

Which she really wanted, didn't she? If not, why the hell had she given up a nice weekend she could have spent alphabetizing her spice jars or bleaching the grout in her bathroom tiles?

"You're smiling," Alan said. "What's tickled you?"

With inexplicable candor, she told him.

He chuckled. "Regretting already? I haven't done a thing except make a cup of tea."

"And get me to sit and drink it naked."

He nodded. "There is that too, but I'm enjoying that!"

She bet he was! "How about we make it even? Shouldn't you get naked too?"

"Later. Jane, my love, that's the point—you do what I want, and I want you naked and available." He reached over and cupped her breast, stroking her nipple with his thumb.

Her breath caught, she couldn't help it, and as he rolled her now-hard nipple between his thumb and forefinger, she sighed.

He took his hand away.

Chapter Four

Jane bit back the moan.

"Patience, love." Alan reached across the table and took her hands in his. "Remember, nothing, and I mean nothing, will happen you don't want. I want to give you pleasure, show you the thrill of submission, the joys involved in giving up power, but the minute you want to stop, we stop."

"I say 'stop' and you stop. Just like that?"

"Not quite like that." She should have guessed. "In the middle of playing, the heat of arousal, you may well say, 'No' and mean 'Yes'. Or 'No more' when what you mean is, 'It's so incredible I don't think I can stand it.'" True enough, but… "This is what we do—You want me to stop, say your name, your full name."

"Please, no!"

"Why not?"

"I question whether I can manage 'Jane Margaret Amelia Beatrice Winston' in the heat of passion."

He let out a low whistle. "Good point! Tell me, how did you acquire that list?"

"I was the first female child on my mother's side of the family after seven assorted brothers and male cousins. My parents didn't want to slight any ancient female relatives, so I got the lot."

"Let's settle for 'Jane Winston'. Think you can manage that?"

"Yes," she paused. "You really mean it? I say my name, you stop."

"I'll stop. Of course, I may start right up doing something else, but I won't harm you, Jane, that's a promise. All I ask of you is the willingness to experiment, to explore your own erotic nature."

The same erotic nature that had been on overdrive since she met Alan. "How willing am I supposed to be?"

"Completely. You follow my lead in everything." His hands eased up her arms and across the tops of her breasts. "I tell you to stand, you stand. I tell you to kneel, you kneel. I tell you to lie down, you lie down. If I forbid you to move, as I will, you don't move a muscle."

"What about the manacles, chains and floggers?" To say nothing of the stuff in the hall cupboard, and the blue butt plug still sitting in the middle of the shortbread.

"We'll have some fun before I take you home Sunday afternoon."

Instinct and sheer commonsense told Jane she'd be a different woman when she walked out of here Sunday afternoon—if she lasted that long. "Alan, have you any idea of my misgivings multiplying right now?"

"Of course." He stood. "Coming?"

It was impossible to refuse his outstretched hand.

Or almost. "Kiss me."

A corner of his mouth twitched. "Giving *me* orders, Jane? I think something's muddled."

She stood up. "Nothing's muddled, Alan. I'd just like to be reminded why I agreed to come down for the weekend."

"A-hah!" He stepped close, resting his hand on the nape of her neck, sliding up to her hairline. "Want a reminder do you, woman?" She nodded, her throat tightening as she looked up at the heat in his eyes. "I'm going to have to take care of this forgetfulness of yours."

His mouth came down, hot, hard and demanding. Pulling her head towards him so she had to rise on tiptoe, he all but forced her mouth open with his lips. As she gasped, he thrust his tongue against hers. Seemed as if liquid heat replaced blood in her veins, and wild raging desire eliminated thought and reason. Jane leaned into him, the buckle of his belt and every button on his shirt brushing her naked flesh. His erection pressed against her belly. He was as aroused and needy as she. She whimpered as his tongue caressed hers, stirring her passion higher and driving her wilder with need. She wrapped her arms around his strong back. Leaning in so her breasts were plastered against his chest, Jane let desire flood her mind and body. Alan was more than a lover. He was her desire, her need, her want.

Feeling his erection grind into her belly, she gasped into his mouth, hardly conscious of her breathing, aware only of his fingers in her hair, his knee between her thighs, his lips on hers, his tongue possessing her mouth and his other hand splayed between her shoulder blades.

He was all and everything, and she couldn't help herself. She pressed into his erection, rocking her hips against him, little moans accompanying her rhythm of need.

"Alan!" she cried out, as he pulled his mouth away.

"Shh!" He brushed his lips on the corner of her mouth. "Don't complain. You'll get what you want, but not just yet." He took her hand in his. "First you need a shower to get the grime of travel off you."

She hadn't exactly traveled by camel or steam engine, but who in their right mind would refuse a shower with Alan?

Chapter Five

They crossed the carpeted landing to a vast bathroom. It took quite an effort on Jane's part not to gape. It wasn't just the red carpeted steps leading up to the enormous, sunken black marble whirlpool in one corner, or the black and white tiling from floor to ceiling everywhere, or the matching black loo and bidet and red wash basins, impressive as they were.

What mesmerized Jane was the red and black freestanding shower, big enough to hold half a dozen quite comfortably. That and the rail across the middle of the shower, and the chain and manacles swinging gently.

"What do you think?" he asked.

"That you have manacles and chains all over the house."

"Just these two, for now anyway." He looked around, "Like it?"

"Not your standard builder's bathroom."

"Heavens no! It has several special features. Come over here."

Deep breath time. Very deep breath. "You're going to tie me up."

"Not completely. I'm going to anchor your hands over your head. Your legs will be free, but you'll have to stand there while I wash you, and you won't be able to touch me."

Sounded straightforward, but the five or six different showerheads weren't and the fittings on a couple of the hoses looked decidedly non-standard.

"Alan..."

He shook his head. "Jane, time to stop questioning and start trusting. I'm giving you a shower—that's all. Either step inside and hold your hands up to be restrained, or we go back downstairs and I take you back to the station."

Jane took three steps forward. Not stopping to consider the alternative, she looked Alan in the eye and raised her hands. He didn't speak. Just as well, as her throat sort of seized up as he reached for the manacles.

They were soft against her skin and not the least tight. Her arms weren't uncomfortable over her head, but pulled just enough to make her concentrate on keeping her feet planted firmly.

"Good girl," Alan murmured, as he stepped back, brushing her breast with his fingertips. "You'll learn, darling. Won't be easy for you, but you'll learn."

As she stood there, looking at her herself in the mirrored wall opposite, Alan stripped. Slowly.

The sight of Alan naked didn't exactly take her breath away, more like jammed it up tight into her lungs so she had to remember to breathe. Why had she ever had reservations? She wanted him.

Unthinking, she reached out to him—or tried to. Throwing her weight forward unbalanced her. Alan leapt forward and caught her round the waist.

"What are you doing?" he said, steadying her back on her feet.

"I wanted to touch you!"

"You will, love, soon, but first, a little soap and warm water, and an exercise in patience." He stepped into the shower, turning his back to treat her to a fine view of his arse as he leaned over and fiddled with the taps.

When Alan turned back, he had the shower spray in one hand, and a soapy washcloth in the other. "Close your eyes."

Behind the darkness of her lids, flickers of light danced and skipped as warm water cascaded down her back, over her shoulders and down between her breasts. The spray hit the small of her back and the backs of her thighs. A faster, finer spray prickled her belly and teased between her legs. As the warm water hit her clit, she shifted her hips, angling them best to feel the full force of the spray—and damn the man he moved it right away!

She opened her eyes and glared. "You did that on purpose!"

"Of course," he agreed. "Keep still! Shut your eyes, Jane and don't move. It will be worth it. I promise."

Jane closed her eyes again and waited. She heard water against the tiled wall behind, but none of it reached her. "I'm getting chilly." Complaining, yes…but darn it!

"Patience, Jane."

In the dark, she smelled lavender. The wonderful roughness of a wet loofah stroked down her spine to her tailbone. The scent filled the room, like a summer garden. "Lovely!" she murmured.

"Thought you'd like that. Pays to obey, doesn't it?"

For now at least! "Mmmm." Seemed a shame to waste effort on words, when she'd rather concentrate on the sensations in her body. Alan was tracing tiny circles all over her back, working downwards over her bum to the backs of her thighs. He used short, straight strokes—thigh to the back of her knee, back of the knee to ankle, up and down before shifting to her other leg.

A shiver of pleasure jerked her shoulders and her spine stretched and curled as she pulled against the overhead restraints. A sharp tap on one bum cheek stilled her.

"I know you like this, Jane, but please control yourself."

A darn sight easier said than done! But nothing if not willing, Jane took a deep, calming breath. It might have worked, if Alan hadn't moved and was now anointing her breasts with lavender. Was it bath oil or shower foam? Did it matter? Hardly. But thinking about it distracted her, for a second or two. Did she want to be distracted? Wasn't concentrating on the sensations in her body far, far better? She sighed and sagged against the restraints. Steadying herself as her shoulders pulled.

Alan nudged the inside of her thigh. Without thinking, Jane shifted her legs apart. She stood squarely, but it wasn't easy to keep still as he ran the loofah up and down the inside of her legs. "I like that."

"I know." Damn him! He stopped.

Not for long. He was now drawing circles on her belly, holding her steady with his other hand on her waist. Her legs were getting wobbly, pleasant enough really, if she hadn't been worried about losing her balance. Her arms were beginning to ache. How much longer? She flexed them to ease the hurt.

"Getting tired?" Alan asked.

"Yeah."

"Won't be long now, I promise."

Once again, warm water cascaded over her body. From two directions—front and back. Between both, her body rocked and arched. She couldn't not move, it was too much, too wonderful. One spray washed over her face, warm, soft and caressing, while stronger, harder jets coursed down her back. It was wonderful, incredible and finished!

"That should have you nicely relaxed." Alan held her round the waist, his thigh against hers and his erection brushing her arse as he reached up and released the manacles.

Her arms dropped, tingling with pins and needles, and he spun her around to face him. He was smiling down at her, his body glistening with drops of water.

"Think I'm clean enough now?" she asked.

His mouth twitched at the corners. "You'll do! But you do have trouble keeping still, Jane."

"It's a bit difficult with you hard beside me!"

"You just have to make more effort, love. Let's get dried off."

As she stepped onto the deep pile mat, Alan wrapped a large bath towel around her shoulder, before pulling on a toweling robe himself. Jane started rubbing herself dry but he stopped her. "Let me do that."

Each pat, each rub of thick towel against her skin, sent a little thrill deep into her cunt. He took far, far longer than necessary drying her breasts, her belly and the sensitive skin on the underside of her butt. Not that she'd complain. She could stand here all evening, but didn't want to. "Are we going to be here all night?"

"Oh no, dear. In fact it's time you did a little something for me."

"Want me to dry you off?" She wouldn't mind running a towel over his nice bod.

"No, dear. I want you to suck my cock. On your knees, love!"

Jane knelt. Heart racing, a snap of indignation gone in the thrill of being eye level to his cock—his decidedly wondrous cock. Perhaps not as large as some she'd seen, but perfectly proportioned—long, firm, upstanding, uncircumcised, the smooth pink head nestling in a little cap of foreskin. Looking up at his dark eyes, his face still damp and his hair smoothed back and glossily wet, Jane smiled. "I'd be delighted."

Gently she reached up, eased back his foreskin and licked the smooth head with the tip of her tongue. He'd played her. Now was her turn. He wouldn't last long, she suspected, but while she had the chance...

Jane flicked her tongue all over the smooth skin, until his hand closed on the back on her head. "Swallow me!" She opened her mouth wide and took him in. Her belly tightened with excitement as her heart sped inside her ribs.

Alan might think he was getting the ultimate thrill, having her naked, on her knees before him. Did he realize the charge it gave her? The power she felt with his cock—the very essence of his masculinity — between her lips, between her teeth. Did he ever worry about her biting or hurting his most vulnerable part?

Like a blast of heat, the thrill engulfed her as she curled her tongue around his hard, hot flesh. His hands on her head moved her mouth up and down his cock, but it was her lips that brushed the rim, her tongue that flicked the tight ridge of flesh on the underside of the head, and tasted his sweet bead of moisture. As her mouth enclosed him, her mind adored the cock that would soon fill her cunt. She smiled around his erection, sighing as her clit started a slow, soft throb in rhythm with her mouth.

"Enough!" Alan eased her head away. "I want to fuck you, Jane." She'd be utterly delighted. "But do me a favor, love, nip back downstairs and get the butt plug."

Talk about switching the mood! Jane had her mouth open to complain but caught his eye. This was what he meant by obedience. At that thought, something tightened between her legs. Need? Desire? Whatever. It was too damn wonderful to waste time wondering. "Okay if I wrap the towel back around me? It's a bit chilly downstairs."

He grabbed a second bathrobe off a hook. "Turn around."

He held the robe for her, wrapped it around her and tied the belt. "Stay warm," he said, "and come back as quickly as you can. I'll be waiting next door."

"Okay." She turned towards the door.

"Oh, and Jane…"

"Yes?" She turned back to him, taking in the sight of his familiar face, his gleaming eyes and his hair, dark and shiny as coal.

"While you're downstairs, bring me up the blue flogger you brought with you. High time you got a taste of it."

Her throat tightened, her heart raced and a great pool of wetness gathered between her legs. "Please, no!" As the words came out, Jane understood about safewords. If he took her refusal at face value, she'd be hideously disappointed.

"Oh, yes, Jane. Be glad it has wide tresses. The thin ones hurt much, much more."

She'd take his word for it!

How she made it downstairs and back, she never knew. Was she sick, twisted? Didn't bear thinking about. Truth was, the thought of the flogger sent her desire peaking. She had to be barking loony to want this. Or was she? Hadn't Alan always been the consummate lover? The time he'd held her hands down over her head, she'd had the climax of her life. When he whispered in her ear about tying her to the bed, she got wet. Even the discomfort of standing in the shower, hands stretched over her head, had aroused her. Hell, it *still* aroused her. And just a glimpse at the chain and manacles suspended from the sitting room ceiling, had her wishing he was putting his earlier threat into action.

"What are you doing?" Alan called from upstairs.

"Just a minute!" She grabbed the flogger and crossing the kitchen, she popped the hard, rubber plug into her pocket and turned to go upstairs, to her waiting lover, and a session with soft suede.

Chapter Six

The sweet smell of lavender still hung around the open bathroom. Alan wasn't there, but there was only one other door upstairs. Jane turned the brass knob and opened the door.

And almost ran.

This was no ordinary bedroom.

There was a bed, a large four-poster, at one end, but…sheesh, it looked as though someone had taken down walls and made the entire upstairs one huge space. In the middle of the vast room, Alan was waiting in all his lovely, naked glory, wearing a leather mask that hid the top half of his face. Her stomach did a little flip. Something about the way he stood, hands on his hips, sent a cold thrill of fear down her gut and a flutter between her legs.

"Why did you bring me that flogger?" he asked

"You asked me to."

"Why?"

She took a deep breath. "You're going to use it on me, and…" Her voice petered out.

There was no letup. "And what, Jane?"

"You say I'll enjoy it but I'm not entirely sure I believe that!" It came out in a rush.

The mouth below the dark mask smiled. "You doubt my word, Jane?"

"I doubt myself!" Was that it? If so, why was she standing here in this odd room? With the vast bed, the enormous chair by the wall and a couple of other unusual bits of furniture, one of which looked like the vaulting horse she remembered from gym lessons in her school days. To say nothing about the table by the bed covered with things she didn't want to look at and the shuttered windows blocking out the light. Wall sconces and candles around the room, gave an eerie, flickering light. She used to think candlelight romantic. She wasn't sure anymore.

"Jane, love!"

Alan crossed the room and drew her into his arms, holding her tight against his chest as he kissed the top of her head. "Doubt me, Jane. Doubt my ability to satisfy you. Doubt the sun rising or the night falling, but never doubt yourself. You're my dream come true. Haven't I told you that before?"

"Frequently."

"Believe me." It would be hard not to. "We're made for each other, two halves of the whole. I need you to obey me, every bit as much as you yearn to submit."

Was he right? Did it matter? Not now at least. "I'm still scared."

"I know." He should get thumped for his smugness—or should he? "A little bit of fear all adds to the fun." Alan tilted up her face and dropped a soft kiss on her mouth. "Did you bring the plug?" Jane nodded and reached into her pocket. His hand closed over hers. "We won't need that for a little while." Never, she hoped, but at least it was out of sight, for a few seconds. He put the plug down on the small table. Right next to a tube of lubricant and a bottle of massage oil. "While we're at it, give me the flogger."

Dropping it on the bed, he took her hand. "Still scared?"

"I think I'm beyond scared at this point! I've given up worrying." Not entirely true, but it sounded like a brilliant idea.

"You can stop me, Jane. Don't ever forget that." He brushed the side of her face with his hand. "I won't ever harm you. Do you believe me?"

"Yes!" She did, utterly.

"Good. Time we started. Take off that dressing gown and lie face down on the bed. Now!"

The last came as an order. Her hands fumbled with the belt. He'd tied a damn tight knot, but she got it open and the robe off her shoulders. "Where shall I put it?"

"On that hook over there." He indicated a large black iron hook halfway up the wall. Somehow, she suspected it wasn't designed to hold clothes. It was far too sturdy, and there were too many of them at odd heights.

No point in dwelling on their use. Face down on the bed, Alan had said.

She crossed the floor, her bare feet sinking into the soft pile of the carpet. Hesitating just a moment at the foot of the vast mattress, Jane climbed up on the bed. The sheets were fine cotton—soft, sleek and sensual. They'd be lovely for sleeping in, if and when she got the chance.

She stretched out, the expensive cotton feeling gorgeous against her skin. She relaxed, or at least tried to, and waited.

His hands closed over her ankles. "Over to the side a bit. I want to be able to reach all of you." Alan tugged her towards him, and to the right. "Much better. Now, Jane, I want to try this without restraining you. I'll tie you down tomorrow, I think, but for now. Just lie there, and don't say a word, whatever I do, understand?"

She lifted her head and nodded, pleased she'd not made that mistake.

"Brilliant, darling." His hand trailed down her spine, his fingertips brushing her skin. "Keep still."

She sensed he moved, but not away. A heady, spicy scent filled the room as something cool ran down her spine. She closed her eyes to better savor the sexy scent as he spread the oil over her shoulders. He had magic hands, kneading her flesh, smoothing over her skin, covering her back, butt and legs with the perfumed oil.

Lying still and letting him do what he wanted was no hardship. Jane relaxed under his touch as muscle by muscle, he eased out the knots and tension. She lost track of time. When he finished, she was loose and relaxed, and utterly contented.

"Feels nice, doesn't it?" Lifting her head to nod was an effort.

"It feels like heaven!"

"Good, now grab this." He handed her a loop of heavy rope, tied to the head of the bed. "Keep hold of it, don't let go. If you do, I'll tie you down."

Her cunt tightened. What now?

"Want to ask anything, love?"

"Yes!" Damn, she'd forgotten to nod.

"That's okay. What's the worry?"

"What are you going to do to me?"

"I'm giving you a taste of the flogger. If you can't stand it, just let go."

"But you just said, if I didn't, you'd tie me down!"

"Then don't let go, Jane. You're nicely loose, stay that way, and by the way, don't you dare climax!"

As if she was likely to in the middle of getting flogged!

She grabbed the rope and waited.

His hand came down first, stroking her bum, caressing the curve of her hip and trailing up her back.

He kissed her shoulder.

A sweet shiver rippled through her as the soft tails of the flogger trailed down her spine. Jane sighed. 'That feels wonderful!"

"Not so bad is it?"

Bad? It was glorious! This time, her sigh dragged out as the flogger caressed her shoulders. Her entire body came alive. Nerve endings she never knew she possessed, responded to the kiss of soft suede. And she'd worried so much. Jane smiled into the pillow—she was limp, warm and utterly content.

The tresses snaked down her back again.

"You like this?"

"I love it!"

"Then try this, my love!" The flogger came down harder. Not enough to sting, just a sweet tingle as the ends hit her shoulders, and a wonderful caress as they trailed down to her thighs.

Again and again it descended, and again and again the strange, sweet pleasure thrilled her. Jane tightened her hold on the rope as her neck arched off the bed. "I can't keep still!"

It was impossible. She wanted her entire body to feel, to respond to the wild thrills coursing through her.

"So I see." The tresses came down again, teasing the insides of the thighs. Her hips jerked. "Yes," Alan said. "Time you rolled over, sweetheart."

It took a few moments for her sensation-fogged mind to understand. When she did, she let go of the rope and rolled on her back. Every stimulated inch of her skin warmed even more as her sensitized flesh brushed the sheet. She looked up at Alan. He stood on the bed, looming over her. What caught her attention wasn't the black mask or the flogger hanging loose from his right hand, but his cock—hard, aroused and aimed straight at her.

She licked her lips, the deep warmth in her cunt increasing to a gentle throb at the very obvious proof of his arousal.

"Not yet, Jane," he said. "Patience! You'll get to suck me, but not until I'm ready."

"You look pretty damn ready to me!"

The eyes behind the mask glinted, "That's no way for a submissive to address her master. I think you need to try harder!"

Comments about how hard he was obviously weren't in order. She smiled up at him, her eyes taking in the stern set of his mouth below the dark mask. "What next?"

"What's next is you grab the rope again."

Easier said than done lying on her back. She felt around the pillow behind her until her fingers closed over the rope.

"Good! Ready to feel my flogger on your lovely breasts?"

She heard herself swallow. Her pulse throbbed in her ears. Damp pooled between her thighs. "I'm ready." She took a deep breath. "For whatever you want to do to me." The words sent a wild thrill right down to her cunt. What was this he did to her? Why did she want, no, *need* this?

"Close your eyes."

Her lids blocked out the sight of his beautiful nakedness, but not the image seared in her brain. The flogger never came down. It came up, caressing between her thighs, up over her pussy, tickling her belly, stroking her breasts like a hundred loving fingers.

She'd been so worried and this was sheer and utter pleasure. At the back of her mind, she knew the same tresses that caressed could also sting, but for now, she lost herself in the sheer thrill of the sweet stimulation and the unfamiliar emotions flooding her mind.

Every inch of her body tingled. It was as if she were coming alive, losing herself, finding her real self, forging a bond with Alan as he wielded and she received.

Jane heard sighs, moans and whimpers like distant echoes inside her head. She was wrapped in a cocoon of sensation. Sensation that built and swelled, growing like a wild possession, spreading across her skin and gathering hot, wet and pulsating between her legs. Her hips rocked, sighs became moans. "Alan, Alan," she muttered, unsure what she was asking, not knowing what she needed.

He knew.

"Righto, love!" There was a clunk as something hit the floor. His hands were on her hips, raising her to him. Jane arched her back in anticipation, and then he was hard, hot and firm in her softness. He plunged deep and Jane cried out, a wordless greeting, a joyous welcome as he drove home.

He paused.

She waited, suspended between sensation and pleasure, until he moved. His cock withdrew, returning with force and wild power. He worked her with a sweet, loving rhythm, as if marking her deep inside, taking her with him to the heights. She was climbing, her mind and body one with his. Following his lead until she came, screaming her climax to the world, throwing her head back and arching her spine as a wild crescendo of joy broke across her consciousness. She'd have sagged, worn and spent on the mattress, but he didn't allow it. He held her to him, clasping her hips with his warm hands as he took her higher, dragging her into the wildest, fiercest climax she'd ever known. It wasn't *a* climax, but a chorus of them. Her body reached, soared, flew in a thousand directions as he held her there by his presence, by his hard cock sealing her heart and possessing her body.

When Alan finally withdrew and lowered her to the mattress, she was limp, sweaty and utterly satiated. He lay beside her, leaning over her, reaching over her head where her hands seemed fused to the rope. He eased her fingers open. "You held this too damn tight."

"You told me not to let go."

He kissed her fingers one by one. "I did, didn't I? My mistake. We'll arrange things better next time."

"Better?" That seemed impossible. Her cunt still rippled with the fading sensations of her multiple climaxes.

"Better and better," he promised as he kissed her cheek, and wrapped his arms around her.

Chapter Seven

She must have slept. The light in the room had changed. How long had she been out? She was rested, but her body still thrummed with the sensations of Alan's cock driving deep. She'd dreaded that flogger, but with it he'd given her the climax of her life. The rest couldn't be as bad as she feared.

Jane shut her eyes, snuggling under the covers to concentrate on her sensitized body. Her skin still tingled in a few places, but best of all was the sweet thrill deep inside. It was as if Alan had touched her very being.

As she lay there, aromas of cooking wafted upstairs. She was hungry and thirsty. Throwing off the duvet, she sat up, turning so her feet touched the floor, looking around for a dressing gown or T-shirt before remembering Alan's prohibition on clothes. She hoped he wasn't planning on eating in the garden.

As she walked into the kitchen, Alan looked up from the stove and smiled. She grinned back. "Hello."

"Hello, beautiful." He crossed the room to her, drawing her close so her breasts rubbed the soft cotton of his shirt and his thigh eased between hers. "My love," he whispered into her hair. Jane clung to him, wrapping her arms around him, aching to recapture the incredible closeness of their lovemaking. "You're alright?" he asked.

She looked up at him, glad he was no longer wearing the mask, and nodded. "I don't think I've ever felt better."

His face lit with sheer joy. "You mean it?"

The anxiety in his voice astonished her. Alan doubting himself was hard to credit, but... "Alan, you've always been a wonderful lover, but this afternoon was phenomenal. I can still feel you inside me and…"

His mouth came down, hot and ardent, stealing her last words, jumbling her thoughts. She gave up trying to think, let her need drive her response and kissed him back. "It was good then?" he asked, as he lifted his mouth. "I wanted that fuck to be wonderful, and needed to see if you were what I thought you are."

"What did you think I am?" Did she really what to know? Yes!

"Sexy, passionate, fantastic in bed and gloriously submissive."

"Thanks for the compliments of the first three—but where did you get the submissive bit?"

He dropped a soft kiss on her forehead. "Don't look so affronted. You are truly submissive. I suspected so when I first met you, got inklings of it the past few weeks and this afternoon proved it."

"What exactly do you mean?" She'd backed away. Did she want to be close to him if he thought she was the doormat sort?

"I'm not insulting you. It's a compliment, Jane. This afternoon, you did submit. You gave over control. That takes courage and strength, not weakness. By handing control to me, you had, by your own admission, the best climax in your life, and I got the thrill of dominating you. We're made for each other, Jane. Think about it."

She obviously was thinking. Alan repressed a smile as her brow creased and her eyes clouded with confusion and uncertainty. He'd set her thinking. It was now up to her to sort it out.

He stepped close and kissed her, brushing her lips gently. She responded immediately. Sweet Jane just couldn't help herself. Mind you, he was pretty much in the same state. "Have a seat while I finish cooking." He pulled over a stool. "Want a glass of wine?"

"Thank you."

He reached for a glass and poured from the bottle he'd opened earlier. "Here." He indulged himself by letting his fingers touch hers. She felt the connection too. He saw it in the flush of her cheeks and her hesitation in taking the glass. He turned away, half-afraid she'd read all he felt in his eyes and go running. Hell! He was almost ready to run himself. He scraped the onions to one side of the pan and threw in chopped red and green peppers, stirring briskly, as he pondered Jane Winston and what she did to him.

He'd never had it this bad. Ever. He wanted her with a need that hurt. It went deeper than the sex and he certainly agreed with her on that being phenomenal. While she was close, he felt happy. Silly, simple, grin-makingly happy and he wanted to stay that way.

"What are you cooking?"

Took him a good twenty seconds to filter her words through his hormones. Looking over his shoulder, he couldn't keep himself from smiling. How many men had the sexiest woman in creation sitting naked in their kitchen on a Friday evening? "Beef in garlic sauce, with extra onions and peppers."

"You remembered."

"Of course." Hell! Even her sighs were sexy.

"What about pudding?"

"How about whipped cream off your luscious breasts?"

The idea appealed, if the glint in her eyes was anything to go by, but she pursed her mouth up, shaking her head. "I'm going to have trouble licking my own breasts, perhaps I'd better put some on your cock!"

He laughed aloud. She was wonderful! "Think you should, do you?"

"As long as you don't mind, and something tells me you won't."

Time to reestablish who was running this show. "I certainly won't, but you will be on your knees with your hands tied behind you when it happens." He let her think about that while he stirred the pan. It was cooking nicely. And Jane, with a bit of luck, was stewing deliciously.

When he glanced back, she was sipping her wine. She looked him in the eye. "You're really serious about this 'I dominate, you submit' business aren't you?"

"Definitely. Jane, I like to dominate the women I love, and I love you." She stared, jaw gaping, as he turned back and reached for the thin slices of seasoned beef. "Won't be long now," he said. "Do me a favor and light the candles on the table." And while she was at it she'd see exactly what he'd done with the butt plug. He bet she'd never seen one in a butter dish before.

"Is this thing purely ornamental?"

Would she ever cease to surprise him? Or was she masking worry with sauciness? "You mean the anal plug, Jane? No, it's certainly not ornamental. I planned on pushing it up your arse this afternoon but decided one new experience at a time was enough, and you responded so well to the flogger."

Bless her, she was scarlet.

"You really go for this, don't you?"

"Don't you too?"

She went dead silent for ages. Had he pushed too hard?

"I'm not sure, Alan. I'm really not."

Damn! He *had* pushed too hard. "Don't sweat it, Jane and don't forget, you can stop it any time. Be a love and hold the plates for me while I dish up the food."

That much he'd managed perfectly—rice fluffy and firm, the meat cooked just to the point, veggies still crisp, and the sauce delicious, even if it had come out of a jar.

He poured Jane another glass of wine, the last she was getting. He wanted her relaxed but still completely aware.

She speared a mouthful of meat and vegetables and chewed slowly. "Mmmm, Alan Branis, you are a darn good cook!"

"Think I'll make some nice woman a good husband?" Damn! Too soon again. She swallowed the mouthful half-chewed.

After she took a good swallow of wine, she gave him a look. It wasn't hurt, indignant or even surprised, just perplexed. "The beef's marvelous," she said after a long silence.

Better backpedal and stick with safe topics, like religion, sex and politics. "So, Jane, the flogger wasn't as bad as you feared?"

"No." She frowned as if thinking. "It wasn't, in fact..." She looked up at him, fork poised, "I liked it and yes, it did get me aroused, but is it always like that?"

"You mean arousing, or that gentle?"

"That gentle."

"You know the answer already, don't you?"

She let out a sigh, "I can guess. But does it always arouse?"

"It does me, and it will you, unless I'm very much mistaken."

"Why, Alan? Why does something that should be awful, feel so wonderful?"

She was more open than he'd ever hoped this early. More honest, more desirable. Better get back to her question. "Jane, I don't honestly know. I think it's the way we're hotwired and I'm just glad we found each other."

A little smile curled the corner of her mouth. "So'm I."

"Want some more to eat?"

"I think I'll wait for dessert."

"How about a bit of butter?"

He loved the way she looked — irritated and intrigued at the same time. "You've been bouncing that thing in front of me since we got here. I'm beginning to think it's merely a table decoration."

"Certainly not." He stood up. "Let's clean up the dishes, and I'll show you where to put it."

"What about a promise of whipped cream and a chocolate condom?"

She was wonderful, coming right back, even when unsure and nervous. "You pick, Jane. Butter or cream?"

She took a very deep breath, looked from him to the butter dish and back again. Thinking, worrying, daring. "Oh, hell! Let's go for butter!"

He'd found the woman of his dreams!

She had to be utterly mad! Sex mad! She could have had him licking whipped cream off her breasts. Instead she was bent over the arm of the sofa, face in the pillows while Alan buttered—or rather lubed-up her arsehole. He had yet to insert the damn butt plug that had alternately fascinated and repelled her all evening. He seemed to much prefer playing with her areshole with his finger. He'd told her not to move, and when she wiggled, slapped her on the rump. Not hard, but enough to sting, and since then he'd held her still by pressing his free hand between her shoulder blades.

She should be forcing herself off the furniture and objecting to the indignity of him playing with her arsehole, but some deep, twisted part of her loved it. Suddenly, he rammed in harder and she let out a soft moan. She might be sick, perverted or bent—maybe all three, but she loved this, and wanted more…

"Ever been buggered, Jane?" Alan asked conversationally as he withdrew halfway and pressed back deep.

"No!"

"Want to be?" A gasp sort of froze in her throat. Did she? His hand pressed harder between her shoulder blades. "Well, Jane? Answer me."

"Yes!" Hell! Why not? She'd fantasized about it often enough. But did she really want Alan's big cock up there?

Seemed she was committed. "Brilliant!" he said, removing his finger. "Time to get the plug in. It's bigger than my finger, so you'll need preparation."

The lubricant was cold but soon warmed in her body. Alan appeared to be having a fine old time, pressing the gel in deep and slathering it over her arsehole. "I think you're ready now," he said at last. Before she had time to object, complain or even think about changing her mind, the hard rubber slid home. "How does that feel?" he asked putting his arms on her waist, raising her up to standing and turning her to face him.

Would be easier to reply if they weren't eye-to-eye. "Odd."

"Not uncomfortable?"

Good question. "Not exactly. 'Odd' is the best description. I've never had anything that big up there!"

"My cock is a lot bigger, Jane."

Her throat tightened at the thought. With a bit of effort, she swallowed. "I know…" Her stomach seemed to know as well. Heck, every inch of her responded at the prospect.

"Oh, Jane. Don't look so worried." He traced her lips with the pad of his finger. "It will meet all your wildest fantasies and more. You have my word."

She'd be a fool not to believe him. "With a money-back guarantee?"

"If you're not completely satisfied, I'll repeat it until you are!" His hand smoothed over her hip and round to stroke her arse. "Sure the plug feels okay? I want to leave it in about twenty minutes."

"What are you planning on doing for the next twenty minutes then?"

"The washing up!"

She should have expected that, given how much he enjoyed tossing the unexpected in her direction.

Chapter Eight

Jane sank deep into the scented bubbles—jasmine if the big bottle by the side of the bath was anything to go by. "A nice soak will help you relax," Alan said when he turned on the taps, filling the large bathroom with steam and scent, after he'd made her bend down and touch her toes as he removed the plug. He'd been right. She was relaxed. Sort of. When she wasn't wondering what exactly he was doing in the bedroom.

At her agreement—no, request, Alan Branis was going to bugger her. Right. Why get so het up? Hadn't she had countless fantasies of just that happening to her, and hadn't Alan proved himself a considerate lover? She'd been so worried about the flogging, and sheesh... She got warm just remembering. And even hotter looking at the larger-size butt plug he'd plonked down on the side of the bath. "Just so as you don't forget what's waiting."

As if she could! Or forget his wicked grin as he said it.

Jane gave a big sigh and sank deeper into the scented bubbles.

"Ready, love?"

Her readiness might be moot. His was obvious. She half-suspected he wore the black silk boxers just to showcase his erection tenting the front.

Not to be outdone, she smiled up at him. "I think so."

"I hope so." He held out a hand.

His fingers closed over hers as she stood and stepped out onto the mat. He wrapped a vast bath towel around shoulders and gently patted her dry. "Come on," he said, turning to lead the way.

"Wait." Jane caught his arm. Looking down at the impressive bulge in his boxers, she licked her lips. "I'd like a taste first."

"Jane!" He'd raised his voice only slightly, but it came out like a snap. "Remember what I said earlier? You follow my directions. Time to get things straight, my dear. I've been a little too indulgent. Yes, you will get to suck my cock. When I give permission. No more lewd suggestions from you. I decide what happens and when. You do as I tell you, or, my dear, you'll feel more than you want on your bottom!"

How could threats and admonitions excite her so? She was almost shaking with anticipation. "I'm sorry, Alan."

Without thinking, she dropped to her knees on the plush mat. "Forgive me," she begged, hanging her head. Just saying the words sent a thrill down to her pussy. It didn't ease in the slightest her ache to take his cock in her mouth, but she could wait, she would, she had to.

"You're forgiven," he replied. "This time. Just stay there on your knees until I call you to get up and follow me."

A strange thrill zinged through Jane as she watched Alan walk away. It wasn't just the sight of his broad shoulders and nice arse. It was anticipation. This man was the answer to her wildest dreams. Very soon…

She took a deep breath.

"I'm ready, Jane, get in here!"

She jumped up at his voice, and all but dashed down the hallway, pausing just inside the door to look at Alan standing at the foot of the bed.

"Staying in the doorway all night?"

"No."

She took three steps across the cream Berber carpet and knelt at Alan's feet. The weird thrill caught in her chest this time. She made herself breathe slowly and waited.

Alan moved. She could see his bare feet and his strong ankles as he paced from side to side. "My dear Jane, you know, without being told, exactly what I want. Perfect. Now get up and come over here, and let me bugger you." She wobbled as she stood. It wasn't fear, more a strange, twisted excitement she didn't want to think about.

"Scared?"

"No. A bit worried, but..."

"Don't be. Come here."

He drew her into his arms, pressing his mouth on hers, kissing hard and fast with an urgency that betrayed his need and fired her own. She reached up, wrapping her arms around his neck and returned the kiss—lips, tongues, arms meshed and joined. Jane heard an echo of a gasp, followed by a whimper as he pulled away. And that was it. Alan swept her up in his arms and deposited her on the bed. At once, he loomed over her, hands either side of her shoulders, one knee on the bed, as his mouth came down again.

If he'd forbidden her to respond, she'd have failed utterly. He matched her need, wild kiss upon wild kiss, hands exploring, stroking, caressing. His mouth now on her breast, teasing and tugging as his lips tightened on her nipple, hurting just slightly. Her body responded, heat flashed over her skin and wild wetness gathered between her legs. He moved to her other breast. "Yes!" he whispered triumphantly as she whimpered in anticipation.

Jane cried out as his lips and teeth pulled on her already sensitized nipple. It was too much! It was wonderful! Alan shifted slightly, kissing between her breasts, before nipping his way down across her belly to her pussy. She was squirming on the bed by the time he parted her bush and opened her pussy lips. "Be still!"

She made every effort to obey. She succeeded, lying still as possible, waiting for his mouth to descend and...nothing! Just a long, long pause, while he blew on her wet pussy, his fingers searing like brands on her sensitive flesh. "Please," she begged, "Alan, please!"

"Please what, Jane?" he asked into her pussy.

"Please kiss me there."

"If you want me to eat your pussy, then say so." She never used that expression. "Kiss" was so much nicer but...

"You don't want it, Jane?"

Dear heaven, she did! "Oh! Please, Alan, eat my pussy!"

He obliged.

Opening her thighs wide, he lay between them, hesitating a moment as he spread her more open, then the full flat of his tongue came from fore to aft—slow, wet and warm. She let out a moan as he repeated the caress, time after time, back and forth. When she thought she could take no more, he pressed closer, his lips covering her cunt and this time, his tongue penetrated her.

She all but rose off the bed. Would have, but his hands on her thighs held her down. If only this could continue forever!

If only she could lie here and have him worship her pussy like this. Her moans and sighs echoed off the low ceiling. Her hands grasped the sheets under her as her body rocked with pleasure.

He shifted again, this time his lips returned to her clit and she all but screamed as his fingers penetrated her cunt. Her groan rose to the heavens as her desire peaked. His fingers curled inside her, driving her need higher. If he kept this up much longer, she'd climax.

Jane whimpered as he withdrew, crying out as a finger penetrated her arse. It was tight, hurt a little, felt odd, but suddenly... "That feels so good, Alan." She pressed down trying to bring his finger deeper, but it was gone.

Alan kissed the side of her mouth as she protested. "Soon, Jane, soon I promise, but you still haven't earned that privilege."

Privilege was it? Maybe. Whatever it was, she wanted it! More and more and... "Alan, please..."

"Of course, dear." He'd shifted, moving up the bed so he knelt astride her. "Very soon, Jane but first you have to suck me." He shifted closer, lifting her head and tucking one of the thick pillows behind it. "That should work nicely. Now is your chance to demonstrate how much you want this cock up your arse. Please me now and it's yours!"

Nothing ever equaled the thrill of taking him into her mouth. As he moved closer, looming over her, bigger, stronger and more powerful than ever, she lifted her head, opening her lips to embrace him. "Hang on, love." Another pillow felt better, raising her so it supported her neck. "Comfy?" Alan asked.

Her reply was to open wide and cover the smooth, sweet head of his cock with her mouth. A great shudder of pleasure rippled deep inside. Her clit almost hurting with need as she drew him deeper, brushing her tongue over his hard flesh. He was immense, male, strong and hers. He filled her mouth. Thinking about the selfsame cock stretching and stuffing her tight arse, caused a frisson of fear, anticipation and delight.

She would not falter, would not fail. She'd please Alan and he'd satisfy her fantasy.

She gave up thinking and let her body take over, desire, thrills and an illicit delight driving her on. She savored the taste of the pre-come seeping from the tiny opening, relished the contrast between the smooth skin on the head and the ridges along the side of his cock. Using her lips, she played his foreskin, easing it back before flicking her tongue over the sensitive spot on the underside of his cock, just below the head. Swallowing him as deep as she dared, before slowly withdrawing, just a little. She whimpered in disappointment as he withdrew.

"Hush." he said, stretching out beside her and pulling the duvet over them. "Sssh. Lie still." He was behind her, his hand cupping her breast, stroking it with a sweet gentleness that made her sigh.

"I love you, Alan!" Cripes! She'd said it.

"I know, Jane, I love you too." His hand came down to rest between her legs before his fingers entered her wet and ready pussy, pressing deep. "I love you, and I'm making your arse mine," he said, easing out his fingers. "Lie still."

She went as limp as she could as his hand stroked her arse and gently parted her bum cheeks. She panted with anticipation as he pressed against her muscle, and one finger entered. Deep.

"Breathe," he said. "Breathe slowly."

She obeyed, making her muscles relax, until all she felt was mild tightness. This she could take but it was only one finger. His cock was so big, so...

"Easy, Jane darling, lie still. You'll be alright. I'm going to stretch you with the plug."

First came the lubricant—cold, slick and smooth, warming as he worked it inside her. Then came the plug—hard, stretching her, opening up her tight hole. Jane gasped as it pressed past the tight ring of muscle and made herself relax. If she lay still, it felt better, less tight, but not exactly less big. It hadn't felt like this before.

"Which one is that?"

"Does it matter?"

"Yes. I want to know whether to panic or not!"

His lips brushed her shoulder. "It's the big one. Just lie still and get used to it. I have to open you enough to take my cock." As he spoke, he pushed her knees up towards her chest. "Stay like that. It opens you more."

Perhaps it did. The plug felt easier this way. Still large, still hard but...her pussy was throbbing and responding more than ever. This was beyond her wildest dreams and his hand caressing between her legs took her a pitch higher. She rocked against him, wanting to feel the strength and security of his broad chest, and brushed back on his very erect cock.

"Easy, love. Almost there," he whispered in her ear. The plug slipped out of her arsehole and his erection took its place. He pressed into her, pausing as he met the ring of tight muscle.

Jane all but froze. Alan went still, his arm around her waist holding her against him, his other hand gripped her shoulder, steadying her. He paused on the threshold of her last virginity, pressing gently, waiting.

A low, slow moan came from her lips. Alan might be entering her arse, but her pussy didn't feel neglected. She throbbed deep within. As he pressed against her arsehole, her cunt responded. Was as if they were connected, one stimulating the other.

"Push back on to me," he said, his breath brushing her neck. "You press down. I'll stay still. That way you take me in as much and as fast as you want."

Nothing could delight her more!

Jane eased back, pausing as the pressure increased, wondering how he could penetrate her, wanting him deep, needing him hard inside her. She leaned back again. This time it hurt, but she stilled. Waiting, letting the hurt fill her, letting the discomfort transmute to pleasure. As if in unison she pushed, he pressed and with a gasp, Alan was in. He paused again, as her body accustomed itself to the intrusion.

"All set, my love?" he asked after a few moments. "Ready for the rest of my cock?"

"Yes!" As she spoke, he grasped her shoulders with both hands. Holding her still, he drove in deep.

It hurt! It was wonderful! The pain, the joy and the thrill mingled as she let out a stream of little cries. She wanted him like this—seated deep in her forever, whenever and however. She'd do anything for him, if he'd only use her like this again. She'd obey any directive, any command, to feel this thrill, this pleasure, this sensation, his total and utter ownership of her.

"I love you! I love you, Alan! I love you!"

"I know, I know, love. Now keep still. I'm going to ream your arse until we both come!"

How could his voice drive her so wild? The promise, the threat, the utter intimacy of their connection, left her awash in desire, hormones and sexual thirst.

He started moving. Gently at first—rocking his hips to ease in and out, never passing beyond her tight muscle, keeping her stretched and filled. As he moved, he stroked her clit, bringing her closer and closer to her peak. Jane pressed back again, wanting him to fill her to the hilt.

She was moaning, gasping, shouting as her climax peaked. Alan kept up the caress as he pumped back and forth, tight and deep inside her. She reached the rim of her climax and screamed, pressing down on him harder than ever, wanting all of him, every single millimeter.

As her wild, crashing climax eased, Alan grasped her shoulders, pumping deep and fast. Jane was too wild with her own climax to notice the full force of his assault. His grunts echoed in her ears, his hands held her fast. She could not move if she cared to. Alan had her, pinioned on his erection, speared, penetrated, marked. Her body leapt again. Taking a second, even bigger climax on the fading ripples of the first. Her cries and shouts filled the room. She thought Alan came too, but she wasn't sure, couldn't be. Her mind, fogged out, caught up in the pleasure, his power, the grip of his hands on her shoulders, and the force of his cock within her, and the succession of little climaxes that shook her very soul.

Alan's hands gave up their grip. He sagged against her. She lay limp on the mattress, sweat between her breasts and a river between her legs. He stroked her hair. "I love you, Jane. You're all my dreams come true."

"Oh, Alan!"

Talking any more was beyond her. She was worn, used, buggered and blissfully content. They lay still joined for several minutes as his erection eased. When his softened cock slipped out, Jane whimpered with disappointment and satiation.

"Sleep, my love," Alan whispered, as he pulled the duvet over them. "Sleep."

She had no trouble obeying that directive.

Chapter Nine

Jane woke to morning sun streaming through the window and a cold bed. As she sat up, she noticed a bright blue dressing gown spread over the end of the bed, with a note pinned on it— *Wear this, love. Last night you earned the privilege of clothing.*

Gossamer-thin silk hardly fitted her idea of "clothing" but she wasn't complaining. She slipped her arms into the sleeves, the silk brushing her sleep-warm skin as she wrapped the gown around her like a soft cocoon.

The sun was high. Hardly surprising, the bedside-clock said eleven. She opened the door and the scent of coffee wafted from downstairs.

The kitchen was empty. The back door stood wide open, a crooked rectangle of sunlight warming the quarry tile floor. "Alan?"

"Jane!" He stepped through the doorway, silhouetted by the sun like a brazen statue in the light. "Sleep well?"

She'd forgive him the very satisfied smirk. She probably had one herself. "Very well. What about you?"

The smirk spread to his eyes. "My cock gets hard remembering your tight arsehole."

She couldn't help the blush, but she was not going to let it bother her. "I can still feel where you filled me."

"Dear Jane." He pulled her close, covering her face and eyes with kisses. "Lovely," he said into her hair. "Luscious, delicious. You smell like a well-fucked woman." He licked the side of her neck, sending a shiver right down to her cunt. "Taste like one too!"

"You had a good taste last night!"

"What about you, Jane, dearest? You all but deep-throated me!"

"Not exactly. I've never quite managed it."

His eyebrows shot up. "Do a lot of oral sex, do you?" He almost growled it out.

"Not every day, no!" He looked so indignant she had to keep back the chuckle. What did he think?! "Stop scowling, Alan. You didn't think I was a virgin, did you?"

"Your arse was."

"The rest of me wasn't. Besides, you didn't get that good at oral sex without practice." Damn! This was degenerating into a squabble.

His shrug conceded the point. "I wish I had been your first though, Jane." He sounded almost wistful.

She reached up to kiss him. Hitting his chin, she tried again and landed square on his mouth. "You don't," she said as their mouths parted. "You really, really don't. The first time I ever had sex, I tried to be nice and helpful afterwards and caught his cock in his zipper." Alan grimaced. "He recovered, married and had five children so I didn't do any lasting damage. But the very first time I sucked a cock, some time afterwards I might add, I got so nervous I bit a hole in the condom."

Alan threw his head back, his ribs shaking as he roared with laughter. "Heaven protect us! Sounds like it's time I kept you to myself and preserved the rest of mankind from injury." What exactly did that mean? The question was on the tip of her tongue but... "Bet after all that wild sex last night you're hungry?"

"Ravenous actually!"

"So'm I! I waited for you but I'm about ready to chew the tablecloth, or the nearest condom!"

Alan was never going to let her forget that one. He lifted the coffeepot off the heater. "Grab the tray with the croissants, love. I'll get the coffee and come back for the rest."

The "rest" was a plate of ham, salami and cheese, jars of apricot and gooseberry jam, marmalade and Marmite, and a great slab of golden butter.

Not a low-fat, low-carb meal, but with steaming mugs of aromatic coffee, Jane couldn't imagine anything nicer. Add the morning sunshine, Alan sitting across the small table, the birds in the trees, and the stream running beside the cottage, and it was close to idyllic.

Jane was on her second croissant and third cup of coffee, when she asked what she was dying to know. "This isn't your cottage, right? You said you borrowed it?"

"Yes. It belongs to a good friend of mine."

A kinky friend obviously. "It's lovely but not your average weekend cottage for rent."

Alan grinned. "I've know John for years. Went to school with his younger brother. He and his wife lived in town but used to come here a lot. She died a little over two years ago. He seldom comes anymore, but he can't bear to sell it. So he lends it out to a few trusted friends."

First "a friend", then a "few" of them, and they were all into whips and chains, she presumed. She had been missing something all these years! "When you see him next, tell him thank you from me."

"If you like, you can tell him yourself."

She wasn't sure she did like, but... "When?"

"We could visit him. He lives in the west country right now. After Adele died he gave up his job in the city and moved. His family has land there, and his parents were getting on. I'd like to see how he's doing. Could you take off for a long weekend in the next few weeks?"

"I'll have to fit it between deadlines, but...yes."

"You could always scout out story ideas in the west country." She could think of a lot better things to do in Alan's company. "Jane!" He shook his head and tutted. "Thinking about sex again aren't you?"

She was not going to blush, not if she had anything to do about it, which it seemed she did not. Her face burned. Too bad. "Something wrong with that?"

"Not in the slightest, sweetheart. I love your preoccupation with sex. It matches my own."

"Does, does it?"

"Thank heaven, yes." He reached for the coffeepot and topped up her cup. "You know," he said as he refilled his own, "when I glimpsed you across the crowd in the boutique, I saw the interest in your eyes. I thought to myself, 'She looks sexy, intelligent, sensual. I wonder how she kisses and what her breasts look like.'"

"Oh! Really? Took you a while to see them."

"A week! I have operated faster, but I didn't want to scare you off. I sensed then that you were what I was looking for."

"What were you looking for?"

"An intelligent, beautiful woman, who liked sex, and above all, liked my sort of sex. You do, don't you?"

With a mouth full of coffee, Jane nodded as she swallowed. "Yes, Alan, against all my better judgment, I do."

"I'm so damn glad!" He reached across the table and brought her free hand to his mouth, kissing the tip of each finger, before turning her hand over, kissing her palm and closing her fingers over his kiss. "I love you, Jane."

Before, she'd treated that declaration as seduction talk but in the bright of morning, she sensed the words came from his heart. How to reply? She still hardly knew him. "Oh, Alan!"

"Alright then. What do you want to do today?"

"I thought I was following orders?"

"That's right, you did agree to obey me, didn't you? Good. Fetch your dress from the hall cupboard, get a quick shower, and meet me in the car in thirty minutes. We're going out. There's an antique show near Horsham I want to see."

Chapter Ten

After the show they wandered around antique shops and drove on to another, smaller show, somewhere deeper into Sussex. It wouldn't have been Jane's choice for a prelude to, or aftermath of, wild sex, but being close to Alan brought its own contentment. Wandering from room to room and shop to shop, looking at jewelry and old china while Alan prowled and poked at Georgian silver and old children's books, convinced Jane spending time with Alan was infinitely more interesting than mooching around on her own.

Alan Branis could definitely become a habit. A very good habit—that is if she wasn't already addicted to him. Just catching his eye across the room had her thinking of nakedness and sex, and a glimpse of his smile got her damp between her thighs. She was turning into a sex maniac and loving every minute of it.

Alan came up behind her as she looked into a display case of Victorian jewelry.

"Like them?" *Heck yes, but…* "Try one on?"

Why tempt herself? "I'm not buying jewelry now." She was still paying for her new bedroom furniture and last year's trip to Machu Picchu.

"They caught your eye, Jane. I can tell besides, I need to buy you a birthday present."

"Alan, my birthday was back in March."

"And I missed it! Sorry, dear. I must get you something to make up for it. Try on a couple and see if you like them."

She tried on an amethyst, an opal surrounded by tiny diamonds, and a cameo, but it was a dark garnet surrounded by seed pearls that caught her fancy.

"Get it," Alan urged. "From me, Jane. A memento of this weekend."

"You needn't worry about me forgetting!" She'd have said more but the stall-holder hovered hopefully.

"Beautiful piece," the woman said, putting a little sigh in her voice. "Really suits your hand, it does."

Alan handed over his credit card.

When Jane objected, Alan gave her a wry smile. "Remember our agreement?"

And she'd thought it was only about sex! He got his way, bought the ring and a matching pair of earrings the stall-holder produced when she realized Alan was an easy sell.

What now? Kinky sex she was perfectly happy with, but buying jewelry took it to another plane entirely. A place where Jane was not entirely sure she wanted to go.

"What's biting you?" Alan asked a while later, sitting in the garden of a village pub they'd stopped at on the way home. "Teed-off at me?"

Was she? "Not teed-off really. More...off-kilter."

He thought about that a moment or two. "Because I bought you a ring and a pair of ear studs?"

"Maybe because of all the loaded connotations that go with a gift that expensive."

Alan tilted his beer to his mouth and drank. Obviously giving himself time to come up with a good reply. "Am I rushing you?"

"Yes!" That was easy but the ensuing silence was anything but easy. She sensed his hurt and confusion because they mirrored her own. "Alan," she began, "I didn't mean that quite the way it came out."

"Jane," he said, reaching over to squeeze her had. "Sorry, love. At my age I should handle things better."

"You're not exactly in your dotage, you know!"

"I'm seven years older than you, Jane. And I know what I want. Have for years. It just took me this long to find you. I suppose I'm stone-cold scared I'll lose you."

It was her turn to squeeze hands, meshing their fingers. Had she ever seen a man so vulnerable? Alan, the dominant lover, admitting he was scared of losing her. "Alan, I have to be honest. I'm scared witless too."

"Of me?" His eyes widened and he shook his head. "Don't be! I'll never harm you. Ever. Jane, I wouldn't!"

"I know that, Alan. What terrifies me is how you make me feel—incredibly sexy, helpless and powerful. It's a rather heady mix. One I've never tasted before."

"One you want to taste again?"

"Oh, yes." Her innards clenched at the admission, but she could no more lie than tell the nice family at the next table that she was sitting there without knickers.

Relief shone in his eyes. Shock, tenderness and an illicit sense of her power over Alan, all jostled in her mind.

He leaned over the table and kissed her, much to the amusement of the three children at the next table. "Jane, let's make a pact, I'll make no secret of what I want—you permanently in my life. I'll settle for what you are comfortable with, weekends, evenings together. Maybe, if I'm extraordinarily fortunate, a week away somewhere. We'll go at your speed, Jane. No faster than you want to." He paused and grinned. "They always say the submissive holds the real power in our sort of relationship..." He let out a slow breath. "Never realized how damn true that is."

Now she was more confused than ever. Or was she? He'd been clear enough. She knew exactly what he wanted. All she had to do was decide what she wanted.

"I love you, too, Alan. It's just I'm sometimes scared of what you make me feel."

"What do you want?"

Time to put her heart and mind to the sticking point. "I want to go home with you and take my clothes off."

His entire face lightened. "And, Jane, what then?"

"Whatever you want?"

"I want to tie you hand and foot to my bed. Do you consent?" Her breath caught. Trying hard to still the wild excitement rising in her gut, Jane nodded. "I can't hear you, my love."

She swallowed. "I consent."

He stroked the back of her hand, tiny circles that stimulated nerve endings in other parts. "You'll be helpless, only the safeword will deliver you from what I have in store for you this evening."

It was only a little caress, but stirred memories of other touches, other demands. "I know."

"You'll submit and accept my dominance."

Dear heavens! She was going wet at the lightest of touches and his voice alone. Much more and she'd be reaching over the table and ripping his shirt off. "With pleasure!"

Alan nodded, his wide mouth curling at the corners. "I'll hold you to every word of that, Jane. Every single word." He pushed her half-empty glass towards her. "Drink up." She drank down the last of the G-and-T as he stood up. "Let's go then, Jane."

On the drive back, Jane had ample time to change her mind. She never considered it. She was too keyed up, too horny and too ready to do anything to sustain the wild arousal overtaking her senses. She hadn't needed that gin. She was already drunk on Alan Branis—a sweet intoxication with no risk of hangover.

It was dusk by the time they drove up the lane to the cottage. The windows were dark and the evening air sent a chill up her bare legs to her pussy as they walked, hand in hand, up to the front door. "The house should be warm enough," Alan said as he held the door open. "If you're chilly, you may keep your dress on but I trust you to remove it the minute you're comfortable, temperature-wise that is," he added with a smile. "A little discomfort with nudity is fine. It stretches you."

"Stretches" was not the verb she'd have used, but did it really matter? "What do you want me to do?"

"Watch a video with me."

It couldn't be that easy, but she walked into the comfortable lounge and curled up on the sofa. Alan followed in a few minutes with two mugs of tea. It was warm, wet, and very welcome.

She almost spluttered it all over the place when Alan handed her three videos. None of them were likely to be Oscar contenders: *The Story of O*; *Naughty, Dirty Schoolgirls*; and *Desires of the Flesh*.

"A hard choice?" Alan asked sitting beside her.

"Sort of. I'm not sure whether to go with one I've seen or pick the one I haven't."

His face was worth a photo. Nice to know he wasn't immune to surprise. "Which ones have you seen?" He actually put a snip in the question.

Jane managed to hold back most of her smile. "The schoolgirl one looks a bit yucky. Why not stick with *The Story of O*? I've seen that before." She wasn't about to admit exactly how many times she'd watched it, or how she'd recently replaced her jerky-around-the-edges, much used video. Not yet anyway. She curled up on the sofa beside Alan as the intro music began. "Jane, love," Alan whispered in her ear, "I want you to sit on the floor, at my feet."

Second time she nearly spluttered tea. "Now?"

"Yes. I'll hold your mug until you get settled. Take a cushion with you if you like. I want you comfortable."

He also wanted her between his thighs. Once settled, it was comforting to be enclosed by his legs and rest her head on his strong thigh. Arousing and stimulating too, surrounded by his body and male presence, and his cock just inches from her face. Jane settled against her lover to watch a video that turned her on, at the same time wondering exactly what Alan had in mind. Once upon a time, O had been a wild fantasy. Now it touched on what he professed to want from her.

"Alan?" she began as she watched O chained in the dungeon at Roissy and beaten by the valet, "Is that what…"

"Good Lord, no, Jane!" he replied, stroking her head. "This is fiction. I'd never abandon you in Roissy—if such a place ever existed. Let's stick with reality. The reality of my hands and your body." She yearned for that reality. She wanted his hands on her, touching, caressing. "Remember my promise," Alan said, "to tie you hand and foot. Do you still agree?"

"Yes."

"Strip, then. You should be warm by now."

Her arms shook as she stood and pulled her dress over her head, giving it to Alan as he held out his hand. "Walk across the room, then turn around and come back towards me."

That she managed, holding her head high and her spine straight to counteract the urge to slump her shoulders and hide.

Alan stood up and reached out to palm her breast. "Lovely, Jane, but I think you'd look even better in a corset. I'll buy one the next time we're in town together." Alan wasn't asking if she wanted a corset. He was telling. Her mouth went dry as her heart raced. "You like the idea of being laced tightly. Don't you, Jane?"

Why lie? "I find it exciting."

"So do I. I think we'll get a dark blue leather one. It will suit your fair skin." He paused, as if considering the thought of her laced into dark blue leather, before barking at her, "Bend over and touch your toes."

Her hesitation earned a slap on her rump, not enough to hurt, but enough to have her bend over at once, head inches from the carpet. What now? More spanking? She was utterly exposed. He'd promised bondage, not spanking but… Jane took a deep breath and waited as Alan gently stroked her arse. "Yes, love, a nice leather corset to nip in your waist and expose your luscious arse." His fingers trailed down her crack. "Want to get fucked here again?"

"Yes, but not tonight, please." She wanted him in her cunt. She needed a slow, deep fuck and by the look of things, he was going to make her wait for it.

"Since you asked so nicely, we'll save that repeat pleasure for next time. Stand up." She managed that without too much wobbling. "Come upstairs." Alan held out his hand. "Time for you to learn the joys of helplessness." He led the way. Jane watched as she followed him up the narrow, twisting stairway, admiring his broad shoulders and tight bum. But Alan was a so much more than very nice bod or an innovative lover. He was...

"Jane," he paused on the top step. "Sure you want to do this? You can back out. We can go out and have dinner down at the Seven Bells, and no hard feelings?"

"Alan, I'm naked. I'm wired up. You'd better not even be considering letting me down having brought me to this point!"

"I'll be tying you down, Jane. Not letting you down." Her cunt clenched at his words. "Just want to be sure you agree. Complete obedience. Utter submission. You may use your safeword, but other than that, once you cross that threshold, you are mine to do whatever I want with. Agreed?"

She swallowed, looking into his dark eyes. "Yes." He grabbed her by the waist, swung her off her feet, tossing her over his shoulder and strode through the open doorway. "Hey, Alan!" Her wriggles earned her another slap on her rump. This one stung.

"Keep still or you'll get more!" Alright for him to say. He wasn't bent over, blood rushing to his head and his hair falling over his face and obscuring what little of the carpet was visible.

He crossed the room and deposited her, quite gently she had to admit, in the easy chair between the two windows. Brushing the hair from her face and kissing her before he drew the curtains to shut out the evening. "Sit there, Jane, and watch while I get things ready. If you have any pertinent questions about what I'm doing, ask. I'll explain what things are for. If you don't understand anything, I expect you to ask. Is that straight?"

"Yes." She hoped.

Without another word, he turned his back on her and walked out the door. *Smashing! What next?*

Chapter Eleven

Alan was back in moments, naked except for silk boxers —
midnight blue ones this time. Hands full of a startling
assortment of straps, scarves, a black leather whip and what
looked like a bundle of red fur. He deposited the lot on the bed.
Sorted though them without as much as a glance her way, and
then turned to her, something dark and soft-looking in his hand
and long ribbons trailing the ground as he came towards her.
"Hold out your hand."

Jane hesitated only a second or two before obeying. Alan
wrapped the black velvet band around her wrist, fastening it
securely with a snap of Velcro that sent her pussy tingling.
Without being told, Jane held out her other arm. "Nice," he said.
"You are very amenable. Good." His approval sent a warm flash
across her face. "Now your ankles."

As he knelt at her feet, the excitement deep inside her
stirred and swelled. Jane looked down at the crown of his head,
and the curve of his broad shoulders. Alan's fingers, warm and
confident, closed around her ankle. He bent his head and kissed
the soft spot beneath her anklebone, before wrapping the velvet
strap tight around her ankle. She was close to shaking as she
offered her last, unbound limb.

"Enjoying this?" Alan asked as he stood. She now looked
up at him. "Scared? Excited? Getting wet between your legs?"

"All of them." She'd ignore the little tremor in her voice. It
echoed the flutter in her stomach.

"Perfect. Know what these straps are for?" He gathered up
the loose ribbons hanging from her wrists

"To tie me down on the bed."

"Definitely, Jane. You'll be helpless, held down by velvet and ribbons, while I do whatever I want to you. You won't even have to obey. You'll be utterly at my mercy."

One look at his eyes showed exactly how that prospect pleased. Jane swallowed. "I know." Where did that come from? Somewhere deep inside where her libido and needs roiled and swirled. Why didn't he just get on with it and tie her down?

Because stringing her out like this was his notion of fun.

He patted her on the head, as if she'd been a good, obedient child and turned back to the bed, standing at an angle that gave her full view of his hands and the collection on the bed.

Without looking back at her, he picked up a whip. No, a whip and a flogger and they were as different as night and day. One was bright red. The tresses looked like fur, or at least a good faux. The other, the one that dangled from his right hand, was unmistakably leather—shiny, hard, black leather, with one long tail that trailed the carpet. The nice, friendly, bunny fur one, he dropped on the bed. Holding the not-in-the-least-friendly-looking one, Alan stepped sideways towards the middle of the room. Keeping his back to her, he raised his right arm and brought it down in a smooth movement, slapping the tail against the bedpost.

The sound went straight to her pussy. Jane let out a long, slow moan, the echo hanging in the low-ceilinged room

Alan glanced over his shoulder and raised his eyebrow. "Enjoy that?"

"I don't know!"

"I think you did."

He turned his back to her and slapped the whip onto the floor. It was a different sound—more muffled, longer and it left marks in the carpet. Jane was whimpering as his bare foot smoothed over the ridges in the pile.

This time he grinned, cracked the whip one more time and dropped it on the floor beside the bed.

She'd taken more deep breaths in the past fifteen minutes than she normally did in a day. What next?

He picked up something else from the heap on the bed and came towards her. "Know what these are, Jane?" He opened his hand. Two dewdrop pearls, each on an inch or so of chain lay curled in his palm.

"Earrings?" Obviously not, no clips or posts but what the hell were they?

"Wrong!" He sounded like the headmaster of her prep school, who used to scare the willies out of her. Not that Mr. Evans ever made her feel sexy.

"What are they, then?"

"Nipple rings, Jane. To adorn your luscious tits." He opened her hand and dropped them in her palm.

She could not stop staring. Seeing them up close, she noticed a tiny ring at the end of each gold chain. She'd read about nipple piercings. The thought did *not* turn her on. She was half-ready to say the damn safeword, grab her dress and run. "How do you put them on? You're not piercing my nipples!"

"Don't worry, Jane. I certainly won't, not today. Let me show you how these go on."

Alan took her left nipple between his thumb and forefinger and gently pulled. It was already hard with need and his touch firmed it up completely. He took one pearl from her outstretched hand, neatly hooked the circle over her upstanding nipple and gently adjusted a little spring on the ring. "Does that hurt?"

"No."

"Sure? You're not being brave or noble on me are you?"

She grinned. "I'm feeling neither brave nor noble right now. You've got me pretty stirred up, but no, it does not hurt."

"It would if I tightened it." She held her breath. "But I'm not going to. This time. I want you to get accustomed to the idea of the weight. Another time, I'll use tit clamps. They are tight.

They cut off the circulation so your nipples go numb. When I pull them off, the returning blood will feel like massive pins and needles. The sensation may well send you into a climax."

She'd take his word for it!

While he talked, he'd attached the second one without her noticing. The weight pulled her nipples. It didn't hurt, just felt odd. He tapped the pearls and the gentle swinging made her catch her breath.

"Sure they don't hurt?"

"It's not hurt exactly, it's…" What the hell was it?

"A novel sensation?"

She'd remember that. No doubt the phrase would prove useful in the coming months. Her thoughts snagged a moment. She was thinking months! Heck! Alan had her snagged and tied! She giggled.

"Alright?" He sounded, and looked, worried.

"Yes. What's next?"

"Eager, my dear?" He all but smirked at her.

"Curious, shall we say?"

"You know what curiosity did to the proverbial cat?"

"I'm not a cat!" Only with her nasty cousin Muriel, and…

She didn't bother to remember who else. Alan was on his knees between her thighs and had two fingers up her cunt. Jane leaned back in the chair, spread her legs wider and closed her eyes.

He pulled out, just when she was beginning to need a nice stroke to her clit.

"Open your eyes." She watched as he sniffed his fingers and put the tip of one in his mouth and sucked. "Essence of Jane." He leaned towards her. "Taste!" She took his outstretched finger in her mouth and brushed the tip of her tongue over his finger. It was more texture than taste—an odd, unfamiliar sweetness. "Like it?" He withdrew his finger.

"I'm not sure." What did he expect her to say?

"I'll make you sure before long, Jane. You'll learn to love your taste—just as I do. By the time we go to sleep tonight, you and I will know your body inside and out. You'll go to sleep, dreaming of my cock inside you."

If he kept this up, she'd be begging long before he got that far. "Alan?"

"Where do you want it first?" he asked standing up, but keeping a hand on her shoulder so she remained seated and looking up at him. Since his cock tented his boxers, she couldn't help licking her lips. Funny how her mouth went dry as her cunt flowed.

"Where?" he repeated.

"My mouth." Her throat closed up, goose bumps raced down her spin and she shivered.

"On your knees, Jane."

The carpet brushed her knees. She barely noticed. Couldn't think of anything but the wondrous cock waiting. For her. Jane reached up towards the fly, but he caught the ribbon hanging from her wrist and yanked her arm up. "No hands, Jane. If you want my cock as much as you claim, put your hands behind your back. Let's see how much you want to suck me."

Playing games wasn't in it. This was torture! But if he thought she couldn't manage, he was in for a surprise. Quite a nice one in fact! She eyed the dark silk that so tauntingly concealed his cock, and brought her mouth down to the lowest point. Couldn't be that hard to ease her tongue inside the fly and latch on to him. That was a misapprehension. Her tongue soon discovered the row of tiny buttons fastening the placket. Smarty-pants, was he? She worked her mouth up and down his bulge, molding her lips around his erection. If he was playing games, she'd do the same. The quiver in his thigh pretty much told her she'd succeeded. He was as needy as she. Just seemed he was stronger willed.

She gazed up and down, from the loose hems brushing his strong thighs, to the gathered waistband that hung just below his navel. Gathered with elastic. Bingo, Alan Branis! Stretching her neck, she leaned forward and fastened her teeth on the elastic. Gritting her jaws together, she pulled back and down. Hard. The elastic came with her, and surprise—success! His stalwart erection popped out, just as her jaws lost their hold and the elastic snapped back.

He yelped. Forgetting the prohibition, Jane grabbed the elastic with both hands and yanked the boxers down. "Sorry, that wasn't intended!"

"That I'll believe! Don't think you wanted to put me out of action, did you?"

"Let me kiss it better!"

Taking the roar of laughter as consent, she swallowed him. Her lips caressing every millimeter of his glorious length as her tongue curved along the hard shaft.

Alan grasped her head with both hands and took over, sliding her back and forth, controlling her completely. Easing her forwards, so his cock entered deep. Pulling her back, so he slid over her tongue to-and-fro through the soft circle of her lips.

Shivers of excitement rippled through Jane. She wanted to do this forever. To kneel here until dawn. For him to work himself within her mouth for hours. She clasped his thighs with her arms and pulled him closer.

He went still, his cock almost touching the back of her throat. "No hands, Jane, let go."

"Sorry, I forgot!" His erection muffled her words, as she joined her hands behind her back and he resumed, his hands tunneling through her hair and cupping the back of her head. She was hotter than ever, needing more. Little sighs, silenced by his cock, grew into moans and her body took up the rhythm, rocking as he moved her head.

He stopped and withdrew. Cries of loss, disappointment and frustration echoed in the room. "Alan!"

"That's enough for now, dear. You and I have to last a lot longer." His hands grasped her upper arms, lifting her to her feet. As she steadied herself, he flicked both pearls and watched them swing. The sensation wasn't unpleasant. Just…odd, and echoed across her body.

"Very nice," Alan said, watching her face. "Get on your hands and knees!"

"What?"

"You heard me, Jane. I'm not repeating it."

She had heard, yes, but hearing and understanding were two very different things. It took her a long minute to actually process his order. She was down on all fours in seconds, ribbons flying behind her, one caught under her knee. She shifted to release it.

"Don't move!"

She froze, trying to stay calm, while wondering what on earth he had in mind. Not much it seemed. At least at first. Alan stepped away and slowly circled her, his bare feet not making a sound. She moved her head to watch his feet, and got a gentle swat on her arse.

"I told you not to move, Jane! Keep your head down. Move again and I'll blindfold you."

How would that feel, in the dark, unable to see anything? Uncertain, a little scared. Not all that different from how she felt right now! But at least she could watch him from the corners of her eyes. He'd moved towards the bed. For one of the whips? Something else?

Something caressed her thighs. She could no more have held back the long, sigh than flown. It was the furry flogger, and it was incredible. Back again, he brought it. Jane arched her shoulders as the tresses kissed her skin.

"Keep still!"

He'd whisked the flogger away. She froze. "It's damn hard to keep still!"

"I know." She could hear the smile in his voice. "You must try harder, Jane. Much harder. Apply yourself!"

Easy for him to say. Damn difficult to do when he flicked the tresses back and forth between her open thighs. The end of one tress caught her clit and her hips tightened. "Sorry! When you touch me there I can't help it!"

"You'll learn to," he replied, reaching under her with the flogger and flicking the ends to hit her breasts with a slap of soft fur. Her neck and shoulders reared up as the thrill coursed through her. "Jane, love," he spoke gently, stroking her back. "This won't do, dearest. When I say don't move, I mean it."

"You're deliberately touching my sensitive spots."

"I'll just have to help you." He reached for the ribbons hanging from her wrists. "You leave me with only one option." He tugged on them until she was kneeling up. "I'll have to tie you down." There was nothing rational about the cold thrill of excitement surging deep in her pussy. No sane reason whatsoever, but sensation burst like hope between her legs. "You do understand the necessity, don't you, Jane?"

This was a game, a wild sexual play, and she was caught up in his voice, his presence and the promise of restraint. Her throat was so tight she had to moisten her tongue and lips to reply. "Yes, Alan. I understand." Dread and arousal mingled deep in her being as she looked up at him—at the heat in his eyes, the slight curl at the corner of his wide mouth and the strong hand that held the two ribbons twisted round his fist.

She didn't understand a thing—except that she wanted whatever was coming.

"Good." He put his free hand under her elbow. "Stand up and walk over to the bed." It was just four steps across the thick pile carpet. Her heart skipped and her pussy throbbed each time she set her foot down. Alan followed close, the ribbons still tight. Her knees brushed the foot of the bed. His knees pressed her thighs just above her knees. "What do you see on the bed?" he asked.

"Pillows and a bottom sheet." The rest of the bedclothes lay in a heap to one side.

His free hand reached forward and swished the nasty-looking whip. The mattress bounced as leather hit the bed. Jane swallowed, unable to take her eyes off the nasty-looking tail. This one was definitely not soft bunny fur. "What do you see on the bed?" he repeated.

Deep breath. Two deep breaths. "The butt plug from last night, a silk scarf and a feather duster." It couldn't be a duster — it had to have another name, but...

"Not a duster, Jane, but I'll accept that answer. Now..." He nudged her behind one knee. "Climb on the bed, crawl up to the head, and lie down on your back."

Sounded easy enough, but the mattress gave under her weight, the movement sending the pearls swinging and pulling at her nipples. They must have tugged her nipples before, but she'd been too wound up with his touch and the caress of the whip to notice.

Turning onto her back swung the pearls harder.

"Alright?" Alan asked at once. She hadn't realized he'd been watching her that closely and saw her wince.

"They pull when I move."

"They hurt?"

Truth needed here. "Not hurt exactly but they're bothersome."

"Want them off?"

He was asking? Yes. Now she had to decide. "Please."

"Alright love, let's make a switch. I take them off and put on a blindfold instead."

She looked sideways at the silk scarf dangling from his hand. How would it feel to be helpless in the dark? Her pussy had a pretty clear idea! Was she nuts? She trusted Alan and that was that.

"Okay," she agreed.

Chapter Twelve

He didn't have to look quite so pleased, or did he? Gently he eased a ring off her left nipple. The other he tugged and made her wince, so he kissed it better. "They may not be the thing for you," he said. "We'll experiment and see what you like, I like, and I can teach you to like. For now, let's see how you respond to bondage."

She made herself go limp as he tied her right hand to the bed-head, leaving a little slack. She could move, but only a few inches. As she tested the limits of movement, Alan grabbed her left wrist and tied that down so her arms were spread wide. After tugging both knots, to make sure they were secure, presumably, he sat on the side of the bed, and ran his hand over her face, down her throat and over her breasts, pausing with his fingers splayed over her belly. "Feeling alright?"

Hotter than Hades! "Wondering what comes next."

His raised eyebrow, and his slow, considered, "Oh, really?" had her questioning the wisdom of her cheeky mouth. He traced slow circles over her belly. "Wondering are you, Jane? Better ease your uncertainty, hadn't I?" He moved fast to the end of the bed, and grabbed the ribbons from her ankles. In seconds, he twisted both ribbons around the posts at the foot of the bed, and tied her securely with a nice, neat knot.

"There we are!" He smiled. "You're helpless now, my love. Apart from a little leeway I was good enough to allow you to avoid cramps, you can't move, can't sit up, can't turn over, can't do anything but lie there and take whatever I choose to do with you!"

He bent over and as he stood upright, held the wicked, black leather whip.

"No!" she cried out, panic rising. "Not that!"

"Oh yes," he replied, cracking it in the air.

The sound sent her pussy flowing, the prospect made her stomach clench and the look in his eye sent a thrill of horror racing. "No!" she yelled, tugging at her wrists. He was damn right! She was helpless and he loomed over her with a whip like an evil ringmaster. She tugged again, just in case, and got the distinct impression she was tightening the knots. "Alan!"

He moved to the side of the bed, his hand stroking her face until she calmed. "It's alright, Jane, my love. It's alright. Want to use your safeword? That's what it's for."

Did she? "No." She didn't sound that sure even to herself.

"Sure, dear? You do remember your safeword?"

"Yes. Jane Winston."

"Good, Jane," He brushed his lips over her cheek. "I promise not to harm you. You don't like my heavy whip do you?"

"No, I don't."

"I'm not going to hurt you, Jane, but you are going to feel it on your skin."

She'd not thought it possible to go cold and hot at the same time. She'd been dead wrong. Jane shuddered as sweat broke out over her face.

"You worry too much, dear," Alan wiped off her face with a hand towel from the bedside table, "You will learn to trust me and accept what I want. There's no need to think, worry or try to second-guess what I'll do. All you have to do is submit."

Maybe it was his gentle voice, the touch of his hand on her face or the sheer proximity of male chest, male voice, male scent and male strength, but she nodded. Hell! She even smiled at him, meeting his eyes as she forced her body to relax, accept and wait.

His right arm moved. Seeing the heavy black handle in his hand, she bit back her protest and waited, willing the desire to overcome the fear and mounting dread.

Alan wound the black leather tails over his hand, so a large loop of plaited leather curled from one side of his closed fist to the other. "Steady, Jane," he said as stroked the leather over each breast and down her belly.

She shut her eyes, to better lose herself in the strange and unfamiliar caress. If this was all he was going to do, she'd have no complaints! Over her belly he stroked, brushing the tops of her thighs, down to her bound ankles, and up along the inside of her legs, pressing the leather into the cleft of her pussy lips, before easing down the other thigh to her ankle.

"Like that?"

"Yes!" she exhaled, unaware she'd held her breath.

"So, Jane, you like the nasty, scary whip, do you? Like the feel of the hard, plaited leather against your tender skin?"

"Yes, I do!" And what's more, wanted more of it. She was nuts but didn't care. She just needed more.

"Good! I knew you'd see reason." He stood up, uncoiled the whip and cracked it in the air.

He stifled her shriek with his mouth. Pressing his lips on hers until she calmed. "Hush, love," he whispered into her mouth. "You've got to get used to this. It's one of my favorite toys. I love the sound of it."

"I don't!"

He lifted his mouth away, but kept his chest pressed into hers, pinning her down. "Whether you like it or not, has nothing to do with it, Jane. I like it and you will learn to like it. I'm going to get you used to it and there's nothing you can do about it."

His last few words seemed to rattle in her mind. How right he was! She could do nothing. Nothing at all. A sweet shudder of anticipation rippled from her shoulders to her hips. Jane looked up at Alan's dark eyes and sighed.

"Brace yourself, Jane!" The mattress dipped to one side as he stood on the bed, and then stepped astride her. His strong legs seemed to go up forever. At this angle, he seemed bigger, more powerful and far, far sexier than ever. She inhaled deeply and caught the scent of aroused male.

"Ready, Jane?" What the hell for? She knew enough not to say it aloud, but as if he'd read her thoughts, he replied. "This!" and raised the whip.

She should be terrified, fighting the bonds, yelling the dratted safeword or...waiting with shallow breathing as he raised his right arm, lifting the nasty tail off the bed. Was this how a mouse felt when faced with a snake, or a small creature caught in an owl's claws? The oddest calm enveloped her as the tail rose higher and with a flick of his wrist, it came down, the knotted tip resting between her breasts.

She took a deep breath and exhaled very, very slowly.

The tip of the whip circled each nipple, before tracing the rise and curve of each breast, ending in a neat figure eight before trailing down her sternum. Stimulating her belly, in a slow, precise, spiral that finished with the knotted tip in her naval.

Alan!" she gasped as a swift adjustment of his wrist brought the tip to the topmost point of her slit.

"Like it?"

"Yes!"

He threw back his head and laughed, the shaking of his body, shifting the knot lower. Jane tilted her hips to move it just that little bit lower so it brushed her clit, and damn him, he whisked it away.

"Jane, Jane, Jane," he tutted, shaking his head. "Good little submissives don't try to get what they want. They wait until it's given to them."

Maybe, but she wasn't feeling like a good little submissive. Horny woman was a hell of a lot more accurate. Jane shut her eyes, took another deep breath and willed herself to be patient.

"Like the dark do you, dear? That's right, you agreed to blindfolding, didn't you?"

Obviously a rhetorical question. Alan jumped off the bed, grabbed a scarf and in moments, a double band of purple silk blocked out most of Jane's vision. Fringes of light seeped around the edges of the blindfold, but that was it. She wasn't just in bondage, she was blind to the world, unable to even guess what was coming next.

Warm oil in a thin stream ran between her breasts and down her rib cage. Alan's strong hands smoothing it over her breasts and across her belly. She sensed he was between her legs. A thigh nudged hers, or was it a knee? And a soft flutter of silk brushed her skin. More shifting as Alan moved on the bed. He breathed on her skin and it heated up, warmed wherever his breath touched—across her belly, over her breasts, around her nipples and slowly but certainly down over her navel, to the top of her pussy.

He had her sighing and moaning, fighting to keep herself from arching her hips to meet his mouth. "Like that do you?"

"Wonderful."

"Want more?"

Jane paused, suspecting a trick question. "I want whatever you will give me."

"Good."

The mattress tipped to one side, but Alan was still between her legs. He'd reached for something perhaps? His fingers parted her pussy. Jane sighed in anticipation of his kiss, relaxing on the pillow as he held her pussy lips open and shoved something cold and hard deep in her cunt. It was the red glass dildo.

Her gasp gave way to little sighs of delight as he worked the cold glass back and forth, as his thumb put gentle pressure on her clit. She was ready to go into orbit. Her hips rocked in the rhythm of his thrusts, her senses concentrating on the depths in her body and the hard intrusion that filled her with joy. She wanted Alan fucking her, yes, but this was different—glass hard and cold, but slowly warming with the friction of her body.

"Good, Jane, my sweet horny love. Go, go, take it all!" With this permission, she rocked faster now, shifting her hips and using the slack in her arms to arch her back. It was tremendous, wonderful! Her sighs came faster and louder as her arousal peaked. Alan's hand descended warm and flat on her belly, holding her to the bed. As swiftly as he'd inserted it, he withdrew the dildo, leaving her empty, bereft and aching with unfulfilled need.

"Alan!" she yelled but didn't care, "Why did you stop?!"

"Because it's not time for you to come yet. There's more."

His shoulders brushed her thighs, pushing her legs farther apart. He held her wide open, his warm breath brushed her cunt lips. She was gritting her teeth, clenching her fists, anticipating, longing for the supreme kiss that never came. "Please," she begged, "Alan, please!"

"Please what, Jane?"

"Kiss me!"

"Okay."

He dropped a soft kiss on the inside of her thigh. "That's not what I want!" His hand closed over her thigh. What now? Damn the blindfold and the wretched restraints! She yanked her arms and grunted.

"Jane, relax. You'll get what you want but only if you settle down. You'll get nothing if you carry on like this."

She bit back the recommendation that he go to hell. She wanted more, needed more, was hurting deep inside and Alan was the only one who could ease her raging desire. With a whimper she made her body calm, forced her hips to settle on the bed, let her arms go limp against the restraints and waited. Listening to her heartbeat and the sound of her own breathing.

How long she waited, she'd never know—thirty seconds, a minute, ten... She just lay there, trusting Alan not to leave her like this, knowing he'd promised her satisfaction. Another deep breath, and something warm and soft wafted over her right arm. Another silk scarf? The furry flogger? It was too light for the fur. Again it came, down her left arm, over her breast, up and down the inside of one leg, then the other. Whatever it was, it was marvelous, stimulating her skin and triggering gentle sensation. So different from the oil and the after-warmth, less intense than the whip, but nonetheless rekindling her arousal. Each touch making it harder and harder to stay still until she let her body rock with the sweet touch.

He stopped, again. She bit back the protest, pulling her muscles tight as she made herself lie there and wait.

"Brilliant, Jane! Absolutely bloody brilliant! You can do it! You're magnificent. Keep that control and you'll get your reward!"

His praise worked more like an aphrodisiac than a calmant, but what matter! Soon he'd give her what she wanted. Hell! What they both wanted. He had to be as aroused as she.

Damn he was! His erection brushed her belly as his mouth closed over her breast. The sigh wasn't hers. The next was though. His tongue teased her nipple as his breath reheated the remaining oil.

"Oh! Alan," she murmured, "you're wonderful!"

"Flattery will get you everything, my love, even a nice hard fuck!"

"Please!" At that promise, her hips rocked, pressing her belly into his erection. Hard! The man was like rock! Perhaps it hadn't been the dildo after all. Except Alan's cock was never that cold.

"You're such a nice-mannered submissive, Jane."

Damn! He moved again. Why now?

With a gasp, she knew why. His mouth closed on her clit and this time she did leave the bed. Only his hands on her hips held her still. It was glorious, wonderful, incredible! His tongue darting and flicking drove her higher and higher. She wanted him inside, but she'd not complain about climaxing like this. Her back arched. A succession of grunts and moans eased from deep in her lungs until he lifted his mouth off. "Not yet."

"Alan, I'm ready. I'm on the point of coming!"

"Jane, you're not ready. You need more. Trust me."

"Alan, I want your cock in me! Hard!" She was all but shouting and didn't give a damn. This was torture!

He pulled the blindfold off. As she blinked in the light, he loomed over her. "Jane, let's get this straight. I decide when you're ready and I say you're not!"

The wail seemed driven by the throb in her clit and the ache in her cunt, but he didn't budge a millimeter. "I can see, Jane, I'm going to have to teach you patience. For that noise, you're going to wait even longer."

"That's not fair!"

"Who said anything about fair? You accept, just as right now, you suck my cock." Alan shifted forward on his knees, straddling her chest and pulled his cock from the dark silk. Her tongue licking her lips was pure reflex. "Open wide!"

She needed no second bidding. Lifting her head, she took him deep. His hands supporting her neck as her lips and tongue worked him. Lying there, bound and helpless, with her lover's cock seated deep between her lips, her body sang, her cunt flowed and the deep thrill in her clit flared throughout her belly. She held Alan's cock between her lips, his power and strength against her tongue and she was his, utterly and completely his.

"Enough, Jane. Can't have you coming just yet."

She really didn't see why not, but wisely kept that to herself. At least she could see him now, but that stirred her need even more. She looked at up him, feasting her eyes on his face, his wicked smile and the beauty of his body, not forgetting the magnificent cock that stood proud and hard. She longed to reach out, and curl her hand over hard flesh, and smooth her fingers through the curls at his groin but she was tied secure and helpless. That thought sent her senses into overdrive. "I love you, Alan! I love you!"

"I love you too, Jane, but you still have to wait."

"I need you!" Damn him! Couldn't he see that?

"I know you do, dear, but it'll do you good to wait. I'll let you know when I decide you're ready." Two fingers thrust deep in her cunt. If he didn't see she was ready, he was barking! No, he was driving her wild.

She tossed from side to side on the pillow as his fingers pumped her. As her need rose once again. His thumb brushed her clit and she let out a slow sigh. "Yes," she whispered as his fingers continued their rhythm, easing her up the peak of her desire. His sweet stimulation drove her higher and higher until it all came together—her body and her mind linked with her need and she was reaching, ready to... "Damn, you!"

He pulled out yet again. Jane cussed and swore and the only thing that stopped her spitting was his hand on her mouth.

"Do I have to gag you, love?"

She sobbed into his hand unable to form the words, incapable of thought. Every nerve ending hurt. Her entire body was primed to climax and he denied her.

Alan wiped the tears from her eyes. "Wonderful and mine. You know that, don't you, Jane? You're mine, my captive, my love prisoner, my submissive, my sex toy. Everything I have and need is here in bed with me."

She was not in the mood for sweet talk. She needed a good frigging!

"I know, darling." His kiss was slow, deep and gentle. "Now, Jane..." He stood up beside the bed. If he was walking out on her, she'd... He wasn't! In seconds, he stripped off his boxers and was back between her legs, kneeling between her thighs, lifting her hips and driving into her with force and love.

Her sigh was a slow keening as he eased his cock deep into her cunt. "This what you want, Jane?"

"Yes! Yes! Yes!" As he drove in deep, pumping with all his strength, her cries echoed off the low ceiling. Jane lost track of place and time. She arched her back, wanting to take all of him

165

into her cunt. She wanted his heart, his soul, his mind, all of them penetrating her, spilling power into her, driving his love deep into her soul and his will into her mind.

She was shouting, screaming her love. The power between them mounted and peaked. His thrusts deepened and increased. Alan grunted once, twice, three times. Jane screamed as her orgasm burst, shattering into shards of pure ecstasy and joy.

His climax broke seconds after hers, yanking her sated mind and body even higher, until she collapsed into a sweaty heap of happy woman, with the weight of her powerful lover pressing her into the rumpled bed.

"That was incredible," Jane croaked, her throat sore and her mind almost too fuddled to shape words.

"We are," Alan agreed, rolling off her. "Hold on." He reached up and released her hands.

Jane promptly wrapped her arms around him. "Alan," she rasped, her voice still hoarse, "I love you so."

"Love you too, Jane. Hope this helps convince you."

"I'm convinced." She had just enough strength left to smile.

"Just a tick." He kissed her and brushed her hair off her face, before getting off the bed and releasing her ankles, ripping open the Velcro so she could move—if she could summon the strength. Spreading the duvet over her, he climbed back in beside her.

"You're mine, Jane," he said. "Never forget that."

She doubted she'd ever have the inclination to.

Jane woke alone. As she watched, the bedside clock flicked over to 11:53. Almost noon.

She sat up, still feeling utterly relaxed, her cunt still echoing the last ripples of that incredible climax. Or rather climaxes.

Alan might be a bossy so and so, but darn, he'd been right about waiting intensifying pleasure. She didn't want—at least not right now—to think about how she'd enjoyed being tied up and teased mercilessly. She'd found the lover of her dreams and he wanted her around. Permanently. That would take some considering.

The same blue silk dressing gown lay across the foot of the bed. Jane pulled it on and padded down to the bathroom. Alan was singing downstairs.

"Morning, Alan!" she called down the stairs.

"Morning, sweet fuck!" he called back. "Sleep well?"

Cheeky bugger! Not that he wasn't entitled to be proud of his prowess. It had been a very sweet fuck. "Not bad at all!"

"I'm making a fresh pot of tea. Want to get a shower while I put the kettle on?"

Darn good idea. "Be down there in a couple of ticks."

It took her a little longer than that. The water was so warm, the floral shower gel too darn sybaritic and the matching body lotion Alan left out, just the crowning indulgence she needed. As she dried her hair, and put back on the robe, tightening the sash around her waist, Jane noticed the shiny white box from their shopping yesterday afternoon. She snapped open the lid and stared at the ring and ear studs nestling in the soft lining.

She fixed a stud in each ear. They were beautiful and they suited her. He'd been so right to insist on buying them. How could she not wear them? Why had she considered refusing his gift? She'd wear them now, and for as long as he wanted. The ring she hesitated over. Alan had made no secret where he wanted it worn. That she was still not ready for, so she slipped in on her right hand.

Pausing only to pick up her crumpled towels and give her hair a last smoothing, Jane crossed the landing and walked down the narrow staircase to where her lover waited.

It was only a few steps from the open doorway to where he stood by the stove. She crossed the distance and knelt at his feet. "Alan Branis, I..." she hesitated. Did she love him? Or did she love sex with him? Only time spent with Alan would sort that out. "Alan, I'm yours," she said.

About the author:

Madeleine welcomes mail from readers. You can write to her c/o Ellora's Cave Publishing at 1337 Commerce Drive, #13, Stow, Ohio 44224.

Also by Madeleine Oh:

Party Favors anthology
Power Exchange
Tied With a Bow anthology

South Beach Submissive

By Jennifer Dunne

Chapter One

"For your next assignment, I'd like you to review something a little different." Bryce Fontaine, editor of *South Beach Sun Daze*, smiled charmingly, and waved a sealed envelope enticingly before his nightlife reviewer, as if she was a bloodhound and he was giving her the club's scent.

Sassy Davidovitch wasn't biting. Bryce was only charming when he expected resistance. Whatever he wanted from her, it was something he didn't think she'd want to do. Since she was the paper's resident party animal, willing to do just about anything that promised a fun time, that meant whatever he wanted was going to be boring, stuffy, or both. No way was she signing up for that duty.

She leaned back in the leather and aluminum frame guest chair in Bryce's office and casually swung one leg, making the LEDs in the heels of her sneakers wink on and off in time to her movements. The bright Florida sunshine slipped through his angled blinds to sparkle off the rhinestones spelling out "Princess" on her T-shirt.

"How different?"

"I want you to join a dating service."

Sassy blinked. That didn't sound like *Sun Daze* material. They reviewed the hottest, hippest, happeningest clubs and restaurants, with plenty of photos, innuendoes and name-dropping, reassuring the beautiful people that they were as important as they thought they were, and offering wannabes the lure of pretending that they were part of the in crowd. The beautiful people didn't need dating services. By definition, everyone wanted to be with them.

She frowned. "Are we expanding our coverage?"

"No. This is an A-list dating service. Membership gets you invited to exclusive private parties, and the next one is coming up this weekend. I want a review of that party. So you have to join the dating service."

He extended the envelope toward her, clearly expecting her to take it. Still, Sassy hesitated. A party review was well within the range of her normal assignments.

"That's all you want?"

"I'd rather have a feature article about the dating service." Correctly reading her mutinous expression, he held up one perfectly manicured hand to ward off her protest. "Think of it as an opportunity to become a serious journalist."

"I don't want to become a serious journalist. I just do the reviews so I can get in to the clubs."

Bryce dropped the envelope in front of her, then planted his palms on the desk top and leaned toward her. "Okay, I'll level with you. We need someone to go undercover to do an exposé on the South Beach dating scene, and you're the only one on the staff who's both single and straight."

"Tony's not gay. And he's a real reporter."

"His girlfriend would kill him."

Sassy picked up the envelope and turned it over in her hands, but didn't open it. The return address was imprinted with an Art Deco style red and black logo of a thorny vine studded with roses, and the name and address of Briar Rose Introductions.

"You can't open the metro section of the *Miami Herald* without seeing half a dozen ads for dating services. Hell, I've typed up the classified ads for more than that in our own paper, both gay and straight. What makes this one worthy of an exposé?"

"The clientele are top-drawer. Actors, actresses, fashion models, rock stars, heirs, heiresses, you name it. Our readers want to know what it takes to get a date with one of them."

She opened the envelope and withdrew a three-page questionnaire. It seemed straightforward enough. Name, address, vital statistics, and were you a dominant, submissive, or switch.

Sassy jerked her head up and stared wide-eyed at Bryce. "Oh, no. No way. I'm not dressing up like a dominatrix to 'whip up' a story for you."

She stuffed the questionnaire back into the envelope and shoved it across the desk to Bryce. Folding his arms, he leaned back, refusing to accept it.

"Then go as a submissive."

She snorted. "Yeah, right. You hired me as a reviewer because I was outspoken and opinionated. What makes you think I could ever be submissive?"

He ran his fingers through his gel-stiffened dark hair, breaking apart the artfully disarranged curls into a tousled mess. "I'm not asking you to have sex with anyone. Just fake your way through the interview, get an invitation to the party, and then write about what it's like. If people think you're a submissive, they won't question you standing on the sidelines, watching the action."

Reluctantly, Sassy picked up the envelope again. "An A-list party, you said?"

"The best. Better than Friday nights at Privé."

"And I don't have to go on any lame dinner dates with self-important bores for the dating service, just attend the party?"

"Fun all the way."

"Okay. I'll do it." She started to rise out of the chair, then fell back with a thump, her eyes widening. "What the hell am I going to wear?"

Bryce's forehead furrowed. Of course, he looked gorgeous, as usual, in a black Armani Exchange suit over a pale lavender collarless shirt. Her office attire consisted of glitter-bedecked T-shirts and jeans.

"You go to clubs all the time. You practically live in them. You must have a clubbing wardrobe."

"Sure I do. In dramatic jewel tones, lamé prints, and rhinestones, glitter, and anything else that sparkles. Not a single submissive thing in the batch."

"Black is always a good choice."

"Hello? Weren't you listening? I don't *own* anything black."

He stared at her. "How can anyone not own black?"

"Because it's boring. *Everyone* wears black. I like my clothes to have personality." She shook her head. "I'm never going to convince anyone I'm submissive."

* * * * *

Sassy spent the afternoon, when she wasn't typing up classifieds, surfing the net for information on dominance and submission that would let her fake her way through an interview. In deference to the early morning meeting—she was usually still in bed at 11 a.m.—she skipped the party at Automatic Slim's that night. The next morning, wearing a commemorative T-shirt from a Miami restaging of *The Rocky Horror Show* bearing the slogan "Thrill Me, Chill Me, Fulfill Me" in red print over a glittering pair of lips, she showed up at the Art Deco bungalow housing Briar Rose Introductions promptly at eleven, awake and alert for her interview with Eveline Summers, owner and proprietress of the dating service.

She'd expected to be grilled regarding her theoretical background history as a submissive, since she'd filled out her application form by randomly selecting things she was supposedly interested in. Stress positions, piercings, and acts involving bodily fluids were out. Everything else, she'd answered either "experienced" or "interested".

Oddly, however, the sticking point appeared to be her employment as a secretary. Not wanting to reveal herself as "Sassy D.", the *Sun Daze* reviewer, she'd used her real name on the application, Alexandra Davidovitch, and listed her occupation as secretary. She spent most of her time at the *Sun Daze* offices typing and answering phones, so it seemed a close match for the job description.

Eveline tapped the offending line with a blood-red fingernail. "You do realize that Briar Rose is an exclusive service? And clients pay for that exclusivity?"

"Are you asking if I can afford your fees on a secretary's salary?"

"Membership is ten thousand dollars a year, payable monthly."

Sassy's eyes widened slightly. Bryce better be expecting that charge, or he'd go ballistic when she turned in her expense account. "It's covered. The secretarial job is only part-time, and not my only source of income."

Eveline nodded and smiled. "We have a number of aspiring models in our membership. According to the terms of the dating service agreement, you're not allowed to use the parties to try and solicit modeling assignments. They are for social interaction only."

It wasn't the first time Sassy had been mistaken for a model. She was thin—her food budget was regularly supplemented by cruising for free samples in the supermarket, and dancing burned an enormous number of calories—and had the classic bone structure of her Russian aristocratic ancestors. She wasn't beautiful, but youth, health, and a *joie de vivre* attitude made her more than passably pretty.

"Understood. Now, about these parties. They're the only function of the dating service?"

"No. Your profile will be forwarded to any men who we feel would be a good match for you, based on your stated interests and experience. They'll contact you according to your preferred contact method, either by phone or email. You can expect about five or six contacts over the next month. The parties are a conducive setting for you to meet people whom you've corresponded with in person. And, of course, to mingle with like-minded people who may become friends."

Eveline withdrew a thick cream-colored invitation from a desk drawer, and handed it to Sassy. The Briar Rose logo was embossed on the cover, and a pile of multicolored papers had been stuffed inside.

"This is your invitation to our next party, on Saturday, as well as a ticket to the Sunday morning buffet after the party. I've included a guide to the flower symbols—you'll be given a white rose, as a submissive looking for a partner. Look for men wearing a single deep purple rose. That is the symbol for dominants without a partner."

Sassy found the list, and scanned it quickly. There were also flower codes for gay and bisexual dominants and submissives, switches of all orientations, and preference for various types of activities, like edge play, piercing, and Ponyboys or -girls. The variety made her head swim.

"Do I have to memorize all of these before the party?"

Eveline laughed. "Only the ones you're interested in. Directions to the party are included in your packet. It's at the Eleanor penthouse. There's a private elevator from the parking garage, staffed by one of our employees, so you can dress in whatever manner makes you comfortable. For legal reasons, we do ask that you refrain from complete nudity, however."

The Eleanor penthouse was one of the city's prime party locations, reserved for launch parties of new fashion lines, wrap parties for Hollywood and TV filming, and private functions of the elite. Briar Rose was a serious player.

Sassy grinned. "I can hardly wait."

* * * * *

Eveline had said to wear whatever made her comfortable to the party, but Sassy figured that didn't mean showing up in jeans and a T-shirt. Since there wasn't anything in her closet that she thought looked submissive, she decided to try for demure, and wore a calf-length white sundress printed with clusters of cherries. Beadwork and sequins subtly accented the fruit, adding a bit of sparkle without being ostentatious. Plus, the double meaning of wearing cherries to her first BDSM party amused her.

She stuffed the invitation, apartment keys, tissues, and lip gloss into a matching clutch bag, and walked to the Eleanor. If the bouncer at the elevator saw her ten-year-old Ford Aspire, with the scars and scrapes that came from being parked late at night on the street in front of bars and clubs, he'd know she didn't belong with this crowd. But it was less than a fifteen minute walk from her apartment on Eighth Street over to Collins then up to the Eleanor. Used to dancing the night away, she had no problem walking that far in her strappy heels. She'd barely started to notice the heat before she was enveloped in the airy cool of the Eleanor's lobby, diaphanous white drapes belling softly in the breeze that flowed from the ocean to the pool side courtyard.

A reception clerk gave her directions to the private penthouse elevator, where she presented her invitation to the tuxedo-clad bouncer. Her spirits rose with the elevator. Whatever else this party proved to be, it was going to be fun like she'd never had before.

In the penthouse foyer, she joined a short line of people trading their invitations for prepared corsages. She recognized two local actresses flanking the owner of a string of nightclubs. He was wearing black leather pants and an open vest. The women wore matching black leather bras and miniskirts, and black leather collars Sassy was willing to bet were studded with stones a hell of a lot more expensive than mere rhinestones. They were either small diamonds, or extremely well-cut cubic zirconium, but they caught the light in a dazzling sparkle when one of the actresses tossed back her hair.

The actress touched the man's arm, leaning forward to whisper something to him, and he turned to face Sassy.

"My slave says you've been staring at her. Is there something I can help you with?"

Sassy's cheeks flamed. She wasn't even in the door yet, and she'd already been caught out as a fraud. "I was admiring her collar."

The man smiled. "Kristin, show the lady your collar."

The actress obediently stepped closer and tilted her head to display the stones encircling her neck.

"Three carats total weight," he continued. "Done by a leather artist and jeweler in San Francisco. I could give you his name if you like."

Sassy lowered her eyes, so he couldn't see her expression. There was no way she could afford a three carat diamond collar, not when she only ate dinner out if the newspaper was picking up the tab for a restaurant review. But her heart beat faster at the thought of that much glittering jewelry surrounding her neck.

"No, thank you."

"Ah. You're a submissive. Do you have a master yet?"

"No." Sassy was still talking to her shoes. This submissive routine was easier to fake than she'd expected. You just had to be mortally embarrassed.

"Well, when you get one, have him see me and I'll give him the name. I'm Carl."

"Alexandra."

"A pleasure to meet you, Alexandra. I'm sure I'll see you around."

The man and his two slaves retrieved their flowers and moved away, and Sassy stepped forward to trade her invitation for her own corsage. The expected white rose was flanked by sprays of baby's breath.

The woman who handed her the flower smiled at her. "I see this is your first Briar Rose party. Welcome. Dancing is on the patio. There are hors d'oeuvres and a bar in the dining room. Role-playing and costumes are allowed in the living room, but all scene play must be confined to one of the two designated play spaces. The scheduled scenes will be occurring in the den, and are all public. Impromptu scenes may be staged in the bedroom, and may be either public or private. A sign-up sheet has been posted by the door. The second bedroom is reserved for participants in the scheduled scenes. Do you have any questions?"

Sassy shook her head. "No, thank you."

She stepped away from the welcoming table and into the penthouse proper, pinning her corsage to her dress as she went. Idly, she wondered where the women in the leather bras had attached their flowers. They wouldn't have put a pin through the leather.

One of them strolled by, carefully carrying three drinks from the dining room to the living room. Her white rose, trailing the silver ribbon that indicated she was in a relationship, was attached to the strap of her bra with a pair of safety pins. Their master had obviously come prepared.

Drawing upon her long experience as a club reviewer, Sassy made her first pass of the party. The trick was to get a quick overview of the tone and feel of a place, then identify the hot spots where something interesting was liable to happen later.

The dining room was crowded with over two dozen people collecting drinks or tiny plates of snacks, their clothes dramatic accents against the white carpeting, white walls, and stark white furniture. She spared a glance for the snacks, half expecting the hotel to have supplied all white foods, then stopped for a better look. They were all sexually explicit. The breadsticks were shaped like penises, the rolls shaped like breasts, and cubes of cheese and fruit were arranged to form an erotic mosaic. The avocado dip was innocuous, although the carved avocado gracing the bowl left nothing to the imagination. And the chocolate-covered strawberries were painted in tiny bondage outfits. The rest of the foods, such as the asparagus and oysters, were well-known aphrodisiacs.

She picked up a bondage strawberry on her way past the table, closing her eyes briefly to savor the exquisite flavor. The chef had used first quality table chocolate and ripe, sweet berries. She went back and grabbed a second berry before continuing her survey.

Most of the people at the mirror-fronted bar waiting for drinks wore white roses, although some dominants were carrying multiple drinks back to where their submissives waited. The clothing ranged from barely there leather and chain mail, through elaborate Victorian costumes and skintight PVC catsuits, to modern designer clothes. Sassy's practiced eye counted four Armanis, two Versaces, a Vera Wang, and a Moschino.

Faint music drifted through the French doors leading to the patio, and she followed the sounds to the dance floor. A DJ was spinning an eclectic dance mix of salsa, reggae, and swing, at an unusually sedate volume. Swaths of white draperies tented above the patio blocked the worst of the Miami sun during the day, and now illuminated the dance floor in the gentle twinkle of white fairy lights strung among the fabric.

Another dozen party guests lined the waist-high wall of the patio, swaying gently to the music, but only two couples were on the dance floor. The first, a nubile woman wearing a costume of leather straps connected by chains and a man wearing a futuristic quasi-military costume, were doing what would have been considered a $50 lap dance at most strip clubs. The other couple, dressed in a scarlet Vera Wang gown and a navy Versace suit, were dipping and sliding gracefully in a well-choreographed swing dance that would not have been out of place at the Governor's Ball.

Fascinated, Sassy studied the dancers' expressions, finding the same combination of intense concentration, pleasure and arousal on them all. The moves differed, but clearly the intent was the same, and sooner or later both couples would be dancing horizontally.

The guests lining the walls seemed evenly mixed between those enjoying the music, and those enjoying the show put on by the dancers. Judging by the bulge in the front of one man's Armani suit, he was enjoying the show quite a bit.

She wandered back into the main party, snagging another of those delicious bondage berries as she passed the hors d'oeuvres table. This time, she headed for the den, and the promised staged scenes.

Somewhere between thirty and forty guests congregated around the walls, their attention toward the center of the room. The furniture normally provided by the hotel had been removed, and replaced with pieces of leather and wood that defied Sassy's ability to identify them, although one looked a bit like one of those horses used in gymnastic competitions, and another seemed like the sort of rotating platform that circus knife throwers used as a target. The only thing recognizable was a portable black leather massage table currently in use.

A woman, naked beneath a partial covering of dried wax, was strapped to the thickly padded leather table. Looming above her, a man in full Victorian garb of deep purple velvet frock coat and top hat dripped candle wax onto her already colorful body to the muted strains of the overture from *The Phantom of the Opera*. He was surrounded by tall candelabras sporting a rainbow of half-melted candles, from which he chose the instruments of his torture.

Hot wax splashed onto the woman's already colorful breast, and she gasped, her eyes closing as her body arched against the restraints.

Despite her best intentions, Sassy found her journalistic objectivity deserting her. She stared in frank bewilderment.

Obviously the woman was enjoying herself. Given the rapidly escalating pitch of her gasps, the next well-placed blob of wax would send her over the edge into an orgasm. And the candle artist's eyes gleamed with fervor as he chose and applied drips of wax, covering her body with colored drips, splashes, splatters, and pools.

Sassy glanced at the crowd surrounding the couple. Some guests watched avidly, their rapid breathing and surreptitious licking of their lips indicating they were enjoying the performance nearly as much as the participants. Other guests watched with near clinical detachment, murmuring softly to each other as they discussed the finer points of the artist's technique. She recognized many of the faces from the jaded Monday after-midnight crowd at Tantra.

Her attention was caught by a pair of vivid gray eyes. Unlike everyone else, he wasn't watching the couple in the center of the room. He was watching her.

The man's dark hair was pulled back with a leather band. Lean and about six feet tall, he showed off his pale gray Armani suit to good effect. The deep purple of his unadorned rose stood out in stark contrast to the gray of his lapel.

His lips curled upward in the hint of a smile as he nodded to her, acknowledging her appraisal of him. Slowly, he slipped through the crowd of guests to reach her side.

"I'm Michael," he said, his low voice pitched softly enough that his words would not disturb the scene unfolding before them or the interested crowd around them.

"Sass— I mean, Alexandra."

The gasps of the woman undergoing the wax treatment reached a fevered pitch, until she gave a final cry of satisfaction and subsided into limp quiet. The man in the frock coat dripped a little more wax onto her, whether to try and rouse her again or to complete his artwork, Sassy wasn't sure. His partner made no more sounds, and the man eventually blew out his candles, switched off the CD player, and bowed to the assembled guests. They applauded enthusiastically, including the man beside Sassy.

As the guests began filing out, she glanced over at Michael. "Why is everyone leaving? I thought all the scenes were in this room."

"They are. But it will take some time to clean up from this scene and set up for the next one. Have you tried the hors d'ouvres yet?"

"The chocolate-covered berries are excellent."

"Then allow me to offer you another serving."

"Okay." Sassy grinned at him, the delicious thrum of sexual attraction tingling through her bones, and jumped into her role with abandon. Flicking her gaze over his flower, she added, "You're the boss."

His lips curved again with that hint of a smile, and he put his arm around her to guide her out of the den and back to the living room. She could feel the heat of his hand against her hip, the strength of his forearm braced against her lower back. Instinctively, she curled into his touch. He responded by tightening his grasp, pulling her tight against his side and spreading his fingers over her hip.

His fingers flexed, drawing up the skirt of her dress a barely noticeable quarter of an inch. Her breath hitched, her imagination filling with the image of him tugging her skirt up all the way, then sliding his hand between her legs to feel her growing hotter and wetter for him, until he pushed his fingers inside her. He'd be a three-finger man, she was sure, forcing her to stretch to accommodate him, making her tremble and clench his unfamiliar breadth.

"What are you thinking of?" Michael murmured in her ear.

"Of you lifting up my skirt and putting your hand inside me," she answered truthfully.

"And you'd like that?"

"Oh, yeah."

They passed a slender blonde woman, with a variety of silver pins and studs piercing her nose, eyebrows, and ears, lounging on the plush white couch and chatting with another dominant. A pair of men in loincloths and steel armbands knelt on the floor at her feet, thin steel chains running to the rings piercing their nipples. More chains hung from the nipple rings, disappearing beneath their loincloths. She didn't want to know what the other ends were attached to.

Sassy realized with surprise that one of the men was a well-known real estate developer, and the other was an accomplished chef currently negotiating for his own show on the Food Network. Michael's insistent pressure against her back moved her past the tableau to an empty pair of chairs flanking a small round table.

"Sit." He released her, and gave her a slight push toward one of the chairs. "And while you're waiting for me, I want you to clench and release your inner muscles, over and over again, as if my hand was really inside you, and you were trying to climax."

Sassy sat, sinking into the soft white chair, and obediently clamped her legs together. She tightened her vaginal muscles, then released them. Tightened again, feeling her ass muscles clench as well this time, then released. When she tightened them the third time, a tremor rippled through her, and her breath escaped in a shaky exhale.

Michael stroked her cheek with one finger. "Good. Keep it up."

Her gaze remained glued to him as he strode over to the buffet table, collected a plate, and filled it with strawberries. All the while, she continued clenching and releasing, trying to draw his imaginary fingers deeper inside her. Her panties grew damp, and her breasts began to ache.

She could stop at any time, and let the fierce need building within her dissipate. Her burning gaze tracked Michael's movements through the room as he left the buffet, waited in line at the bar, and eventually returned with a tall glass filled with ice and an effervescent clear liquid. At first, he'd glanced her way frequently, but the looks had grown further and further apart, until she hungered for his attention nearly as much as she hungered to have him inside her, and feel his mouth on hers.

That thing with the wax? That she didn't get. But this? Oh God, yes, she understood the appeal of this.

Michael's softly worded instructions had her trembling with eagerness, anticipating the moment when he would fulfill his implied promise to touch her that way in real life.

Michael pulled the second chair next to hers and sat down, placing the glass and the plate of bondage berries on the table before them. His gaze skimmed her body, before returning to her face, and he smiled at her.

"You're flushed, Alexandra."

"I've been doing what you told me to."

"Very good." He picked up one of the berries and held it to her lips.

She opened her mouth, and Michael teased her lower lip with the chocolate-coated berry. He rubbed it back and forth across her lip, sliding it in and out of her mouth in tantalizing mimicry of the joining she still ached for.

He paused, the berry pressing lightly against her lip, the sweet taste of melting chocolate awakening her tongue. "Did you like following my instructions?" Michael asked.

Sassy nodded. Closing her lips around the berry, she watched his reaction as she sucked lightly, pulling it from his loose grasp. His eyes darkened, his breathing deepening as he reclaimed the stem of the berry.

"Bite," he ordered.

Obediently, she closed her teeth on the berry with a sharp snap. Michael's quick inrush of breath echoed hers. He reached for another berry, and held it just out of her reach.

"What else would you like?"

"You. Inside me. Between my legs, between my lips, everywhere."

"Show me."

He held out the berry, and Sassy loved it with her mouth. She licked the smooth chocolate coating, running her tongue

187

around the base of the strawberry, and flicking the cleft at the bottom. She heard Michael's sharp intake of breath, and teased the cleft again, tickling it with her tongue, as if she really was probing the slit of his cock.

"Oh, that's good," he whispered. "What else?"

Sassy kissed the melting chocolate of the berry, then slid it into her mouth. Working her lips around the stem, she brushed his fingers. Then she started licking and sucking the berry in earnest, the sweet chocolate even sweeter as she imagined it was his cock filling her mouth.

Reluctantly, she let the now wet and glistening red strawberry slide over her lips. Playfully, she bit off the very tip of the chocolate-free berry.

Michael groaned softly. "Wait here. I'm going to see when the bedroom's free."

Chapter Two

Michael dipped his fingers in the glass of club soda, rinsing the chocolate from his fingertips, then wiped them on a napkin. Sassy watched hungrily as he rose and made his way through the party to the bedroom of the penthouse, to reserve them a time slot.

What the hell was she doing? She was supposed to be reviewing this party, not screwing one of the guests.

Without Michael's charismatic presence inspiring her, her body began cooling down, rationality reasserting itself. She was here to work. But she couldn't review the party without taking part in the total party experience.

She clenched her vaginal muscles again, quickly restoring her aching need for Michael to fill her. By the time he returned, she was panting softly, her panties wet and the flesh between her legs hot and pulsing.

"Good news." Michael reached down and drew her to her feet. "There's a spot open now. I signed it out for private use."

Trembling, Sassy clutched his lean, muscled arm as she followed him on unsteady legs. She wanted him so badly, she could hardly see. The sounds of the party around them faded into the background, no more meaningful than a gaggle of squawking geese.

Then he was pushing her into the penthouse bedroom designated for party use and closing the door behind him. A black leather massage table identical to the one in the den contrasted with the white fur-covered bed and the stark white dresser between which it was positioned. The flowing white draperies, descending from a fabric-covered ceiling, fluttered in the draft from the hidden air-conditioning vents, alternately revealing and concealing a wooden pillory erected on the other side of the bed.

Michael's hands touched her again, and she lost all interest in her surroundings. He hiked up the skirt of her dress, skimming his hot palms over her bare thighs. Sassy moaned with desire.

He ripped her panties off her, dropping them to the floor and exposing her to his touch. One hand slid between her legs. His fingers slipped over her hot, pulsing folds, and found her wide-open entrance. He thrust three fingers inside her, stretching her opening just the way she'd imagined, then flexed his fingers, stroking the inner walls of her vagina.

Sassy moaned, trembling, and clutched his broad shoulders. She couldn't take much more of this, but it felt so good she never wanted it to end.

"Take off your dress," he ordered, his voice low and hoarse.

Sassy jerked the dress over her head and threw it away, bucking her hips to ride his hand as she did so. God, his hand felt so good inside her.

He moved so that he was directly in front of her, his back braced against the door. Thrusting the hard muscle of his thigh between her legs, he trapped his hand against her wet, hungry flesh. With his free hand, he cupped her ass, nudging her forward until she straddled his leg, driving his fingers deeper inside her.

Sassy shuddered, and moaned again.

He leaned her backward, arching her over his arm and lifting her breasts to him. His mouth closed over the thin white satin of her bra, tonguing and sucking on her nipple in time to the movements of his fingers until the bra was as wet and her breast as aching as her pulsing core.

His fingers flexed within her as he bit lightly on her nipple. Sassy gasped, rocking her hips to urge him deeper and arching backward almost to the point of pain, lifting her breasts as high as she could.

Michael chuckled, a deep rumble vibrating through his chest. "Take off your bra."

Sassy's quivering fingers fumbled with the hooks, the simple action taking far longer than normal. Finally, the clasp gave way, and she tore it from her shoulders and flung the offending garment across the room.

Michael's head dipped and he kissed first one swollen nipple, then the other. Sassy moaned and clutched his dark head to her breast as his tongue and teeth tugged her nipple into his mouth then closed firmly around it.

Her legs trembled, no longer able to support her weight, and she collapsed against the iron strength of his thigh. His fingers stroked and fondled her inner chamber as his mouth claimed mastery over her breasts. She was his, completely and utterly, to do with as he would. She had no thoughts left, lost in the pleasure his skillful actions were giving her.

Dimly, she registered a change in position. Her feet were no longer on the floor. Instinctively, she locked her legs around his waist.

Michael continued to stroke and caress her, his fingers reaching deep inside her, as he carried her across the room. She felt leather against her ass and the back of her thighs, and released his waist.

"Lie back," he whispered.

His words made no sense to her, sound without meaning. Fortunately he understood her problem, and used his free hand to press her shoulders back, until she was lying on the leather table, her legs dangling over the end.

Michael withdrew his fingers, making her gasp at the sudden loss and emptiness.

He chuckled again. "Hungry, are you? We can fix that."

She heard foil tearing, and the spurt of lubrication. Then he was thrusting a thick, condom-covered dildo inside her. Her vagina clenched and released over and over as she struggled to take all of it inside her. She gasped and moaned, but he skillfully avoided touching her clit or moving the dildo enough to give her relief.

Sassy's head whipped from side to side, her fingers digging against the padded leather surface of the table. She pulsed, aching, needing more but not knowing what she needed, only that Michael could give it to her.

He gripped her chin, stilling her restless thrashing, and forcing her to look at him.

"How do you like it?" he asked.

"What?" She blinked, trying to focus on his face.

Michael smiled, and stroked her cheek. "I should have asked you this earlier, when you could still think clearly. What turns you on the most? What toys do you want me to use, where, and how hard?"

"I don't know." Sassy writhed on the table, trying to move against the dildo that was filling but not satisfying her.

Michael put a hand on her hip, holding her still. "No. No more until you talk to me."

"But I don't know what to say! I've never done this before."

His thumb had been idly caressing her hip as he held her down, but now his hand froze. "This is your first time as a submissive?"

"Yes."

"Damn."

She blinked and forced herself to focus on his face. Was he mad at her? Worse yet, was he not going to finish what they'd started?

"Please, Michael," she begged. "Don't stop now."

He chuckled again, but it had a bitter edge to it. "I have no intention of stopping. You've just made things a little more challenging. Fortunately for you, I love a challenge."

His thumb resumed the slow caress of her hip, stroking up and down the sensitive crease of skin leading to her groin.

"You know how this works? About safe words?"

Sassy nodded, eager for him to continue. His gentle caress stopped just shy of tickling her, sending shivers of reaction through her vagina, seizing and releasing the motionless dildo. The promise of more made her body ache with need, hot lubricant dripping between her legs in a futile effort to encourage the dildo to slide back and forth within her.

"If I do anything you don't like, you stop me by saying your full name. No matter how much you beg me to stop, if you don't use your name, I'll think it's part of the scene you're playing. You understand?"

"Yes."

"How will you stop me?"

"I'll say Sasha Davidovitch."

Michael smiled, his eyelids lowered in an expression of supreme contentment.

"Very good...Sasha."

Belatedly, Sassy remembered she'd told him her name was Alexandra. But that wouldn't work as a safe word. Only her mother ever called her Alexandra. She'd been Sasha, or the variant nickname Sassy, since she was old enough to express an opinion. In the heat of passion, that was the name she'd use.

Michael stepped away from her, opening and closing drawers. When he returned, he had a riding crop tucked in the belt of his pants, and held two small black and silver metal objects in his hands.

"Nipple clips," he told her. He watched her face as he demonstrated how the tiny screws moved the two pieces closer together and held them a set distance apart.

Sassy licked her suddenly dry lips, and swallowed. Her breasts already ached for his touch, for his mouth and teeth and tongue. Would the nipple clips be as unfulfilling as the dildo, a teasing presence that stoked her body's fires higher without giving any relief? Or would they be the things that finally sent her over the edge? And what was he planning to do with that riding crop?

He cupped her left breast in his palm, flicking his thumb back and forth across her nipple. Flame shot through her body, and she arched her hips, bearing down on the dildo.

"Please," she begged.

Michael was in no hurry, teasing and tweaking her nipple with his fingers and thumb, then leaning down to take her in his mouth and use his teeth on her. Sassy gasped and moaned, each touch driving her higher. She writhed and wriggled, bucking her hips and arching her back, straining toward a release that was infuriatingly out of reach.

She felt the firm grip of the plastic surrounding her nipple, pressing tighter and tighter as Michael turned the screws. A high-pitched whine echoed through her ears, and she realized it was coming from her own throat. With a final twist of the screws, the clamp latched on to her nipple, tighter than any of Michael's previous touches.

Sassy cried out in joyful release as the orgasm ripped through her, her hips bouncing on the table with uncontrollable spasms. The dildo slipped partway out of her relaxed muscles, and the feel of it sliding over her entrance was enough to start the cycle of tension all over again. Her muscles clenched around it, trapping it from escaping, and she whimpered.

"Please."

"You liked that," Michael said softly, tapping the clip and sending another wave of fire through her. He reached between her legs to grasp the protruding end of the dildo, sliding it further out, then thrusting it fully inside her again.

Sassy moaned, arching into the thrust. Her muscles tightened, holding the welcome pressure of the dildo deep within her, even as she pulsed in time to the throbbing heat coming from her clamped nipple.

When Michael cupped her other breast, the anticipation nearly undid her. She whimpered and whined, urging him to fasten the second clamp. In response, he toyed with and teased her breast and nipple until she thought she'd go insane with need. Finally, when she could no longer see through the haze of desire clouding her vision, he tightened the clamp around her swollen nipple.

Sassy held her breath as the two sides of the clamp moved closer and closer, her body humming with anticipation. Would it be as good as the first one? Could it be?

Then the clamp bit down on her, hitting the flashpoint and triggering another full-body orgasm. Her chest arched up, her neck bending back, as her hips bounced and trembled in a wet wave of fulfillment.

Again, the dildo slid partially out of her loosened grasp, and again, Michael teased her body with it before sheathing it fully inside her again.

"Oh," she whispered. "That was... I... You... Wow."

"That's just the beginning. I'm still warming you up."

Sassy whimpered. She'd had two of the strongest orgasms of her life, and her body ached for more. How much farther could Michael take her? What would the final release be like?

Gently, he rolled her over, positioning her so that her feet were once again on the floor, and she was bent across the table. The leather tabletop pressed against her swollen, clamped nipples, sending another wave of fire through her, and she let out a shuddering moan.

Michael's hands glided over her back, her hips, her thighs, and her ass, stroking and caressing as he arranged her body to his satisfaction. He nudged her thighs further apart, lowering her hips a fraction of an inch and brushing the base of the dildo against the solid bulk of the table.

Sassy moaned, and rocked her hips forward, pressing the dildo against the hungry walls of her vagina.

"No!" Michael snapped.

She froze. She didn't want to displease Michael. If he wasn't happy, he'd stop doing the wonderful things he was doing to her body, and she'd never find fulfillment.

"I'm sorry," she whispered. "What did I do wrong?"

He fondled her ass, arousing her and assuring her that he was not unhappy at the same time. "You're not allowed to pleasure yourself. All your pleasure comes from me."

"Okay."

"Say it, Sasha."

"All my pleasure comes from you." As she said the words, she knew they were true. This is what she'd been missing with her previous lovers. They'd used each other to find their own pleasure. No one had ever been responsible solely for finding and giving her pleasure.

She tensed, suddenly afraid of the other half of that equation. Was she responsible for giving Michael his pleasure? She didn't know what to do. Would he be dissatisfied? Would he want nothing more to do with her?

Sassy was cruising without a road map, here. He had destroyed her preconceptions of what it meant to be a submissive. She'd thought it would involve pretending she didn't have opinions, or allowing a man to feel important by ordering her about. Maybe even getting tied up during sex, or playing a kinky Red Riding Hood meets the Big Bad Wolf game. But this was so far outside of her experience that she had no idea what he expected of her.

She choked back a tearful moan.

Michael's touch softened, moving up to gently circle her back. "Sasha? What's wrong?"

"You do please me. You do! But I'm not doing anything to please you. You won't be happy with me. You won't—"

"Sh." He continued stroking her back. "Turn your head this way."

She complied, resting her cheek against the warm leather of the table. She blinked, clearing her vision, and focused on Michael's face. He was smiling softly, almost indulgently.

"Pleasing you is pleasing me. See the evidence yourself."

She lowered her gaze, to where his erection tented the front of his pants. He hadn't been hard like that when they'd entered the room. Pleasing her really was pleasing him.

As the tension eased out of her, he increased the pressure of his hand against her back, driving her into the padded leather of the table. Her nipples, hard and swollen from the nipple clamps, erupted in twin flames. She clenched tightly around the dildo, almost but not quite finding another release.

She screamed, "Michael!"

The front of his pants rippled as his cock jumped in response to her scream.

"You're beautiful, Sasha." His touch turned gentle again, stroking the sides of her chest, then dipping below and sliding his hands between her body and the leather table to fondle her swollen breasts.

Sassy whimpered, arching her torso upward to give him free rein with her breasts. She wanted him to touch her nipples again, but didn't want the soft caresses to end. Although it didn't matter what she wanted. Michael would do whatever he pleased to her. And she'd love it.

He touched the clamps again, delicately, and she moaned with pleasure. Then he loosened the screws, releasing the clamps from her nipples so that her blood flowed once again. Red-hot knives driven into her chest would hurt less. She howled, instinctively rising to clutch her injured flesh.

Michael caught her arms and held her down on the table, pressing kisses to her shoulders and back until she soothed. Her breasts still throbbed, but the immediate pain was gone.

"It only hurts for a moment," he assured her. "But your nipples will stay extremely sensitive for much longer."

Releasing her arms, he slipped his hands around to her front and cupped her breasts again. He brushed his thumbs across her nipples, the barest whisper of a caress.

Sassy moaned, flames pulsing and shooting through her at his touch.

"Better now?" he asked.

"Oh, yeah."

He chuckled. "Good. But you've got a very strong flinch reaction. We'll have to take care of that."

He released her breasts and stepped away. She felt the heat of his presence by her hips, then heard a rasp of fabric, followed by a metallic click. Something soft touched her lower back. Before she could figure out what it was, Michael tightened the strap, belting her securely to the table.

A tremor rippled through her. Now she really was at his mercy. She couldn't get away even if she wanted to.

He slipped a pair of padded jogger's wristbands on her arms, then pulled her arms forward, not straight over her head but far enough that she was stretched across the table. He expertly attached the bands with other straps, binding her arms and upper body in place. Belatedly, she realized they weren't regular wristbands, but some kind of extremely comfortable manacles.

Behind her, out of her range of vision, she heard the tear of foil, followed by the rasp of his zipper, indicating that he was putting on a condom. She shivered, wondering when and how he'd slide his cock inside her. A second slow zip suggested his cock was staying inside his pants, at least for now. Sassy breathed out a disappointed sigh.

Michael glided his hands over her shoulders, back, and ass, subtly asserting his complete domination of her body. The gentle pressure against her still throbbing breasts caused another aching wave of need to grip her. She moaned softly as more lubricant trickled down the inside of her thigh.

"How does that feel? Anything too tight? Any pinching?"

"I'm fine."

"You're sure? Tug against the bonds."

Sassy tried to move her arms, or stretch against the strap pinning her lower back to the table. She was immobile. But not painfully so.

"I'm sure."

"Good." His palm slapped her ass.

She yelped in surprise, instinctively tightening her ass cheeks and jerking forward. Her muscles clenched around the dildo, just as the base of it bumped the table and rocked it inside her. She moaned with pleasure.

Michael slapped her ass again, rocking the dildo, then did it a third time. He found his rhythm, slapping her and driving her against the table with a steady motion. Soon she was panting with excitement, bearing down hard with each slap then relaxing her muscles and allowing the dildo to slip partially out of her, until the next stinging slap pushed her against the table and forced it inside her again.

He paused, and she moaned in despair. "Don't stop, Michael. Please."

"I think you're forgetting who's the master here."

"You. You are! I'm sorry."

"That's not good enough. You need a lesson."

Sassy trembled, terrified at the thought of him teaching her a lesson, more terrified that he might stop and never give her the satisfaction she craved.

He reached between her legs and grabbed the base of the dildo. She moaned, hoping he meant to replace it with his own hard cock. He jerked the dildo free, pulling the fat head of it over her throbbing entrance, and she cried out. Her knees sagged, and if she hadn't been strapped to the table, she'd have fallen.

Her thighs were sticky with lubricant, which he smeared with his thumbs as he pushed her legs wider apart.

"Your body is mine to control," he lectured her. "All your pleasure comes from me. However I decide to give it to you."

She felt his hair brush the inside of her thighs. Then his mouth closed over her pulsing, hot flesh, and his tongue stroked along her folds and plunged deep within her core. He suckled, pulling on her until she came in a shuddering rush, filling his mouth with her juices as she cried out.

He bit lightly on her swollen labia, and she moaned, unable to contain her pleasure. When he stood, he kept one hand cupped between her legs, stroking and massaging the hot, slick folds. She whimpered, and sagged against his hand, letting gravity thrust her against his fingers.

"Where does your pleasure come from?" he asked, slipping one finger between her folds and flicking it across her clit.

She gasped. "You. All my pleasure comes from you."

"And who knows best how to pleasure you?" He flicked her clit again.

"You!" she cried.

His finger hovered just above her clit, so close that she could feel the heat of it, but tantalizingly out of reach. "And what will you do?"

"Whatever you tell me to, whatever you want. I'm yours to command."

"Good girl." He rubbed her clit briskly, almost savagely, thrilling her with the agonizing pleasure. Then he took his hand away.

Without his support, the straps binding her to the table took her full weight. She grunted, but made no protest. She was his to command. He determined her pleasure.

Michael cupped and caressed her ass, his gentle, kneading strokes reminding her of how tender she was there after his earlier spanking. His fingers felt cool against her hot skin, and she imagined she could feel her blood pulsing over the globes of her ass. Pulsing for him, because of him.

She sighed. "Michael."

Something else brushed her tender ass, a square of something soft and pliant. Her muscles tightened. The riding crop!

He swatted her lightly, softer than he'd been spanking her. Sassy's muscles tightened. Without the dildo to bear down upon, her vaginal muscles clenched tighter than they had before, tighter than when she'd been priming herself for Michael's domination. The crop fell again, striking her other cheek, and she whimpered softly. The rhythm of strokes built, falling faster and harder, until she couldn't catch her breath. The pain and pleasure combined, blending and blurring, until she couldn't say where one ended and the other began. She was floating on a cloud of pure sensation, without definition, without explanation. It didn't need any. It only needed to be experienced.

A brilliant light flashed through her mind, as all her nerve endings seized up and screamed in joy at the same moment. She might have cried out, or she might have slipped silently beneath the waters of consciousness. She was too far gone to know.

When she came to, still shuddering and shaking with the aftershocks, she was lying on her side on top of the room's bed. Michael lay next to her, cradling her body against his, and gently stroking her hair.

Her cheek rested against the brushed cotton of his shirt, and she realized he was still dressed. Skimming her gaze down his body, she confirmed that he was completely dressed. Worse, he was no longer aroused.

She tipped her head back and glanced upward, meeting his indulgent gaze. He didn't look unhappy.

Hesitantly, she asked, "Did I please you?"

He smiled, and trailed a finger over the curve of her ear. "I came when you did, Sasha. You pleased me very much."

She closed her eyes, sighing gently as she settled against his warm chest, her ear resting above the steady thumping of his heart.

"How about you? Did you like your first time as a submissive?"

"Oh, yeah. It was… I don't know how to describe it. More intense than parachuting and bungee jumping combined."

Michael shook back his sleeve and glanced at his watch, a multifunction digital watch that seemed at odds with the cool elegance of his Armani suit.

"Our time slot is almost over. We'll have to return to the party soon."

Sassy blinked. She'd forgotten about the party! It was her whole reason for being here, and she'd forgotten about it.

She felt her face flame. "Oh God. The way I was screaming, they all heard me. They'll know exactly what happened in here."

"Don't worry about it." He dropped a light kiss on the crown of her head. "The draperies muffle the sound. But even if any guests did hear you, they'd be jealous, wishing they were having that good a time. This is why people come to these play parties. To play."

His reassurance only made her feel worse. This wasn't his first party. She wasn't the first woman he'd picked up and played with. He'd rocked her world, taken her someplace she'd never been, never even dreamed existed, and she'd been just another fun time for him. Maybe not even all that fun. After all, she was the one who'd been doing all the shouting and screaming.

His arm tightened around her, and he tipped her chin up so that he could read her face. A slight furrow creased his forehead.

"What is it, Sasha? What's bothering you?"

"Nothing."

His gray eyes narrowed. "BDSM relationships are built on trust and truthfulness. Don't lie to me, not even a social lie. What's bothering you?"

"I'm not your first submissive."

"No, you're not."

She shook her head, trying to clear away the last of the sensual haze her time with Michael had instilled. She needed to think clearly.

"I've never been to a pickup party, not even for ordinary sex. I'm out of my league here. Am I your date for the evening after this? Or was it just a fun time, and now we go out and mingle and try to find someone else to have fun with?"

He kissed her forehead and smoothed her hair, until she relaxed and laid her head against his chest again. "This is a play party, not a pickup party. Most of the guests are already in relationships. I came to watch the scenes and talk to friends, not find a new submissive. You were an unexpected treat."

Unexpected didn't begin to cover it, from her point of view. If someone had tried to convince her before she arrived at the party that before the night was out she'd be tied up, begging a man to beat her with a riding crop, and loving every minute of it, she'd have thought the person was crazy. But Michael had taken her on an amazing ride, and she could only guess at the wonders further down the road.

If her life had one credo, it was that you took fun where you found it. She'd found fun, all right, and now she wanted to take it as far as she could.

Sassy looked up hopefully. "Does that mean you'd like me to be your submissive?"

"You let me initiate you into the ways of BDSM tonight. Let me continue to guide your development, and we'll see where this leads."

She'd been hoping for more. She'd wanted to hear that it had been as special for him as it had been for her, that he felt connected to her now and unwilling to let her go. But she'd take what he was offering, because one thing was abundantly clear. Being with Michael would be more fun than she'd ever had in her life.

"Okay," she agreed. "You can be my Yoda."

He laughed. "I'm planning a much more *personal* style of guidance. I'm going to get into your head and under your skin, taking your body every chance I get and making you think of nothing but me when I'm not inside you."

Sassy trembled, her body turning liquid and starting to melt at the heated promise in his words. "I can hardly wait."

"Well, you'll have to. Our time's up. You've got two minutes to get dressed and cleaned up to go back out into the party."

She bounced out of the bed and raced around the room, gathering up her underwear and dress. Michael handed her a moistened towelette to clean between her legs, and swabbed the leather table with an antibacterial wipe that smelled strongly of bleach. The toys went back in the dresser drawer, nestled in their places among a collection that made her mouth water with eagerness to try them all.

Chapter Three

They spent the next two hours watching the scenes, Michael holding Sassy before him with his arms clasped loosely around her waist. Some of what she saw made her flinch backwards against his protective strength, but more often she shifted forward in anticipation, or rubbed her hands restlessly over his arms. Through it all he asked her questions, wanting to know what it was about the scenes that affected her.

They watched a flogging that left her breathless, as Michael probed her feelings about the different whips and floggers, and where each of them was used. A humiliation scene made her wince, and informed him in no uncertain terms that she did not find being disparaged and belittled the least bit sexy. A demonstration of rope dress tying left her indifferent, until his soft explanation of the changes the abrasion and compression were causing to the submissive's body heated her blood.

When a bound, gagged and blindfolded submissive was led to the center of the room and teased with a variety of feathers, furs, and textiles, Sassy's panties grew damp with eagerness to experience such complete dependence on Michael for not just pleasure, but all sensation. Then the dominant performing the scene invited some of the gathered guests to take their turns with the girl. Sassy stiffened with distaste even as the girl writhed in obvious ecstasy.

"You wouldn't want to be shared?" Michael breathed in her ear, tightening his hold on her with reassuring possessiveness. "Many submissives find it the ultimate expression of bowing to another's will."

Sassy turned to read his expression. Did he want to share her with other dominants? Was that what his other submissives had done for him?

"I...I don't think I could. I'm sorry."

"Sh." He brushed a kiss across her forehead, and cradled her body against his, soothing her with his touch. "I won't ask you to do anything you don't want to do. But I have to know why you have a problem with it so I can determine if it's just something you find unappealing, or if it's something you're afraid of, but you could work your way into it with time."

She thought about it, turning in his arms to watch the woman writhing in ecstasy as she was teased and tormented by five unknown dominants, both male and female, while her master stood by and observed the action. Sassy tried to imagine five times the arousal Michael had inspired in her earlier. She failed.

"I think it's because they don't know her. They're doing the things they would do to arouse any woman. She's not special to them."

"And you want to be special?"

"Yes." Sassy glanced over her shoulder at him. "Is that wrong of me?"

"No desire between consenting adults is ever wrong. Some are just more complicated to fulfill than others."

She raised an eyebrow in obvious disbelief. "There must be some limits. What if someone's desire would leave them maimed or disfigured?"

"Would you set yourself up as the arbiter of what is an acceptable range of suffering to exchange for pleasure?"

Michael's voice had not risen from his previous low whisper, but his enunciation grew markedly more clipped.

Sassy blinked, startled at his vehemence. "Well, no. Of course not."

"But you believe someone has that right?"

"I...maybe. I don't know. Let me think." She bit her lip, not wanting to anger Michael, but also not willing to back down from something she truly believed was correct.

"Come on. You can think outside."

Wrapping his arm securely around her, he led her through the assembled crowd and out onto the patio. Ignoring the dancers, who now included the multiply pierced mistress and her two attendants demonstrating some sort of line dance to another couple, Michael guided Sassy to an empty spot along the waist-high wall facing the ocean. She watched the hypnotic ripple of the distant waves, and felt her breathing deepen and slow.

"Take all the time you need," he instructed in the same clipped tone. Her brief feeling of peacefulness vanished. He was mad at her, and struggling to control his temper. But she wasn't going to just roll over on this issue. Not unless she could prove her initial opinion was wrong.

The sultry Latin beat echoing across the patio made it easier to concentrate than the gasps and muffled cries of the submissive. Slowly, Sassy worked her way through the problem.

Speaking as much to herself as to Michael, she mused, "If someone stepped in to prevent someone else from acting on their desires, in order to protect them from the results of their actions, it would be relegating the person to a child status, unable to be trusted to make a decision for themselves. You can't say that applies to only one area of a life. So you'd have to strip all of the rights and privileges of adulthood from them."

She nodded, certain of her reasoning. "So if they were capable of acting as an adult in other areas of their life, it would be wrong to penalize them for their sexual desires. And if they weren't capable of acting as an adult in other areas of their life, that would become obvious, and they could be institutionalized or otherwise treated without basing the decision on their sexual preferences."

Behind her, Michael relaxed slightly, and his voice resumed its accustomed gentleness. "In some places, dominants and submissives are still persecuted for their desires, arrested or sent to counseling until they can act 'normal'. The laws are still on the books in most states, although they're rarely enforced unless we flaunt our behavior in a way that can't be ignored."

Sassy felt the blood draining from her face. She'd been thinking of the review of this party as a deliciously lurid article for *Sun Daze*. But could her review actually get someone arrested? Close down the dating service under some obscure codicil of law?

"Sasha? What is it? You're pale as a ghost."

She closed her eyes and inhaled deeply, sucking in deep breaths of humid salt air. Gradually, her initial panic faded, and she opened her eyes.

"Feeling better now?" Michael asked.

Sassy nodded, but kept her gaze trained on the ocean.

He sighed deeply, tucking her body into his embrace and resting his chin on top of her head. "I was in a relationship last year that turned ugly. There were some dicey moments when she threatened to get the cops involved. Your comment hit a nerve."

"For me, too. I didn't realize how important it was to keep all this secret."

Michael chuckled. "Unless you take out an ad in the paper announcing your new proclivities, you've got nothing to worry about. Miami's pretty laid-back about sexuality."

She shivered. Her review would definitely be advertising her newly awakened sexuality. Everyone who read it would know how she'd spent her evening.

"You're cold. We should go back inside."

She shook her head. "Suddenly, I'm not interested in the party anymore. I've got a lot to think about."

Although she usually stayed and partied until a club shut down, that was because she liked to have fun. She had enough material for her review. If she wrote a review at all.

But if she didn't write a review, Bryce would never cover the expense. She had enough trouble making her rent payments. She'd never be able to repay the thousand dollars Bryce had invested in the Briar Rose membership.

Michael studied her face intently for a moment, turning her chin so that the decorative fairy lights better illuminated her.

"You're frightened. And not in a good way."

Sassy hesitated, then nodded.

"Of...?"

"It's complicated. But it's about my job."

"Worried about what will happen if they learn about this party?"

"If my boss knew what I'd done tonight, I'd be in big trouble." That much was true. He'd question her ability to be objective.

Sassy blinked. Maybe that was it. He wanted an article. Maybe he'd be willing to accept an article about the appeal of BDSM, an eyewitness account of one woman's journey into submission.

"You've had an idea?" Michael prompted.

"Maybe. It might work."

He smiled, stroking her cheek and hair with casual possession. She leaned into his touch, and his smile broadened. "Ready to go back to the party?"

Sassy shivered again, anticipating Michael holding her close, his low voice whispering in her ear, the warmth of his body heating hers with promise.

"Yes." Her throat was so tight, her answer was barely louder than a breath.

Michael bent his head and claimed her lips, his gentle pressure gradually growing more and more insistent as he backed her hips against the low wall of the patio. Her view of the dance floor blocked by his body, she felt isolated and alone with him in this dim, secluded corner he'd found for them. Soft reggae music played from the DJ on the other side of the patio, masking the sounds of other conversations and reinforcing the sense of solitude.

Michael's tongue plunged inside her mouth, tasting and taking. Smoothing his hands over her body, he caressed her back, then cupped her ass. He squeezed, pressing his fingers into the flesh still tender from his earlier spanking and flogging.

The memory of how completely he had possessed her drew a shaky groan from her, and the flesh between her legs began to throb in anticipation. Her nipples tightened, beginning to ache. He shifted one hand up to press his palm into the small of her back, anchoring her against his onslaught. With his other hand, he slowly lifted her skirt, until his fingers could slip beneath the hem. He stroked her bare thigh, then the sensitive skin of her inner thigh.

Sassy sighed into his mouth, clutching his shoulders and shifting her legs further apart. Why had she made the mistake of putting her underwear back on?

His fingertips brushed lightly against her damp panties, teasing her with his faint touch against her pulsing flesh, before dancing away to trace delicate circles up and down her inner thigh. When Michael lifted his head to begin trailing kisses along her jaw, she whispered, "What do you want to do to me?"

"What would you think of my taking you right here, against the wall, in full view of the guests behind me on the dance floor?"

Sassy shuddered, her heart pounding. Her legs quivered, too weak to hold her upright without his strong hand at her back, and her breath puffed in and out in rapid bursts. The thought terrified her. She was the reviewer, the objective analyst who recorded others' outrageous behavior for the titillation of her readers. She didn't want to become the story.

But wasn't that exactly what she was contemplating? Becoming the story for Bryce, exposing her inner self on the page for all of Miami to gawp at?

The idea was darkly seductive. She wanted Michael to make love to her, to feel his cock filling her, then exploding as he found his release. She was growing wetter just thinking about it. And if he did it here, in full view of everyone, he'd relieve her of having to choose to expose herself in print. She'd be the story, whether she wanted to be or not.

Her inner spirit protested. It was one thing to hand over control of her body in the context of a hot bout of sex. It was another thing entirely when her career was on the line.

Michael was still waiting patiently for her reply, watching her expression. She temporized, answering the question he'd asked without answering the question he'd meant.

"I think you'd be announcing to everyone that I'm your submissive."

"And that would make you feel…?"

"Very, very special," she admitted. That was part of the allure. But was it enough?

Michael growled softly, a sound of masculine pleasure, his firm erection pressing into her stomach as he nipped the sensitive skin above the pulse point in her neck. She tilted her head, exposing more of her neck to him. Despite the arousal rushing through her blood, she snickered.

"What?" he asked.

"I feel like I'm in a nature special. 'The alpha dog expresses his dominance by growling, and the submissive dog exposes its vulnerable neck and underbelly.'"

As soon as she said it, she worried that he might not appreciate being compared to a dog.

To her relief, Michael laughed. "You have a very strange sense of humor. That dress is no accident, is it?"

"What, the cherries? Nope. More like truth in advertising."

He nipped her again, eliciting another groan. "You were embarrassed in the bedroom, thinking people would guess what you were doing. If I took you against this wall, they wouldn't just guess, they'd know."

He pushed her wet panties aside with his thumb, and slid a finger along her slick folds. Sassy gasped, the sudden jolt of pleasure making her vision swim.

"Sasha?" he prompted.

"I don't care!" The hell with her job. If Bryce didn't want her story, she'd quit. It would be worth it to feel Michael coming inside her at last.

Her inner muscles tensed and quivered, aching to claim his finger and pull it inside, even as she fought to keep her legs and hips steady. She remembered her earlier lesson. All her pleasure came from Michael, on his schedule, at his whim. She was not to try and rush him.

Her hips shook with the effort not to rock forward and sheathe his finger inside her.

"Why? Why don't you care?"

"Because I need you inside me. Not your fingers, or your tongue, but your hard, hot cock. Making me yours, completely."

His fingers stroked her wet folds, gliding over her hot, aching flesh. Sassy shuddered and moaned.

Michael bent his head and rested his forehead against hers, releasing his breath in a ragged exhale. "I have *got* to learn to ask these questions before you're lost to passion. But your body is like a drug to me. I can't resist touching you."

His fingers probed deeper, finding her entrance. Capturing her mouth with his, he swallowed her soft moan of pleasure, then moved his free hand to the back of her neck to hold her lips pressed to his. He stretched her wide, thrusting three fingers all the way inside her, and flicked his thumb over and around her clit.

Sassy came in a burst, her startled cry silenced by his greedy mouth. His kiss gentled. He slipped his hand away from her pulsing body, tugging her panties back into place, and lifted his head.

No longer focused exclusively on her body's needs, she became aware of the seductive throb of Latin music from the dance floor, and the hushed voices of the assembled guests. They were probably talking about her, getting a hand job out here for everyone to see, the way they'd dissected the scenes in the other room. Her cheeks flamed, and she wished she could jump over the wall and disappear. Unfortunately, given the height of the penthouse, that would be a permanent exit.

"You made no sound," Michael reassured her. "And no one on the dance floor could see what I was doing."

"You're sure?"

"Yes." He dropped a light kiss on her forehead, then stepped away, took a handkerchief out of his pocket, and wiped his fingers. "You're not ready for that level of exhibitionism. But I can still show everyone that you're mine."

Sassy's heart beat faster, her breath turning shallow. All the benefits, with none of the cost. "How?"

"I wanted to say hello to a few of the other dominants before leaving. When we go in, you'll sit on the floor at my feet. Look at no one but me. Speak to no one but me, unless I give you permission." He smiled. "And if you're very good, I'll take you home with me, and we can finish this party in private."

She trembled, eager to leave now. She wouldn't be satisfied until she felt him coming inside her, and knew that she could stir him the way that he stirred her. But to do that, she'd have to be a perfect slave.

She bent her head, and dropped a curtsey to him. "As you command, Master. Let me show you how good I can be."

Chuckling softly, Michael wrapped his arm around her and led her around the dance floor. They passed the blonde woman, also standing on the sidelines, although only one of her slaves was with her.

"Michael! Where have you been hiding yourself all evening?"

"Schooling my new slave," he answered. Nudging Sassy forward, he murmured, "Show your respect to Mistress Melissa by bowing."

Sassy had no wish to bow to the other woman. She had her own slaves. Let them bow to her. But Michael had asked it of her, and she ached to please him. Remembering the way his cock had swollen and jumped every time she submitted to him, she did as he instructed, stepping forward and bowing, never lifting her eyes from the white marble of the patio. In her mind, she bowed to Michael. His hand tightened around her waist, warm and possessive.

"Good for you, right back in the saddle," Melissa purred.

Sassy longed to see the other woman's expression. Was this a sly sexual innuendo, or a comment about Michael's disastrous previous relationship? She almost lifted her head to satisfy her curiosity. Then she recalled Michael's lesson. All her satisfaction came from him. Was that just physical satisfaction or intellectual satisfaction as well? She'd ask him later, when they were alone. After he made love to her. For now, she'd assume it meant everything. She wasn't willing to risk losing a night of incredible sex over a passing curiosity, so, quivering from the strain, she kept her gaze down.

Oddly, the fact that she hadn't wanted to give in, but had done it anyway, filled her with shivering pleasure. She'd strip naked and lay down on the floor at Michael's feet if that's what he wanted her to do. She almost wished he'd ask it of her, so that she could prove her willingness to submit to him.

Michael laughed, pulling Sassy in front of him and pressing his rigid erection into the cleavage of her ass. "And I plan to be riding all night."

Her face flamed, even as her body quickened. She melted against him, happy to accept his absentminded caresses of her hips and thighs as he chatted with the other woman. She paid no attention to his words, since they weren't directed at her. Instead, she enjoyed the way his voice rumbled through his chest, and how the heat of his hands seemed to soak right through her thin dress. The arrival of Mistress Melissa's other slave, bearing a tray filled with drinks, ended the conversation.

Michael took a moment to compose himself, then led her into the living room. After pausing on the threshold to scan the room, he headed for the smaller of the two conversation groupings. He sat in the center of the white leather loveseat, stretching his arms across the curved back. As he'd instructed her, Sassy smoothed out her skirt and sat on the plush white carpeting. She rested her head against his knee and waited.

She heard a familiar voice, and opened her eyes to see a pair of black leather pants in front of her, flanked by two pairs of toned, tan legs. Master Carl and his submissives.

"We met in line at the door," Master Carl finished explaining. "She was quite taken with Kristin's collar."

Michael tipped Sassy's face up to look at him. "Would you like to wear a collar some day?"

She shivered, imagining Michael's strong hands fastening a collar like Kristin's around her neck, telling the world that she belonged to him. She'd seen other collars at the party; some were thin velvet chokers, others embossed leather or gold chain that looked more like jewelry, and still others were heavy leather with studs, spikes, or rings that made them look like dog collars for a particularly nasty Doberman.

"If it was pretty," she answered.

Michael chuckled. "Wearing a collar isn't about what it looks like. It's about how you feel when you're wearing it."

"How would I feel?"

He brushed the back of his fingers against her collarbone in a whispered caress. "Special."

She closed her eyes, leaning into his touch. "Yes."

"You've chosen well," Master Carl said.

Michael's voice turned cold. "I don't think you're qualified to judge."

Carl coughed. "We've taken enough of your time. Enjoy your evening. Come, girls."

Sassy slitted open her eyes and watched them walk away. When they'd passed into the dining room, Michael shook himself and turned his attention to her, resuming his interrupted caress.

"So you'd like a collar, hmm?"

"What was that about, Michael?"

He hesitated, then let out his breath on a sigh. "Remember that relationship I told you about, the one that turned bad? He's the one who introduced us."

She didn't know how to answer that. All she could think about was that Michael obviously hadn't wanted to answer her question. But he had. Because BDSM relationships were based on trust, and he wouldn't lie to her.

An icy knife stabbed her stomach. She reassured herself that she hadn't lied to him. But she hadn't told him the truth. She hadn't told him why she'd come to this party, or that she planned on exposing their relationship on the pages of *South Beach Sun Daze*.

"Have I been good, Michael? Very, very good?"

His fingers glided over her throat and along her jawline. "Very good."

"Then will you take me home with you?"

He glanced around the room, surveying the guests. "There's no one else here I want to talk to. I'd rather spend the rest of the night listening to you scream my name when you come."

She quivered with excitement, hot, aching need melting the last of her icy dread. Softly, she whispered, "Take me home, Michael. Make me scream for you."

His thumb stroked across her mouth, then he tugged gently on her lower lip. "Giving orders now? Do you need to be taught another lesson?"

She could tell from his teasing tone that he wasn't upset with her. He knew she was begging, regardless of how she'd phrased her pleas.

Opening her mouth, she sucked his thumb inside. She caressed the firm pad and smooth nail with her tongue, stroking across the creases of his knuckle.

He groaned softly. Lifting her hand, he placed it over his crotch, letting her feel the heat of his erection. As she pulled on his thumb, swirling her tongue over and around it, his cock stiffened, pressing against her palm.

She whispered, "I live to serve you." With his thumb still in her mouth, her "L" came out like a "W", making her sound like Elmer Fudd. A very sexy Elmer Fudd.

"Then you'd better let go of my thumb, because if you keep sucking like that, I'm going to open my fly and order you to take my cock in your mouth right here in the middle of the party."

His thumb slid out of her mouth with a wet pop. He pressed her palm against his erection, stroking himself with her hand, then groaned and lurched to his feet. Still holding her hand, he dragged her upright.

"Let's go. My apartment is five minutes away. I can wait another five minutes to feel your mouth around me."

"It's Saturday night in South Beach," she reminded him.

He groaned again. With the cruisers out, it could take five minutes just to go five blocks. "Hell. It's a private garage."

Chapter Four

Michael's Ford Expedition unlocked with a click of his key chain. The sound of slamming doors and people's laughter echoed weirdly among the concrete pillars of the garage, coming from unseen hotel guests either arriving or leaving.

He gazed longingly at the cargo area of his SUV, then shook his head. "Not private enough. Get in."

Sassy climbed into the passenger's seat, sinking into the buttery-soft leather, and strapped herself in. He started the engine and pulled out of the narrow space, the tires squealing as he cut the wheel hard to the right.

While he was occupied with maneuvering the big vehicle through spaces designed for much smaller cars, she studied the Expedition and what it said about the man beside her. She wouldn't have guessed he'd be an SUV driver. He seemed the type to drive something sleek and sporty, with plenty of power under the hood. Probably a convertible.

Turning in her seat, she glanced at the cargo area. The beige leather was scraped along the sides and marred with faint black streaks. The SUV wasn't a fashion statement. He actually used it to transport things.

They rolled under the rising security gate onto Collins Avenue. As she'd predicted, traffic moved at a crawl.

Michael growled under his breath. "We'll cut across to Euclid at the next intersection. Traffic should be lighter there."

"What do you do? For a job, I mean?"

He darted a surprised glance at her. "Afraid I'm not qualified to navigate a traffic jam?"

"No. I just wondered what you hauled in your SUV."

"Oh." He inched forward, approaching the intersection, then cursed when the light changed before they reached it. "I'm a photographer. I haul my gear to photo shoots—camera bags, lights, power boxes, cables, that sort of thing."

"A photographer? Have I seen your work?"

"Probably. I did the last Gold Door layout. That was on busses and billboards all over Miami. And my spring fashion spread photos were picked up by *People, Us, Time*...most of the majors printed at least one shot."

Sassy's eyebrows rose. That was a far cry from souvenir snapshots and family portraits for Christmas cards. She'd just been saying the polite thing when she asked if she'd seen his work. She'd never expected the answer to be yes.

"I should have known you'd be talented. You've been so skillful at everything else tonight."

He chuckled. "You've made it easy. Working with models is anything but."

The light changed, and he turned right, the street opening up in front of them. A quick left onto Euclid, then he was accelerating southward.

"I live south of Biscayne Bay. We'll be there soon, now."

Her pulse raced. "Soon I'll feel that strong, hard cock of yours between my lips, swallowing you down as I kneel before you."

Michael's fingers clenched the steering wheel in a white-knuckled grip, and the speedometer spiked upward. Cursing under his breath, he eased his foot off the gas.

"Don't talk like that," he ordered. "Or we'll never get there. I'll pull over and have you do me right here in the Expedition."

Her lungs froze in her suddenly tight chest, but her panties grew damp. She was so hot for him. The idea that he was equally hot for her, that he had to fight to control his reaction to her, made her tremble with excitement. What would happen when they were finally alone, when no one could see or hear them?

They slowed briefly to merge onto Washington Avenue. Then they broke free of the South Beach traffic, and he gunned the engine.

"What about you?" he asked, his voice tight with strain. "What do you do?"

She didn't answer. How could she? BDSM relationships were supposed to be based on trust and truthfulness. She couldn't lie to him. But if she told him she was a club reviewer, he'd guess why she'd been at the party.

"Sasha?"

Now he was getting suspicious. She had to distract him.

She laughed, although it sounded false to her ears. "Nothing as interesting as you, I'm afraid. I'm a kind of secretary."

"A kind of secretary? What kind?"

"No. I mean, I do a lot of what a secretary does—answer phones, type—but that's not my job title." She paused as a new thought struck her. "I don't think I actually have a job title."

Michael chuckled. "Maybe you really are a secretary, then."

At least he wasn't questioning how she could afford the Briar Rose fees on a secretary's salary.

"Do you model on the side?"

Oh, damn. He was. How was she supposed to answer without lying, but without raising his suspicions?

Sassy fluttered her eyelashes at him. "Why? Do you want to photograph me?"

"God, yes. If I could capture that look in your eyes, that you had in the bedroom—that cross between fear, excitement, and total and complete trust and compliance—that picture would keep me hard for the rest of my life."

"Really?" she whispered. An entirely different kind of warmth was curling through her now, a glow that radiated outward from her heart. It had nothing to do with sex, and everything to do with feeling cherished and adored.

"I told you, absolute truth between us."

The warmth vanished, leaving her feeling vaguely queasy. When he found out the truth about her, he'd be furious. That would be it for their relationship. Still, she'd make the most out of it while she could. If they were doomed to split up, that just meant she'd have to milk their encounters for the maximum pleasure and excitement. Michael could have no complaint with that.

Starting now. "Are we almost there yet?"

"Almost."

He turned down a side street leading to a towering oceanfront condominium complex. Half a minute later, he was pulling the Explorer into his designated parking space in the garage. A minute after that, he was leading her through his door.

She barely had time to notice the tiled foyer decorated with photographs, presumably his, before he pushed her through a beaded curtain into a spotless blue and white kitchen, then through the formal dining area into the living room beyond. The thick sand-colored carpet, blue and green chairs, and coffee table of driftwood and glass, made the room seem like it was part of an undersea palace. Even the artwork on the walls was different, sculptures from shells and driftwood instead of photographs.

Michael released her hand long enough to open two sets of French doors onto the wraparound balcony, letting in the humid night air and the restless sound of the surf crashing on the beach below.

"Come here."

She walked slowly to his side. Now that the moment had come, she was inexplicably nervous. What if it wasn't as good as she'd imagined? What if it was even better?

"On your knees."

Sassy knelt before him, the thick carpet cushioning her knees. His suit pants bulged outward, and this close to his cock, she could smell the musky scent of sex and sweat on him.

He ran his fingers through her hair, caressing her with trembling hands.

"Undo my pants."

She reached for his belt buckle, and discovered her hands were shaking, too. She'd given head before, but never like this. Never because she'd been ordered to pleasure her master. More than anything, she didn't want to disappoint him.

The buckle finally released, and she fumbled with the button and zip until the pants were undone. They fell to the floor, revealing his underwear. Boxers. Navy blue with white and green plaid. The underwear was as much of a surprise as his SUV had been. She'd expected sexy briefs, or silk shorts.

Then again, there were advantages to boxers. She could see his straining erection through the gap in the front, although his cock tented the cotton to one side rather than pushing through the opening.

"The boxers, too?" she asked.

"Yes."

Delicately, she stretched the elastic waistband away from his body, then pulled down his shorts, freeing his cock. Meanwhile, he pulled off his jacket and shirt, then kicked off his pants, shoes and socks so that he was standing naked before her.

She admired the dark hair arrowing across his taut stomach, down to the thick nest of dark curls at the base of his cock. His cock itself was long and straight, smooth except for the faint tracery of veins beneath the skin. The head was at a slight angle, reminding her of nothing so much as a jaunty beret.

As she watched, it swelled further, twitching with eagerness. She closed her eyes and inhaled, leaning forward to fill herself with his scent.

Michael's fingers tightened on her skull, pressing her cheek to his cock, burying her nose in the musky curls surrounding it.

"You smell so good," she groaned.

"Time to see if I taste as good as I smell. Do it."

Sassy rubbed her cheek up and down his cock, eliciting a groan from him. His fingers clenched in her hair. She followed by tracing the same pathway with her tongue, licking him from his root to his quivering head.

A droplet appeared at the tip, and she licked that away, too. She teased his slit with the tip of her tongue. He gasped, his cock twitching.

"Take me in your mouth, Sasha. All the way."

Opening her lips, she nibbled delicately at his head, the same way she'd nibbled on the strawberry at the party, working him with her lips while her tongue teased and tortured. He shuddered, groaning with pleasure. His hands opened and closed restlessly, tangling in her hair, but not yet urging her to greater speed.

Her mouth closed over his entire head. She sucked, lightly at first, while her tongue traced the rim. Sucking harder, she worked her way down the length of him, until her nose was once again buried in his musky hair.

"Oh, yeah," he moaned. "That's it."

Sassy stroked him with her tongue as she sucked, then scraped her teeth along his length, all the way to his head, as she pulled back and let him slide most of the way out of her mouth. She took a deep breath, relaxed her throat, and swallowed him in a long, smooth glide.

His soft cry had no words to it, but she knew exactly what he meant. She did it again, then again, faster. His hands gripped her skull, moving her head up and down on his cock in the rhythm he wanted. To brace herself, she reached up and grabbed his ass. She felt his tight ass muscles clench beneath her touch, and she groaned around his cock filling her mouth.

Her world narrowed to his hot, hard cock, slipping in and out of the steamy cavern of her mouth. Beads of cum gathered at the tip with every long stroke. Soon his legs were trembling, his shaking hands no longer able to guide her head.

Sassy increased her rhythm, sucking him harder and faster. Her own breasts ached in sympathy, and the flesh between her legs pulsed in time to her movements. But she expected no satisfaction. This was Michael's moment, her purpose to give him pleasure.

He grunted, hoarse gasps rising in pitch. His fingers dug into her scalp, crushing her face to him as he thrust deep. With a bellow, he came, shooting hot liquid down her throat.

She swallowed, over and over again, determined to wring him dry. Suddenly, hot liquid burst forth between her legs and she shuddered with her own release.

She clung to his legs, kissing and licking his now limp cock. He stroked her hair, once more gentle.

"That was worth waiting for." He sighed in pleasure. "You can stop now."

Continuing to kiss him, she asked, "I can, but do you want me to?"

"Yes. Or we'll never make it into the bedroom."

She gave him one last, openmouthed kiss, then rose to her feet. Momentarily sated, she indulged her curiosity, and studied her surroundings. Her apartment would fit neatly in the space of his dining and living rooms, possibly overflowing into a bit of the kitchen. The open airiness of it made her feel free. Or maybe that was just being with Michael.

In addition to the formal dinner suite, a beautiful beechwood table comfortably surrounded by six matching chairs, inside the apartment, at the end of the balcony outside the first pair of French doors stood an Adirondack-style table and two chairs of weathered gray wood. His tastes seemed to run to clean, simple lines, a unity of form and function. The balcony was completely empty where it ran past the two sides of the living room, with nothing but a decoratively scrolled iron railing blocking his view of the ocean. It would be fabulous in the daylight. Even now, with clouds covering the moon and stars, the unseen darkness of the water pulled at her with a mysterious lure. The distant lights of cargo ships along the horizon twinkled like stars that had fallen to earth.

Enticed by the sound of the surf, she pushed aside the magnetic insect screen and stepped out onto the balcony. He followed her outside, unselfconsciously naked.

"You know what I'm thinking of?" he asked.

"No. What?"

"Coming out here with you during a storm, leaning you against that railing and taking you from behind, pounding into you with the rhythm of the waves pounding against the shore, wet with rain and slick with sex."

He moved up behind her, trapping her against the railing. Sassy shivered, imagining them moving together with the fury of a storm, screaming their release as thunder clapped and lightning shot jagged bolts across the sky. She leaned back, resting against his warm strength.

"I'd like that."

"I can think of a few other things you might like, too."

He nuzzled the side of her neck, lightly nipping first her ear then her collarbone. Sassy melted into his embrace, the familiar aching need already growing inside her. His touch was an addiction. The more she got of him, the more she craved.

"Are you going to share your thoughts with me?" she asked, trying for a teasing tone but too breathless to quite pull it off.

"I'd rather show you."

She offered no resistance as he turned and ushered her inside, shutting the door behind them. After closing the other balcony doors, he returned to guide her through the living and dining areas, to the only interior door she'd seen in the apartment. With a flourish, he threw open the door.

The first thing she saw was the king-sized four-poster bed, covered with a navy and green spread, beneath a huge ceiling fan. She stepped into the room, fully as large as the living and dining rooms, and saw a sitting area to her right. A profusion of hardy ferns in baskets hung from the ceiling, their long fronds waving gently in the current from an unseen air-conditioning vent. Unlike the simple elegance of the bed and matching dresser in smooth pecan, the furniture in the sitting area was all made of leather; futons, ottomans, and oversized square cubes for end tables.

Michael noticed where her attention lingered, and chuckled softly. "Looks quite respectable, doesn't it? But those ferns don't need such heavy hardware to hold them in the ceiling."

Sassy glanced up at the heavy iron hooks in the ceiling. Hooks easily capable of supporting an adult's weight. She licked her lips.

"What do they hold when the plants are taken away?"

"Whoever I want them to."

She pictured herself naked, strung up by chains attached to manacles on her wrists, displayed for Michael's viewing pleasure. Or any other pleasure he might desire of her, since she'd be helpless and at his mercy. She shivered with a mix of fear and desire, a chill snaking down her spine even as her womb pulsed with heat. Michael rubbed her arms, and she moaned softly, leaning back against his warm, strong body. "How would you hook me up? Chains and manacles?"

"You have a vivid imagination. I like it." He nibbled the side of her neck, smoothing his hands over her hips and stomach to mold her more securely against his body. "But no, that's not a safe way to suspend someone. You could hurt your wrists or shoulders. I'd have you wear a body harness, or sit in a suspension sling. That way, you could safely be suspended for hours."

"Hours?" she whispered.

He chuckled. "There's a lot of ways to play with you while you're up in the air. I'll show you some time."

Sassy's mouth turned dry. What other ways would he have of playing with her? And what else would he use?

Cued by the disguised hooks, she paid more attention to the leather furniture. The end-table cubes were about the same height as the table he'd bent her over at the party. And the adjustable futons had leather straps that could as easily tie a person to the cushion as tie the cushion to the frame.

"It's all for sex games, isn't it?"

"Smart girl."

"But why?" She turned to face him. He'd said that Miami was indulgent of BDSM practitioners. But his secret dungeon gave the lie to that theory. "This is your private apartment. Why do you have to hide your equipment?"

"There's private, then there's *private*. My studio and office are down the other hallway from the foyer. Clients can wander in here by mistake. And I entertain casual friends who wouldn't understand. Only the people I trust see beyond the respectable façade."

Sassy's lungs stopped. He trusted her. But he shouldn't. She might still have to betray him.

"Oh, Michael," she cried, and plastered herself to his naked chest.

He bent and scooped her into his arms. She squeaked, automatically clutching his neck. Then she realized he was carrying her to his bed.

The hell with the review or the article. All that was in the future. She'd just enjoy being here with him now.

Melting, she nestled her head against his shoulder, the fingers of one hand stroking his hair while her other hand caressed his bare chest. A low sound of pleasure rumbled through him.

He released her. She squeaked again as she fell, then bounced harmlessly on the thick covers of the bed. From their softness, he either had a down mattress cover, or a down blanket.

"You're wearing too many clothes," he complained. "I like looking at your body. Take them off."

She rose up onto her knees and pulled the dress over her head, then tossed it blindly aside. Her bra followed a moment later. She started to shimmy out of her panties, working them down her thighs, then rolled onto her back and lifted her legs to get them the rest of the way, kicking off her shoes and panties. The shoes tumbled to the floor.

Michael growled and pounced onto the bed, landing between her legs. He grabbed the panties before they could fall to the floor as well. "Mine."

Lying on her back, she gazed up at him as he stared at her exposed sex with raw passion darkening his gray eyes. He traced one finger lightly over her mound, stroking the damp curls. Slowly, he nudged her knees further and further apart, until she was spread as wide as she could be.

He lifted the panties to his face and inhaled deeply. "There's nothing like the scent of a well-pleased woman. How many times have I made you come so far tonight?"

"I don't know. I lost count." She did some quick arithmetic in her head. Three, no, four times in the bedroom at the party. Once on the patio. Did in the SUV count? She'd gotten wet, but hadn't orgasmed. She'd done that when she'd sucked his cock, though. "At least six times."

"Not nearly enough. I'll just have to make you come again." He sighed in mock aggravation. "And again. I'll be at this all night."

Sassy whimpered, her bones turning to shifting sand at the thought of him wringing orgasm after orgasm from her body, all night long.

He stood, then, and walked over to his dresser. He dropped her panties, exchanging them for some other fabric from his top drawer. When he returned, he shook out two fine linen handkerchiefs, folding them expertly and wrapping them around her wrists. He knotted silk scarves around the handkerchiefs, holding them in place, then knotted the first scarf to his bedpost.

"Lie down in the middle of the bed, your arms over your head," he directed.

Remembering how he'd tied her hands at the party, she put her arms out to the sides rather than straight overhead.

"Good girl." He adjusted her position slightly, then tied the second scarf to the opposite post. "How's that feel?"

She tugged at the bonds. There was a slight give in the scarves, but not enough to come loose. Her breath quickened, blood pulsing through her throbbing core.

"It feels like I'm at your mercy. You can do anything you want to me."

"I want to kiss you." He slid his hands beneath her hips, cupping her ass, and tilted her up to better expose her sex. Looking down at her, he slowly licked his lips. "Long, hot, wet kisses. Deep, penetrating kisses."

She shuddered, and felt the lubricating moisture dripping over the throbbing flesh between her legs. Her knees were spread wide, and as he watched her body, she felt her folds spreading for him, too. Then he bent his head, and put his mouth to her.

His tongue stroked and caressed her, spiraling around her entrance. He slipped away to suck lightly on her clit, then thrust his tongue inside her channel, licking and sucking, until she spasmed and screamed his name.

"Seven," he whispered.

True to his word, he made her come again and again, until she not only lost count, she lost the ability to count. At some point he untied the scarves and flipped her over, reinforcing her total submission by taking her from behind where she couldn't even see him as he pleasured her. She was so far gone by then, the experience was like something out of a dream.

He curled around her, then, stroking her gently and whispering to her in a sleepy voice. She was drifting, unable to focus on his words. Something about her, and being good. All she needed to know was that he was pleased with her. She had satisfied him. Completely.

Chapter Five

In the morning, Sassy woke gradually, at first aware only of her aching muscles that protested her vigorous night of clubbing. She must have forgotten to take her usual aspirin and glucosamine nightcap when she got home last night. When she tried to sit up, she discovered the sheets had tangled around her in the night, pinning her to her uncomfortably warm bed. She shoved sleepily at the offending bedcovers, and discovered it was a man's arm that weighed her down.

Memory returned in an instant. She hadn't gone home. Michael had exhausted her so thoroughly, she'd fallen asleep in his bed.

His arm tightened, drawing her closer to him.

"Morning," he mumbled, nuzzling her neck. When no further caresses were forthcoming, she realized he'd just been burrowing deeper into the pillow they were sharing.

He'd been insatiable last night, touching and tasting every inch of her. But this morning, he didn't seem the least bit interested.

She propped herself up on one arm so that she could look at him. "Michael?"

He groaned, and covered his eyes with his forearm. "God, don't tell me you're a morning person."

She laughed. "According to the clock on your dresser, it's nearly eleven. That hardly counts as being a morning person."

"It does when we didn't get to sleep until dawn."

"Well, whose fault was that?"

He lowered his arm, a sleepy, self-satisfied smile warming his face. "I think we both contributed."

Sassy dropped back down to the mattress. Cuddling against him, she twined her legs with his and pillowed her head on his firm chest. With her free arm, she stroked and caressed his beautiful body, reacquainting herself with the curves and planes she'd learned so thoroughly last night.

He sighed with pleasure, his cock twitching as it stirred to life. "Waking up like this almost makes it worth facing the morning."

"Almost?" she protested in mock outrage. "I know how to make you want to wake up."

She slipped her hand between his legs, cupping and fondling his balls. His cock stiffened. She stroked light caresses up and down his length before taking him firmly in her hand and squeezing gently.

Michael groaned, his hips lifting to push him deeper into her embrace. But she moved with him, denying him what he sought.

"This is one way to wake you up," she teased, squeezing again. "Or I could get up and make you some coffee."

"You're making me choose between sex and coffee? You're an evil, evil woman."

Sassy laughed. "So? Which will it be?"

"The hell with the coffee."

He rolled over, pinning her to the mattress beneath him. Then his lips found hers, and she forgot about teasing him, forgot everything but the feel of his body moving above and inside her. The brief delay while he found and applied a condom nearly reduced her to tears at the loss of his sweet heat. Then he was back, pressing urgently at her entrance. She opened eagerly for him, her body hot and slick, easing his way. His first thrusts were slow and gentle, feeling her reactions.

Too slow. Sassy grabbed his ass and pulled him down, while lifting her hips up to meet him, seating him fully inside.

Michael chuckled breathlessly. "That's the way you want it, huh?"

"Please."

He moved faster, pumping in and out of her with enough force to push her deep into the mattress with each thrust. They were both panting, straining toward release. Then he shifted his position, resting his weight on his knees instead of his arms, and cupped her ass. He lifted her hips as he thrust deeply, changing the angle of penetration and sending her over the edge.

She shouted his name. He continued pumping, faster and harder, his labored breathing coming in harsh gasps. Then he cried out, his rigid body shuddering as the condom filled with his cum.

He collapsed on the bed beside her, his limp cock stroking her one last time as he slid free. "You're right. That made me want to wake up. I don't, however, want to get out of bed."

"Me neither. Ever."

He laughed, and nudged her toward the edge of the bed. "Don't get too comfortable. I still want that coffee."

Sassy slid out of the bed and stretched, then lifted her hair away from her neck, the cool air welcome against her warm skin. Behind her, Michael caught his breath sharply.

"God, I wish I had a camera with me."

She glanced over her shoulder in a peekaboo pose to see his eyes dark with desire. Her body hummed, the blood pulsing hot and thick through her veins.

"I could get one for you," she offered.

He closed his eyes and shook his head. "Later. First, coffee."

She stopped first in the generous master bathroom, the whirlpool bath and shower unit enticing her with the promise of future wet and soapy lovemaking. Borrowing his comb, she untangled her hair, certain he'd appreciate the improvement once he'd had his coffee and could open his eyes. Then she padded out to the kitchen. She spotted the brushed steel coffeepot at once, holding pride of place in the center of the counter beside the double sink beneath the breakfast bar. A matching toaster oven was positioned beside it. But there was no coffee canister.

Opening and closing cupboards revealed a wide variety of pots, pans, and serving dishes—he hadn't been kidding about entertaining—as well as his supply of glassware and coffee mugs. Eventually she also discovered the pullout shelves of the pantry cupboards, which did contain two boxes of assorted teas and a package of coffee filters, but no actual coffee.

Hands on hips, she studied the kitchen. She'd looked everywhere.

"Where's your coffee can?" she called to the bedroom.

"Back of the refrigerator," Michael's voice drifted out to her. "The filters are in the cabinet next to the stove."

Who kept coffee in a refrigerator? Then again, what did she know? She drank instant.

The fridge was filled with typical bachelor fare, takeout containers, leftover pizza, and beer. In a nod to healthy eating, he also had sport-top bottles of water, bagged salad, cream cheese, and fruit. The open pint of half-and-half was obviously for the coffee.

A folded and sealed brown paper bag behind the water bottles bore a sticker from The Daily Grind, with "French Coffee House Blend" written in bold black ink. She took out the bag, inhaling the aroma as she opened it. Thick and rich, with subtle hints of fruit and exotic spices. Her mouth watered.

Carefully following the directions, she measured three generous scoops into the filter, then filled the carafe with water and poured it into the reservoir. She flipped the switch, returned the coffee to the fridge and got down two large mugs. Then she leaned against the wall until the kitchen filled with the delicious fragrance.

Michael strolled out of his bedroom, sniffing the air appreciatively. He was wearing swimming trunks, with a lightweight beach robe folded over his arm.

"We'll have our coffee outside," he announced, holding the robe out to her. "Beautiful as you are completely naked, that's a sight I want to save for myself."

Sassy pulled on the robe, turning her head to inhale the smell of sunscreen mixed with Michael's own unique scent. The overly large robe engulfed her. She had to turn back the cuffs three times, and the hem hung down below her knees.

While she was fixing the robe, Michael poured out two mugs of coffee, adding a liberal splash of cream and a touch of sugar to his. "How do you like your coffee?"

"A few drops of milk and three spoonfuls of sugar."

He raised an eyebrow, but dutifully sprinkled her mug with droplets of half-and-half, then spooned in two servings of sugar. "There's some natural sweetness to the coffee. Try it with two sugars first, and you can always add more if it's not sweet enough for you."

She wrapped her hands around the warm ceramic of the mug, closed her eyes, and inhaled deeply. Too bad coffee never quite lived up to the promise of its aroma. Then she tasted it.

Her eyes flew open. "It's wonderful!"

Chuckling softly, he opened the French doors and ushered her out onto the balcony. He waved her toward the near chair, with the view of the beach, while he circled around to take the chair with the view of her.

They sat quietly, drinking the heavenly coffee, while the distant sounds of talking and laughter drifted up from the beach, punctuated by the throaty roar of motorboats and personal watercraft. She smiled, watching as the caffeine hit Michael's bloodstream. He straightened, no longer slouching in the Adirondack chair, and his gaze sharpened.

"Great in bed and you make a killer cup of coffee," he teased. "The perfect woman."

Sassy looked down at the nearly empty mug clasped in her hands, the easy camaraderie of the morning destroyed by his words.

"I'm not perfect," she whispered.

In an instant, he was out of his chair and kneeling by her side, lifting her chin up so that she would look at him. "Sasha? What's wrong?"

Now was the time to tell him. Admit that she'd gone to the party under false pretenses, that she was planning on writing an article about everything she'd done with him. Reassure him that whatever her original motives she was here because she wanted to be with him.

Except, after she told him all that, he wouldn't want to have anything to do with her. Hadn't he told her how important his privacy was to him? Hadn't he stressed that the foundation of any BDSM relationship had to be trust?

She shook her head, glancing away from his storm cloud-colored gaze. "I'm thinking about work again."

"Well, stop it," he ordered, tapping her wrist lightly with his fingertips. "You'll feel better after you get some breakfast in you."

"Breakfast? But I looked in all your cupboards, searching for the coffee. You don't have any cereal, or eggs, or even bagels."

"Briar Rose puts on a great spread for their morning-after brunch. It's casual, held poolside, although still invitation only."

"That's why you're wearing trunks. But I don't have a bathing suit with me."

He shrugged. "I can loan you one. I have plenty of costumes for photo shoots. Or we can stop by your apartment."

Show him her tiny three-room apartment? No way. He'd know in an instant that she could never have afforded the Briar Rose fees. He'd want to know who had paid her way, and the whole story would be out.

"Loan me a costume. I'd like to see more of what you do."

Michael gulped down the last of his coffee and led her back inside. They passed through the beaded curtain into the foyer, then through an open archway and down a short hallway that ended in a bathroom. The metal sign on the door bore the discreet logo of the White Star Line. Sassy glanced around the hallway, looking for the matching "This Way to the Lifeboats" sign, but saw only framed photographs.

The photos were all of people, but they were a strange juxtaposition of young musicians filled with vibrant attitude, high-fashion models caught in a moment of alluring humanity, and flamboyant drag queens. Some were clearly studio shots, while others had been taken on location. The hallmark of all of his work, however, was the sense that the camera had captured a side of the people not normally revealed — the sheer, exuberant joy of the musicians doing what they'd always dreamed of doing, the longing of the models to live the fantasy they portrayed instead of the soul-crushing reality, and the vulnerability of the drag queens exposing their innermost nature.

"These are fabulous," she breathed, wanting to stop and study the photos at length. Then she noticed the signatures on the matting. "Jack?"

"My full name's Michael Jackman. One of the first guys I worked with in the business insisted on pronouncing it as two words. 'Hey, Jack, man.' Everyone else thought my first name was Jack. It was less confusing to just answer to that."

He tugged on her hand, pulling her around the corner of the hall to a diamond-shaped patch of carpeting. They entered through the open side of the diamond. The wall to their right contained more photographs, to their left was a door marked "Private", and directly opposite was another beaded curtain.

Michael pushed open the door, and led her inside a crowded office. Padded bags and molded boxes full of gear filled the double-braced industrial wire shelves. Open binders and loose papers were scattered across a cluttered desktop, with other binders and portfolios on the shelves of a combination bookcase-file cabinet.

He opened another door, but kept his arm across the doorway, letting her look but not enter. Unlike the clutter and chaos of his office, the shelves of his darkroom were all in perfect order. Jugs of chemicals were lined up neatly, their labels facing outward. Trays were stowed on their sides, tilted slightly, exposed to the air but safe from dust, while stacks of development paper were safely cocooned in their light-proof coverings. A plastic basket of old wooden clothes-pegs sat beneath a retractable clothesline. Two heavy machines of black and silver defied her limited knowledge of photography, although she could identify the flat plates that must hold the finished photographs, and knew the complex knobs and levers on the sides of the machines must be used to perform adjustments.

"This is the heart of it all," Michael whispered, his voice as reverent as if he was in a church. "Slices of life caught on film and fixed forever."

He dropped his arm and stepped behind her, resting his cheek against her hair and capturing her in a loose embrace. Drawing her back against his body, he cradled her against the heat of his rising cock, and bent his head to nuzzle her neck.

"Let me photograph you," he breathed. "Let me capture your beauty and life on film."

Sassy nodded. If their relationship had to end, at least she would have this slice of time, perfectly preserved on film. It might be all she would ever have of Michael, after he learned the truth. And if his camera could capture her inner spirit as well as he had in the photos lining his walls, he'd know that, whatever other lies and omissions she'd been guilty of, her feelings for him had been real.

"What do you want me to do?"

He pulled her through the beaded curtain into his studio. Just inside the door, reflective white umbrellas arched over the powerful lights. A camera attached to a tripod pointed at the three panels topped by thick rolls of background images that hid the outer wall of the room. Michael muttered to himself as he flipped through the images, finally unrolling a scene of a woodland meadow, with rolling green hills rising in the distance. The images overlapped, forming a continuous picture, and curled onto the floor.

Then he turned on the lights, shining a diffuse glow against the backdrop. Suddenly, it looked real, as if she could run forward onto the grass and disappear into the cool woods.

He paid no attention to the effect. Opening a closet, he pulled out a carpet painted with fake grass, and a basket of silk flowers. He spread the carpet in front of the backdrops, overlapping its edge with the bottoms of the pictures. Then he tossed handfuls of tiny flowers in random cascades across the grass.

Ducking behind the camera, he looked through the viewfinder. He made minute adjustments to the positions of the flowers, then checked the image again. Once more, he shifted the flowers. This time, he was satisfied with the results.

He dug through the basket, pulling out five star-shaped white flowers—lilies or orchids. The sort of flower used in corsages.

Sassy smiled, recalling the Briar Rose flower code. White flowers, to show she was a submissive. But it should include a silver ribbon, indicating that she belonged to a master.

Clearly thinking the same thing, Michael twined a glittering silver ribbon through the stems to make a bouquet. Without looking at her, he said, "Take off your robe and kneel in the center of the meadow."

She pulled off the robe and tossed it against the wall behind the camera, where it would be out of the way. Then she crossed to the strip of flower-strewn carpet, finding it surprisingly soft against her bare feet.

"Which way do you want me to face?" she asked.

"So your shoulder is towards the camera. Either side."

Sassy chuckled. Unlike the models he normally worked with, she was not obsessed with having cameras photograph only her "good side". She didn't even know if she had a good side. Instead, she knelt with her right shoulder facing the camera so that she could continue to watch Michael as he worked.

He came out of the closet with more props, this time lengths of silver chain in various thicknesses.

"Hold out your arms in front of you."

When she did as he asked, he draped the chains across them, then ducked behind his camera to gauge the effect. The chains were surprisingly lightweight, although oddly, the smallest seemed the heaviest. After a moment of careful study, she realized most of the chains were actually plastic, and painted silver. The thinnest chains were real metal, which is why they weighed more.

Michael pulled away all but the two thinnest chains, and wrapped those loosely around her arms, one by her wrists and one in the middle of her forearms. He checked the image again, then removed the thinnest chain. Carefully, he rewrapped the remaining chain, winding it around her wrists and partway up her arms. Then he pressed the end of the chain into her hand, bunching it up and folding her fingers around it, until a four-inch tail showed. He placed the bouquet of flowers in her other hand.

"Perfect." He moved back behind the camera. "Move your back leg forward about three inches. And rotate your shoulders so your chest is toward me."

She did as he said, then followed additional directions to spread her knees further apart, tip her hips forward, lift her arms, bend her elbows, and tilt her chin. She was starting to feel less like an object of desire and more like a giant posable doll. How could he capture his subjects' inner emotions like this?

Then he began to speak.

"Can you feel how you're positioned, your pussy open and ready for me to reach out and touch you? Your breasts aching for my caress? Even now, they're swelling with desire, the nipples beading, tightening into two hard little buds."

Sassy's body quickened in response to his words. A faint draft wafted across her naked body, teasing the damp folds between her legs. Her ass tightened, thrusting her exposed sex forward. Her nipples hardened, aching for his mouth to suck on them. She curled her fingers tighter around the stems of her bouquet and the end of the chain.

"Yes, Michael," she whispered. Her gaze sought his, but he was hidden behind his clicking camera.

"The flowers are an offering," he continued. "You wish to please me, by giving me gifts of beauty. But their beauty is nothing compared to yours. And so, you offer me yourself. Your hand is the one that has chained you."

"Yes," she sighed, wishing it was true. Determined to make it true. She would offer herself to him, give him anything he wanted. Her body. Her soul. Everything she had. And he'd see how much he meant to her, how badly she wanted to be his slave. When he learned the truth about her job, he'd remember her eager willingness, and know that she hadn't lied to him. Not about her feelings, and not about anything else. She just hadn't told him the truth. But he'd be able to see the truth in his photographs.

Michael groaned, snapping off a flurry of pictures. Then the rapid clicking stopped as he adjusted something on the camera.

He pulled off his swim trunks revealing a rampant erection. The trunks were the kind containing pockets, and he pulled a condom package from the pocket with a flourish worthy of a magician pulling a rabbit from a hat.

Watching him roll the condom over himself, Sassy's flesh pulsed hot and wet, eager for him to plunge inside her. He circled behind her, kneeling between her calves, and wrapped his arms around her waist. His solid cock prodded her ass, then slipped forward, sliding between her legs.

They moaned in unison. Michael reached down and guided his cock into her. Cupping her mound, he pressed her hips back as he thrust forward.

"Michael!" she cried.

The camera's click echoed in the room.

"Timer," he whispered, swirling his tongue around the edge of her ear then nibbling gently on the lobe.

He pinched her nipple with one hand while his other squeezed her clit. A lightning bolt flashed through her. She arched her body, driving herself deeper onto his cock.

He thrust into her, again and again, whatever he'd seen through the viewfinder of his camera turning him savage with a need to claim her. His gentle nips along her neck and collarbone grew harder and harder until he sunk his teeth into her shoulder, pinning her like a jungle cat while he pumped his cock in and out of her.

She writhed against him, mindless with need. She needed to touch him, kiss him, caress him. But her hands were bound, his body hidden behind hers except for the one hand still kneading her breast and the other between her legs. Still holding her bouquet, she grabbed his arm, clutching his hand tight to her chest.

"Please, Michael. Please!" she begged.

The fingers of his other hand dug between her folds, finding and squeezing her clit as he pounded into her. Once. Again.

Sassy threw her head back and screamed her release. Her muscles clenched around Michael's thrusting cock, and he bellowed with his own climax, exploding inside her.

He held her close, his cheek resting against her hair, her spread thighs braced against his. She could feel the slight rise and fall of his chest behind her as he breathed, their lungs synchronized in tandem with their thundering pulses. Slowly, hearts and lungs returned to normal.

The rush of blood no longer filling her ears, other sounds intruded. Michael's soft exhalation of breath and low purr of masculine pleasure. The muted whir of the air-conditioning cycling on. The click of the camera.

Sassy stiffened. "You took pictures of us making love?"

"I'll give you the negatives," he promised. "But I wanted you to be able to see what I see."

If he'd asked beforehand, she'd have denied him. *Sun Daze* was a feel-good paper, edgy enough to appeal to jaded locals as well as adventurous tourists, but not so extreme that they'd lose advertising dollars. Paid for by advertisements and classifieds, as well as the revenue from their website, they didn't need celebrity scandals to drive sales. But she'd mingled with enough staffers from other papers at the various clubs and events around town to know how a single incriminating photo could be recycled for years to drive sales. She'd never open herself up to that kind of notoriety.

Except Michael hadn't asked her permission. She'd known the camera was there, known he'd set a timer, and hadn't protested. That had been enough for him. And he'd offered to give her the negatives, as if guessing the possible publicity was the source of her concern, not distaste for the subject matter.

Sassy smiled. When their relationship ended, at least she would have this much of him, something to look at to keep the memories as fresh and vivid as the film.

She relaxed into his embrace. "I'm glad you did."

He kissed her lightly, rewarding her acquiescence. "Developing the film can wait. Time to get dressed and go to the brunch."

Chapter Six

A short time later, dressed in a white bikini patterned with starbursts of silver glitter flaring around her nipples and shooting upward from her crotch, Sassy followed Michael onto the wide pool side patio at the Eleanor. His navy and white Ralph Lauren Polo swim trunks had bulged appreciatively the first time he'd seen her in the outfit, and he'd declared that if she walked in front of him, he'd be unfit for polite society.

She recognized many of the people from last night's party, although they'd all changed into beachwear, ranging from bikinis that were the legal minimum to full-length cover-ups and sun hats. Some retained hints of their sexual preferences, such as the crocheted bikini being worn by the submissive who'd demonstrated rope dresses. Some were completely hidden, like Mistress Melissa's two slaves who wore T-shirts and trunks.

Of course, even though this was a private party, non-attendees could still see them. Neither of the men would want to advertise their nipple rings or other, more private piercings. The reminder of how many people's reputations could be damaged by a full exposé was sobering.

Michael glanced over his shoulder at her. "Something wrong?"

"Why?"

"You slowed down."

Sassy forced a smile. He was too damned perceptive. "Just looking at all the partygoers. Quite a change in dress from last night."

"You can look later, while we eat." He tugged her hand, pulling her toward the first of the buffet stations.

He loaded a plate with melon cubes, pineapple wedges, fluffy scrambled eggs, strips of cinnamon French toast, and bacon slices for them to share. Sassy accepted two frosty glasses of fresh iced tea from the hotel employee manning the beverages. A separate small bar was set up for those who had indulged too heavily the night before, and wanted a hair of the dog, or those who wanted the traditional Sunday morning mimosa or Bloody Mary.

Michael located an empty chaise, white like all the hotel furniture, and sat down. Sassy looked at the crowded patio in confusion.

"But where do I sit?"

"Right here." He patted his thigh invitingly with his free hand.

Careful not to spill the drinks, she straddled the lounge, and slowly lowered herself onto his lap. His rapidly firming erection pressed against her ass. She shifted position slightly, scooting back and easing his cock between her legs, and was rewarded with his sigh of pleasure. She leaned back, against his chest, and stretched her legs out, her smooth, shaved legs looking delicate and feminine bracketed between his lean, muscled legs lightly furred with dark hair.

He put his arms around her, resting the plate of food in her lap, slightly to the side so that he could see it over her shoulder. Spearing a pale green cube of honeydew on his fork, he lifted it to her lips. She opened her mouth and let him slide it inside, feeling the answering twitch from his cock beneath her.

Slowly, they worked their way through the huge amount of food. If Sassy had entertained any doubts that providing for her pleased Michael, he put them to rest most thoroughly. She could feel how his arousal built with every forkful of food he fed to her. That made her hotter and wetter, until her bikini briefs were soaked through as if she'd actually gone into the pool. When she paused for a cooling sip of iced tea, she noticed no corresponding jump in his cock, even though she sucked on the straw in a highly suggestive fashion. No way was she passing up such a great opportunity to turn him on.

"These glasses are sweating," she told him. "I'm afraid I'll drop them. Is it okay if I put them down?"

"Sure."

Sassy leaned over and placed both glasses on the concrete, where they instantly formed twin puddles. Now Michael could serve her drink to her, and they'd both enjoy it. Playfully, she wiped her chilled, wet palms against his warm thighs. He shivered, but his cock jumped upward.

He hugged her with his free hand, pulling her tight against himself. His cock pressed against the thin fabric of her bikini until it shifted to one side, allowing him to push between her plump nether lips.

She swallowed a moan. He felt so good. But it wasn't enough. Her body clenched, eager to pull him the rest of the way inside her. She wanted more than the swim-trunk-covered tip of him against her opening. She wanted the length of him, hard and hot and slick inside her.

"Michael?" she whispered, barely breathing the words so that the people sitting on the chaises to either of side of them wouldn't hear her. "Can you slide out the fly of your swim trunks?"

His arm tightened around her. "Oh God. You have no idea how that makes me feel."

"Yeah, I do."

She rolled her weight from one ass cheek to the other, teasing the tip of his cock a few hairsbreadth deeper. He buried his face against her neck, muffling his groan.

"I can't put a condom on here. And I'm too stiff to get up and go to the men's room."

Sassy growled with frustration. "Well, what if you just don't come?"

His answering chuckle sounded pained. "My control is good, Sasha, but it's not that good. Knowing I'd made you come in the middle of a crowded party would send me over the edge."

The mention of the crowd surrounding them was enough to cool her ardor...until his cock twitched against her throbbing flesh. Her muscles clenched, tightening and releasing in wave after helpless wave, desperate to pull him inside her. He groaned into her neck again, following up with a hungry openmouthed kiss full of tongue and teeth. She writhed against him, tilting her head to allow him free plunder of her neck and shoulder, and cursed the borderline high blood pressure that had kept her off the pill.

"I need you, Michael. Now. Screw the condom."

A deep shudder coursed through him. "No. Your safety is my responsibility."

She heard his breathing shift, slowing and deepening. The head of his cock no longer pressed urgently against her. He drew another two deep breaths, then pushed her forward, off of his softening cock and onto his thighs.

"Get up—carefully—and don't say anything."

Sassy did as he'd told her, knowing he was fighting to bring his body's reaction back under control. He waited a moment longer, then rose fluidly to his feet. Only his white-knuckled grip on the plate still in his hand gave any indication of how much effort was required not to be aroused.

He stalked off, leaving her standing beside the chaise. Not knowing what else to do, she picked up her glass of iced tea and took a long, cooling drink. She stood there for an eternity, scanning the crowd who lounged around the pool. A few couples were sharing chaises, kissing or engaging in some discreet petting beneath loose beach wraps. Latecomers like her and Michael were still eating. But most people had their eyes closed, resting in the sun as they chatted with those around them.

A pair of giggling women slipped into the pool, clinging to the wall and splashing at the man they'd left behind. He let out a roar, and followed them into the water, dunking first one then the other. The women's laughter mingled with their squeals, attracting the attention of other partygoers.

As if this was a signal of some sort, the pool was soon filled with laughing, squealing people, splashing and dunking each other. In the middle of all this Michael returned, his plate piled high with fruit.

"You went back to the buffet?" she asked. She'd been so sure he was going to put on a condom. Disappointment settled in her stomach, destroying what appetite she had left.

"We needed a reason for me to be leaning back and forth, besides the obvious," he whispered, although their nearest neighbors had both joined the party in the pool, and were no longer likely to hear him.

He sat on the chaise, the plate in his lap concealing his hand as he adjusted his swim trunks and liner. Sassy glimpsed the pale white tip of a condom in the opening.

"Sit," he ordered.

Her legs quivered with nervous anticipation as she eased herself onto his lap. His arms tightened around her, and he bent his head to kiss her shoulder. As his tongue stroked lazy circles against her skin, his cock rose and hardened. When he was ready, he nudged the crotch of her bikini to the side, then guided her back until the head of his cock pressed against her opening.

She shivered, her hungry flesh pulsing against him.

"You really want to do this?" he asked one last time.

"Yes," she breathed.

"Then spread your pussy."

"How?"

Michael growled. "Lean to the left a bit."

As she shifted her weight to that side, he cupped her bikini-clad hip with his right hand and stretched the skin, opening her to his invasion. The head of his cock slid inside her. She gasped, her muscles tightening and trying to draw him deeper.

"No," he cautioned her. "You'll have to remain completely silent, if you don't want everyone to know what we're doing."

Sassy nodded, not trusting her voice. Michael leaned forward, his arms around her holding the plate of fruit in her lap. Slowly, he speared a cube of melon and raised it to her lips, the natural flexing of his hips as he moved lifting his cock higher, pressing deeper inside her. She opened her lips and took the sweet honeydew into her mouth, the way she wanted to close around his cock and pull him inside her. He flexed, pressing his cock against the wall of her vagina, and she moaned softly.

"You like the fruit?" he asked, humor lacing his deep voice.

"Oh yes," she whispered. "It's so sweet."

He bent to spear another melon cube and lift it to her lips, his cock nudging the barest fraction deeper. Sassy's muscles clenched, trying to pull him further inside, but it was no good.

"Relax," he told her. "Enjoy the taste of each piece. It'll take a long time to work through the whole plate. A *long* time."

A tremor rippled through her. She wanted him now. But as she'd learned so well, her wants meant nothing. She'd given him permission to satisfy her, and he'd do it his way. She had no doubt that the end result would be beyond her wildest imagining, but getting there would test her patience and obedience to their utmost.

She leaned forward slightly, taking the fruit before the fork reached her mouth. Straightening, she rolled her weight, settling over him, stifling her sigh as he slipped further inside her.

Gradually, they worked out the best rhythm of slowly shifting their weight forward and backward, Michael's cock sliding ever so slightly deeper each time.

Sassy focused on the party around her, watching the cavorting models, actors, executives, and other beautiful people laughing and splashing in the pool. Only by keeping her attention on them rather than the feel of Michael's hard length pulsing inside her could she keep her breathing normal, her body relaxed. She wanted to pant, to tremble and shiver as he pushed deeper and deeper, each agonizing inch a triumph of anticipation that only whetted her appetite for more. But she couldn't. She couldn't give any clue that they were actually having sex on this chaise.

"You are so hot for me," Michael murmured. "I can feel your lubrication flowing down my cock."

Now that he mentioned it, she could feel his damp swim trunks against her ass. She tensed. "Oh God. It'll stain, and everyone will know."

He chuckled breathlessly. "This is a pool party. I'll go for a quick dip when we finish. No one will know."

Michael curled around her to offer her another piece of fruit, sighing gently as his cock finally entered her fully, his balls pressed against the thin barrier of his swimsuit below the opening of the fly. Tightening one arm around her waist, he snuggled her hips even closer, muffling his groan with an openmouthed kiss against her shoulder.

"Now," he whispered. "Tighten your inner muscles. But keep the rest of your body loose."

Sassy clenched around his cock, pressing herself along his length. Breathing deeply, forcing herself to stay relaxed, she clenched again. And again.

She'd waited so long for him to fill her that now she couldn't get enough of him. He swelled, growing harder and thicker.

The party blurred out of focus, bright colors and sharp sounds smearing into a collage of light and noise that grew dimmer and dimmer. Michael's tongue swept back and forth over the tender spot on her shoulder where he'd bitten her that morning, the edge of pain heightening her passion still further.

"Please, Michael," she whispered on a shaky breath.

"Keep perfectly still," he warned. "Completely quiet."

Sassy bit her lower lip, hard enough that she tasted blood. But she didn't move. And Michael did.

Holding her tight about the waist, he flexed his cock, rocking back and forth deep within her. She ground her teeth against her lip, using the pain to focus, keeping her from crying out in passion. He turned his head, nuzzling the side of her neck, then scraped his teeth across her pounding pulse. A soft whimper escaped her.

Carefully, he eased the mostly eaten plate of fruit forward, casually dropping his other hand behind it. Then beneath it. His fingers probed beneath the edge of her bikini and brushed her hot, swollen clit.

Sassy started to arch, remembering at the last moment that she wasn't supposed to move. Instead she forced the movement inside, bearing down and clenching around his cock with all the strength she was capable of. Michael squeezed her clit.

The orgasm ripped through her, blowing her away. The party disappeared in a swirling fog of pure sensation, then even that was gone, leaving her floating and flying far from her body.

She drifted slowly to consciousness, aware of uncomfortable heat along her side. She turned away, seeking the coolness on her other side.

Michael's rich chuckle brought her fully to wakefulness. "Sleeping beauty awakes."

She blinked. He was stretched out on the chaise next to the one she occupied, his dark hair plastered to his scalp and droplets of water clinging to his tanned and muscled body.

"What happened?" she asked, sitting up and running a shaky hand through her hair. The shifting beam of direct sunlight crossing her formerly shadowed chaise had woken her.

The sunbeam had been nowhere near them when they'd started making love.

"You passed out," he answered, his tone smug and full of pride.

She scanned the party. The pool was empty, as were most of the chaises. The buffet tables had been cleared, although the bartender was still available to dispense drinks.

"The brunch is over? How long was I out?"

Michael chuckled. "About an hour and a half. I told everyone that you hadn't slept much last night, and had fallen asleep in the heat."

"But that's not what happened."

"No." He stood and pushed his lounge chair flush against hers, making a double-wide chaise, then stretched out beside her. She curled against him, his pool-dampened skin soothing her overheated flesh. But she didn't want sex again. She just wanted to be near Michael.

"You," she whispered against his chest. "Only you."

She felt more than heard his deep rumble of masculine satisfaction as she acknowledged once again that she was his to control, and all her pleasure came from him, however he chose to give it to her.

He lazily stroked her hair and back. "The party's over. We can stay a little longer, if you want to cool off in the pool, but now that we're losing our shade, you really should switch to a new lounge."

Sassy sighed, stretching her limp muscles. Sex with Michael was better than the best sauna and massage for completely relaxing her.

"I don't want to move."

"You also don't want to fry to a crisp."

The edge of the sunbeam crept further across their chaise, roasting her back until it prodded her into motion. She jumped up and ran across the patio, leaping into the pool with a big splash. The water closed over her with an arctic shock, and she kicked up to the surface, gasping and spluttering. After a moment, she acclimated, enjoying the refreshingly cool water.

Michael strode off, returning a short time later with one of the hotel's fluffy white towels. Sassy climbed out of the pool and stood dripping on the patio, her arms outstretched, as he toweled her dry. He glided the soft fabric over her skin in a gentle caress that ended all too soon. Grinning, he snapped the wet towel against her ass.

She jumped. Her body hummed, remembering the heights to which he'd already taken her, and eager to return.

"Is that a promise?" she asked.

He tossed the towel aside, flinging it across one of the abandoned lounges, and swept her into an embrace, his mouth claiming hers as he bent her over his arm. She was breathless and trembling by the time he lifted his head.

"Sadly, it's a promise that will have to wait," he said, his gray eyes shadowed. "I have something scheduled for this afternoon."

"Business or pleasure?"

"Business. Scouting locations for a photo shoot."

Sassy nodded. He couldn't reschedule. No problem. She could use the free time this afternoon to write up a draft of her first article. She'd at least have an outline to show Bryce on Monday.

Neither of them stepped away.

"When can I see you again?" Sassy asked.

"I'll be working tomorrow and Tuesday, pretty much dawn to dusk. How's Wednesday?"

"An eon away. I'll ache for you every night until then."

He smiled, the familiar warmth kindling in his eyes. "You'll ache for me even more come Wednesday night."

Sassy's legs quivered, threatening to drop her to her knees. Her nipples tightened, and her stomach clenched. She longed to be spread before him, tied to his bed or across a whipping bench, as he wrung scream after scream from her, plumbing the depths of her passion.

He wrapped an arm around her shoulders and guided her back to the lobby of the hotel. "I'll walk you to your car."

The chill of her duplicity shocked her out of her passionate daydream. If she told him she'd walked to the party, he'd want to drive her home. She couldn't let that happen. If he saw where she lived, he'd know she couldn't afford the Briar Rose fees. Then he'd want to know where the money had come from. And she'd have to tell him why she'd gone to the party.

"Sasha?" he prompted.

She'd stopped, forcing him to stop, too. Now he was looking at her with concern.

"I walked to the party. But I don't feel like going home. I think I'll go shopping instead."

"For anything in particular?"

"Mmm, something to wear Wednesday."

Michael laughed. "I know just the place. I'll drive you."

* * * * *

Sassy looked at exotic leather and lace costumes in the erotic boutique Michael drove her to. Her pulse quickened at the thought of Michael kissing and licking her exposed skin, teasing her flesh with gentle lashes and stinging slaps. But even the cheapest outfit on the clearance rack was well outside her price range.

Sighing, she left the store and walked home. Before leaving the brunch, she'd changed into her dress and strappy shoes. Now the humid air caused the fabric to cling damply to the small of her back, and tangle awkwardly between her legs. The thin dress seemed to grow heavier with every block.

She spent the rest of the day working on her article for *South Beach Sun Daze*, struggling to find the right balance between titillation and dry facts. Shortly before midnight, she finally gave up, filled with a new respect for the journalists at the paper. She drifted off to sleep with dreams of a future where her skillfully worded articles of one woman's adventures in BDSM lured both readers and advertisers to the paper, while safely protecting everyone involved behind a screen of impenetrable anonymity. Then she slid into the arms of Morpheus, and dreamed of all the ways Michael had yet to master her.

Monday morning, after her morning yoga stretches worked the stiffness out of her muscles and a thick cup of coffee opened her eyes, she grabbed the pages of her article and headed for the office. She'd type it up on the office computer, then show it to Bryce.

He was waiting for her, bolting out of his office in the back and reaching her desk at the front of the reception area before she'd had a chance to sit down.

"Well? Did you decide? Article or review?"

"Actually, I was thinking I'd do the article."

"Yes!" Bryce pumped his fist exuberantly, earning curious glances from the reporters already at their desks.

"But not the one you'd suggested."

Bryce's glee evaporated. "What do you mean?"

"Instead of an exposé , I was thinking of more of a human-interest story."

"Human-interest? I wanted edgy and provocative, not wholesome family fare. We're trying to gain readers, not put the ones we already have to sleep."

Sassy's cheeks blazed. The background hum of telephone conversations and clacking keyboards fell silent as everyone watched them.

"I can't discuss this here," she protested. "Can we go to your office?"

Bryce glanced at his slim gold watch, reminding her of Michael's pragmatic timepiece. The sudden hunger that gripped her stole her breath away. But more surprising than her physical need for Michael, she was filled with a desperate desire to keep him safe, to protect him. The cops would never call on him because of anything she said in the paper.

Bryce shook his head. "No, I've got a meeting. I won't be free until two o'clock. We can talk over lunch."

"You're buying?"

"If you review the restaurant."

"Deal."

Chapter Seven

By the time two o'clock rolled around, Sassy had typed, proofread, and printed her first draft of the article. It was the story of a submissive, S., and the Master, M., who helped her explore her undiscovered sexuality. Hopefully, readers would assume the S. and M. stood for submissive and Master, rather than their real names. Even so, the style was different enough from her usual smart-mouth attitude as Sassy D. that no one should connect the two.

She folded the papers and tucked them into her purse. She'd show them to Bryce after lunch, after she'd had a chance to warm him up to the idea.

He joined her at her desk. "Ready? There's a new bistro on Ocean Boulevard that's supposed to be a very trendy watering hole."

Sassy laughed. "Everything on Ocean is trendy."

"Ah, but this is trendy for locals, not just tourists."

"Should be good, then."

Bryce drove them to the bistro, easily finding a parking space now that the lunch crowd was gone. Some tourists were still lingering, though, watching the activity in the park across the street. A portable generator chugged rhythmically, cables snaking away from it to power lights, fans, and a variety of black and silver boxes whose purposes escaped her. Beautiful women relaxed in tall director's chairs as makeup artists touched up their faces, listening intently to a tall man dressed in a formfitting black shirt and tight black pants. His black ponytail, bound in a black Hair Glove, reminded her of Michael, making her body instantly hot and eager for his touch.

They took seats at a marble-topped table shaded by a market umbrella where they could face the action.

"What's going on?" she asked their waiter when he brought menus to them.

"They're shooting a perfume ad. For Ocean Breezes."

"Never heard of it."

"It's new. Some movie star is endorsing it. They wouldn't say who, though. It's supposed to be a big secret. Are you ready to order, or do you want your drinks first?"

Sassy glanced over her menu, quickly deciding on iced tea and gazpacho. She needed something cold to counteract the heat that thoughts of Michael were generating.

After they ordered, Bryce turned to her and rested his chin in his palms. "Well?"

"You know who Briar Rose caters to."

"The A-list."

"The A-list who are into BDSM."

"Yeah." He leered at her. "And our readers want the vicarious thrill of knowing what they do behind closed doors."

"What if you got a series all about what exactly went on behind those doors?"

Bryce's eyebrows lifted. "I thought you weren't going to do an exposé?"

"I'm not. My articles would follow one person, starting from her introduction to the scene, and describe everything that happened to her."

"You?" He frowned. "You said you'd review the Briar Rose party only if there was no dating and no sex."

"I changed my mind once I got there."

His gaze dropped to her clinging "Goddess" T-shirt, noting how her nipples had pebbled just talking about the party.

"So I see."

Sassy reached into her pocketbook and withdrew her article, sliding it across the table to him. "Here."

The waiter arrived with their drinks. She traced condensation circles on the table as Bryce read, eventually tearing her gaze away from his expression and forcing herself to look at the activity in the park. He'd tell her what he thought of the story when he finished.

The man in black gestured fluidly with one hand, catching Sassy's attention. She recognized the graceful ease of movement. Then he turned, and she saw his profile. Michael.

Her body kicked into overdrive. He'd said he'd be working, but she'd never thought to ask what he'd be photographing, or where.

His face glowed with intensity, his passion for his art evident in every line of his body. The two models listened to his explanation with rapt attention, their eyes slightly glazed and their glistening raspberry lips parted.

Sassy wanted to go over there and slap them for poaching. He was hers.

But he wasn't. He couldn't be, until she could be honest with him.

As if he felt her eyes upon him, Michael turned, scanning the crowd in the bistro. His gaze passed over her, then returned, his eyes widening. They smiled at each other, the rest of the world dropping away as they traded hungry promises with their eyes.

"This is great!" Bryce brought her back to reality with a snap.

She turned to face the editor. "You really think so?"

"Well, not the writing. That's still rough. But I'll work on that with you. The story, though. That's great. You'll take our readers along on your sexual journey of discovery. They'll be right with you every step of the way. We'll have advertisers wetting themselves to place ads on those pages."

Bryce smiled dreamily.

"It'll be anonymous," she warned.

"Of course."

She lifted her half-empty glass of iced tea, and he clinked the rim of his lemon water against it.

"Deal," she said.

Michael's voice cut through the quiet. "No, no, no! Jeannette, turn to your LEFT, and extend your RIGHT hand. Palm UP!"

Bryce glanced over at the park, his expression quickly sharpening in interest. "Do you know who that it? Jack Jackman. He'd be A-list if he ever went to parties. Rumor has it he's still in the closet."

Sassy stared at her boss in shock. Michael, gay? "Why?"

"There's no shortage of beautiful woman who'd sleep with him in an instant if he'd shoot their portfolio. But he doesn't bite."

Sassy hid a smile behind a sip of tea. Oh, he bit all right. She could still feel his teeth sinking into her shoulder as his cock plowed into her from behind. She shifted restlessly on the hard wooden slats of her chair.

Oblivious to her discomfort, Bryce continued with his story. "Last year, he did finally date one, a hungry up-and-comer that rumor had it would do *anything* to advance her career. A few weeks later, they broke up, and she suddenly had enough money to move to LA and start a career as an actress. The story is he couldn't get it up with a girl, and he paid her off so she wouldn't tell anyone."

Sassy blinked. Michael was insatiable. He didn't have a problem getting it up, he had a problem keeping it down. God, she'd lost count of how many times he'd made love to her over the weekend.

She wondered at the source of this rumor. His friends at the Briar Rose party had clearly known the details of his breakup, and that he was heterosexual. But they'd also called him Michael, his real name, rather than the name he used for his art.

Jack was his cover. A gay man still in the closet. People would think they'd guessed his secret, and not probe any deeper to uncover his BDSM lifestyle.

Bryce sucked in a quick breath. "He's coming this way. How do I look?"

"Fine," she answered without looking at her boss. Instead, she turned toward the park. Michael was heading straight toward her.

If Bryce found out they knew each other, she'd blow Michael's cover. She couldn't do that to him. Bryce lived for gossip. If he knew the truth about Michael, everyone in Miami would know.

She met Michael's gaze as he waited on the other side of Ocean to cross the street. The heat in his eyes both thrilled and terrified her. If Bryce saw that, he'd guess Michael's secret for sure.

Locking gazes with him, she waited until she was certain she had his full attention. Then she hardened her expression and turned her face away. From the corner of her eye, she saw his brows crease in confusion. But he was still crossing the street as soon as the light changed, heading for her table.

She twisted slightly in her chair, turning her shoulder toward him. She couldn't signal any more clearly that she didn't want to talk to him.

Bryce practically stopped breathing when Michael stopped in front of their table.

"Mr. Jackman, I'm a huge fan of your work. The photos you did for A Dozen Dead Rats were inspired."

"Thank you. It's a pleasure working with young, vibrant musicians." The polished response contained none of the passion and excitement that had filled his voice when he discussed his work with her. "And you are?"

"Bryce Fontaine, editor of *South Beach Sun Daze*. We'd love to interview you, if —"

"I don't do interviews." His cold gaze speared Sassy's heart. "Are you a *Sun Daze* reporter?"

"No." Oh God, this was worse than she'd feared. But how could she reassure him without letting Bryce know they were acquainted? "My name's Sassy. I'm the restaurant reviewer."

Bryce chuckled meaningfully. "Oh, she's much more than that. Her new series…"

Sassy kicked him under the table. Belatedly, he remembered that her articles were supposed to be anonymous.

"…is going to be fantastic. A totally different kind of review."

Fury smoldered in Michael's eyes, but his blandly polite facial expression never changed. "I'm sure. If you'll excuse me, I need to check the visual composition of my shoot, and this is the best angle and distance. I'll be out of your way in a moment."

He turned to face the park, lifting his hands before his eyes in a framing square like a Hollywood director. A moment later, he dropped his hands, muttered, "Too much green," and stalked back to the park.

Sassy let out the breath she'd been holding. Michael's quick thinking had invented a plausible reason for why he'd come over to their table. His secret was safe. But her secret was out. She wanted to cry. She'd known their relationship would end if she wasn't able to be truthful, but she'd inadvertently implied something even worse than her real reason for being at the Briar Rose party. Now Michael probably thought she was trying to get material for an interview, to lift herself up through the ranks at the paper.

Her gazpacho settled in her stomach with a greasy chill that had nothing to do with the quality of the food. Now, on top of everything, she was going to have to foot the bill for dinner at the bistro, to give it a fair review.

Back at the paper, she waited for the office to clear out. Most of the reporters only worked part-days, since there wasn't that much news in a weekly paper, even with the additional articles for the website. Bryce had an understanding with the reporters that they could use the additional time to write freelance articles for other papers or magazines, so long as they weren't in direct competition with *Sun Daze*, and they turned in their primary assignments for him on time. It allowed him to keep a higher caliber of writer for the pay he was willing to give them. But while they were in the *Sun Daze* offices, they were supposed to be working on *Sun Daze* material.

Sassy only cared that this gave her relative privacy to call Michael's answering machine.

"Jack Jackman, Fashion Photographer. Leave your name, number and message at the beep, and I'll call you back."

"Michael, hi. It's Sasha. I'm sorry about what happened today. That wasn't how I wanted you to find out. Remember, on the patio at the party, I told you how I was worried about work? They sent me there to review the party, and a *Sun Daze* review names names and gives juicy details. After what you said, I realized that could get people in trouble. But I had to give Bryce something, because he's the one who put up the money for the Briar Rose membership. I convinced him to take a series of anonymous articles about my experience, but I kept your name out of it. If he found out we knew each other, he'd have guessed you were the Master I was writing about. You saw what a blabbermouth he is. I was trying to protect you."

She paused, wishing she could see his face when he listened to the message. Wishing she knew how he was going to react. She sighed, and hurried to keep speaking before the machine cut her off.

"That doesn't have anything to do with why I want to see you again on Wednesday. You set me on fire. Please, call me. Let me know if you still want to see me."

She recited her home and work phone numbers, and fell silent. There was nothing more to say.

The machine clicked and hung up on her, but she continued holding the silent phone to her ear, unwilling to relinquish that last tenuous contact with Michael, until it began bleating its loud, annoying phone-off-hook signal.

She hung up the phone, and tried to focus on her work. Every time the phone rang, her heart leapt, hoping it was Michael. That he'd checked his messages during a break in the shoot and was calling her on his cell. But every time she was disappointed, and it was just people calling to place classified ads, or a video store wanting to be transferred to the advertising department, or a restaurant asking to have the number of copies they received increased.

By the time she went home, she was thoroughly depressed. She tried convincing herself that he hadn't had a chance to listen to his messages yet. After all, hadn't he said he'd be working dawn to dusk? But she was afraid that he had listened to her message, and was ignoring her.

He hadn't called her home number, either. Full dark came, and still he didn't call. She heated up a package of Ramen noodles, then sat picking at the food rather than eating it. When it congealed into a cold, sticky mass, she gave up and threw it out. If she got hungry later while she was out clubbing, she could always chow down on pretzels from a sympathetic bartender.

Opening her closet door, she stared unseeing at the clothing. Tonight was Monday. Tantra. A wild orgy of self-indulgence. Everything would remind her of Michael. She couldn't go.

She sighed, brushing her palm across the soft, breathable fabrics of her clubbing clothes; crushed velvet skirts, silk tank tops, and rayon halter dresses, all brilliantly colored and dusted with glitter or spangled with sequins. She was beginning to understand the appeal of black.

"I just wanted to have fun," she whispered. But this weekend had gone so far beyond fun, it wasn't even on the same map. Now adventures that had seemed wild and daring would just remind her of what she had shared with Michael, and pale to insignificance in comparison.

She glanced at her clock. He would have called by now if he was going to call her.

Her imagination conjured up pictures of the two beautiful models from today's photo shoot, consoling him in his bedroom. One knelt between his legs, sucking his cock, while the other straddled his shoulders, letting him feast on her pussy.

Oddly, Sassy felt neither jealous nor threatened by the mental picture. Michael was a man. If you sucked on his cock, eventually he'd come—it was physical nature. But those women, no matter how talented, couldn't give him what he really wanted, what he really needed. Eventually, he'd call her. Because he wanted what they'd shared as badly as she did. He wouldn't risk losing that because of a misunderstanding.

Cheered, she grabbed a flirty minidress in electric blue, covered with fuchsia and gold sequined flowers. She might not be up for Tantra, but a few hours of dancing at Back Door Bamby would do the trick. And if he did call, he wouldn't find her at home, waiting by the phone like some pathetic high school girl hoping for a date.

When she dragged herself in at two o'clock, exhausted by hours of vigorous dancing, the message light was still dark. But at that point, all she cared about was going to sleep.

She dreamt of Michael. He'd tied her to the giant leather cubes in his bedroom, and was whipping her, chastising her for being bad and not telling him about her real reasons for attending the party. Then he dropped the whip and made love to her, saying she could keep as many secrets as she wanted, as long as she allowed him to punish her for them.

She woke up hot and aching, her pussy wet and needing Michael to fill it. She spread her legs and stroked herself, imagining the fingers pushing inside her were Michael's. Shuddering, she arched upward and cried out, then fell back onto the bed. The orgasm barely soothed her itch, and she started stroking herself again, hoping to coax forth a better one.

It was a hopeless task. She could play with herself for hours and never come close to feeling what Michael made her feel. It wasn't just the physical act with him, although that was great. But it was the mental and emotional aspects that pushed her over the edge. She could never give herself that kind of experience.

Finally, she admitted defeat. Aching and restless, she climbed out of bed and got ready for work. Michael didn't call that day, either.

He didn't call while she was partying herself into exhaustion at Automatic Slim's, either.

By late afternoon on Wednesday, she was beginning to think he'd never call, and wondering if it would seem too pathetic of her to leave another message for him. Her phone rang, and she forced herself to answer with a perkiness she didn't feel, "*South Beach Sun Daze*. How may I help you?"

"Tied to my bed, naked and aching would be a good start."

"Michael," she breathed, all her blood rushing from her hands and face to pool low in her groin. Her panties were instantly damp, her flesh pulsing with needy heat.

"So, you really are a secretary."

"Of a sort. I write up classified ads, transfer incoming phone calls to the right desk, and review clubs and restaurants on the side."

Sassy realized she was babbling, and clamped her mouth shut.

"I don't like being used."

"I didn't use you, Michael, I swear. The minute I saw you, there was this instant chemistry between us. What happened had nothing to do with my review, and everything to do with how you made me feel."

"I know. Or I wouldn't have called."

She hesitated, then decided to risk asking, "Why'd you wait so long to call?"

"I wanted to develop your pictures, first."

The pictures he'd taken Sunday morning. Had he planned to use them as a counter-threat in case she tried blackmailing him like the model had?

His voice dropped to a low purr. "The camera doesn't lie."

"So you believe me." She let out a sigh of relief.

"Yes. But we still have a lot to talk over. When do you get out of work?"

"Five."

"I'll be waiting for you at my apartment. The doorman will have your name on his list."

He hung up, leaving Sassy clutching the dead handset until it started bleating at her again. The annoying noise barely registered.

He wanted her! Anything else was unimportant. She floated through the rest of the afternoon in a haze, at one point realizing she'd somehow combined an ad for a used Jet Ski with one for a NordicTrack, offering to sell a high-performing set of Nordic skis and a like-new JetTrack.

She snorted. The seller would probably get more money for the mythical JetTrack than he would for the thousand-dollar clothes rack of choice. At least it wasn't February. You couldn't give a NordicTrack away at that time of year, when so many people gave up on their New Year's resolutions to eat less and exercise more.

Pointing out the ads she'd worked on after Michael's call with colored tape flags, Sassy carefully reviewed each one, catching only two other mistakes. She'd prefer to look them over tomorrow, when her head wasn't spinning with thoughts of her impending meeting with Michael. But the paper had to go to the printer's tonight.

On impulse, she printed out a copy of her article, proud of the way it had turned out under Bryce's expert editing. She stuffed the printout into her bag to show Michael. There would be no more secrets. No more surprise revelations.

The workday finally ended, and she scampered out. The rush hour traffic was a zoo, but it took less than half an hour to reach Michael's building. She wished she'd been able to go home and change into something sexier than jeans and a glittering T-shirt of golden cat statues, a souvenir of a friend's lucky trip to Las Vegas two years ago. But she wasn't about to keep him waiting. Especially since she was hoping to be out of her clothes pretty quickly once she arrived.

She pulled into the guest parking area, which didn't require a passkey, unlike the parking garage. Her beat-up little Aspire looked completely out of place in the sea of luxury sports cars and SUVs that could stow her subcompact in their cargo spaces. But she didn't care. Michael wasn't interested in her for her car.

Remembering how they'd nearly made love in his SUV that first night, she was flushed and eager by the time she arrived at the building's lobby.

"Sasha Davidovitch, for Mr. Jackman," she told the uniformed doorman who guarded the elevators.

He consulted a list on a clipboard, running his finger down the page until he found her name and checked her off. "Mr. Jackman is expecting you."

The up elevator already contained four people from the parking garage when it opened to let her on. Two of the men wore business suits, one navy and one gray, while the remaining man wore khaki pants and a green golf shirt. The woman wore a black patent-leather short skirt and matching heels with a fuchsia and black silk blouse.

The two men in suits were discussing some aspect of the law as it related to offshore investments, completely ignoring her, but the other two nodded and flashed brief smiles as she entered the elevator and pressed the button for Michael's floor.

By the time she rang his doorbell, she'd convinced herself that she should have taken the time to go home and change first. He was surrounded by beautiful people all day long. The least she could have done was boost herself closer to their level.

Instead, all she'd taken the time to do was pop a breath mint and run a quick comb through her hair before leaving her car.

Michael answered the door immediately, making her wonder if the doorman had given him warning that she was on her way up. He pulled her inside, slammed the door shut behind her, and pressed her up against the wall, covering her mouth with a demanding kiss. She melted against him, sighing against his lips and twining her arms around his neck.

His attack gentled, and he nibbled and sucked on her lips playfully while his hands slipped into the back pockets of her jeans. With a sigh, he lifted his head.

Sassy grinned. "Hell of a hello you've got there."

He chuckled. "I was trying to prove something to myself. That kissing you really was as good as I remembered."

"And was it?"

"No."

"Oh." Her heart dropped to her toes.

Michael bent his head and pressed another swift kiss to her lips. "It was better."

"Oh!" Her heart soared. Much more of this, and she'd need a Dramamine for her internal organs.

He stepped back, looking over her jeans and T-shirt. Rather than being upset at her casual attire, though, he grinned. "Anxious to see me, were you?"

"I thought about going home and changing into something sexy. Regretted it about a million times between the office and your door. But my apartment was out of the way, and I didn't think I could afford the time."

"Doesn't matter. You'll be out of them soon enough."

"I was hoping you'd say that."

Leaving one hand tucked in her jeans pocket, Michael steered her through the curtain into his dining room. A row of potted ferns lined the table.

Heading toward his bedroom, he said ominously, "But first we need to talk."

Chapter Eight

The seating area had been transformed. Two leather chairs had been pushed together at an angle, and the cubes that had been between them moved aside to form a black leather table. What had appeared to be decorative Velcro straps when the cubes were on their sides now rested open upon the table, just waiting to tie her down. A collection of riding crops, whips, paddles and floggers filled the surface of another cube, neatly laid out for use.

But the biggest change was near the ceiling. The ferns had been removed to the dining room, and in their place, a heavy black leather swing hung by chains from the wrought iron hooks.

"Sit down," he ordered, nudging her toward one of the chairs.

Sassy sat, her eyes drawn to the pile of implements. She shivered in mingled anticipation and fear, remembering her dream. Had her subconscious mind guessed Michael's reaction correctly?

Michael dropped into the other chair. "I explained to you how BDSM relationships had to be based on a foundation of complete honesty."

"I never lied to you."

"A lie of omission is still a lie."

She dropped her gaze and shuffled her feet, watching as the LEDs blinked on and off. "Yeah. I know."

"You explained your reasoning, and I can understand why you did what you did. I don't condone it, and won't accept any similar prevarications. But I understand. So I'm giving you one chance to come clean, about anything and everything."

"The job was the only thing. That I was at the party to review it."

"You're sure?"

She hesitated, thinking back over all of their discussions, wondering where she might have misled him either on purpose or accidentally. "Well, you know the paper bought my Briar Rose membership fee. I couldn't afford it. I can't even afford to eat out if the paper's not paying. I'm about as close to broke as you can be without being in debt."

He said nothing, but nodded encouragingly.

"I did lie to Eveline, telling her I was experienced, but I already told you I wasn't. And I tried modeling once, but hated it. The photographer wasn't anywhere near as good as you, and kept bellowing these incomprehensible things, like four o'clock and Position Three, then shouting at me when I didn't move the way he wanted."

She fell silent, racking her brain for anything else. Then she dove for her purse, pulling out her printout of her first article.

"Here. You can see everything I said in the paper. It'll come out tomorrow."

Michael quickly scanned the copy. Unlike *Sun Daze*'s normal style, she hadn't named names, calling Briar Rose "an exclusive Deco District dating service," Carl and his slaves "a music business executive and two young models", and Michael himself simply "a devastatingly attractive dark-haired man".

He looked up, smiling. "Devastating, huh?"

"Oh, yeah."

"So your first article covers up to when we got the room. That would be your second article?"

"Right. I figured I could get at least two months of stories from the party and what followed. Although I'll probably leave out the photo session, since that could identify you." She hesitated. "Unless you don't want me to go through with it? I could keep the story focused on just what happened at the public parts of the party."

He shook his head, folding the paper and handing it back to her. "No. I don't have the right to ask that of you."

"If it's going to cause trouble—"

"It won't. You're discreet. I'll take a look at your future articles, if you like, to make sure you're not saying anything that could be a problem. But you could be doing a big service to people who might be interested in the lifestyle, and not know how to get involved. If *Sun Daze* wants to run a list of contacts—anonymous bulletin boards, chat rooms, and stores that cater to the scene—I can put one together for you."

Sassy felt herself glowing, radiating happiness. She was surprised Michael didn't need sunglasses to look at her. She'd expected him to be furious about the articles, and here he was offering to help her write them.

"So, is that everything?" he asked.

"Well, I didn't really want to go shopping Sunday. I didn't want you to see my apartment. That's everything."

"Why didn't you want me to see your apartment?"

"Your bedroom is bigger than my whole apartment. If you'd seen where I lived, you'd know I couldn't afford Briar Rose, and then the whole secret would be out."

He nodded. "Complete honesty from here on?"

"Complete honesty," she agreed.

"Good. Strip."

She didn't question him, simply standing, toeing off her sneakers, and removing her jeans and T-shirt as quickly as she could. The air-conditioning raised gooseflesh on her skin, but she trusted that Michael would soon have her burning for him.

"You wouldn't have tried to keep a secret from me if you'd understood what it means for me to be your Master. So we're going to practice your complete and total submission, until you do understand."

"Yes, Master."

"Get on the table, face down."

She did as he ordered, discovering very solid wood underneath the padded leather. He adjusted her position, then fastened the straps around her arms and lower back.

The first slap against her ass took her completely by surprise. She tensed her ass muscles, anticipating another slap, but instead the rubber lashes of a flogger landed across her upper back. She jerked in surprise, pulling tight against her restraints.

Michael grabbed a fistful of her hair and pushed her head down onto the table. "I said face down."

"Yes, Master."

He slipped his hand between her legs and fondled her clit. "Good girl. You're rewarded when you behave."

Sassy whimpered. She wanted to spread her legs wider, or press herself harder against his fingers. But she knew that wasn't allowed.

"Very good," Michael purred, rolling her clit between his fingers.

She moaned with pleasure. Then the paddle smacked her ass. Her moan transformed to a startled yelp.

He spanked her again with the paddle, alternating ass cheeks, until the hot skin pulsed with every beat of her heart. The rhythm varied, sometimes hard and sometimes soft, sometimes slow and sometimes fast, so that she could never anticipate it. Unlike the spanking he'd given her at the party, this one seemed designed specifically to keep her from building to a climax.

Then he exchanged the paddle for a riding crop, striking the backs of her thighs. It hurt, but not unbearably so. Still, she winced when two strikes in a row hit the same patch of skin.

Michael paused. "Remember, you can stop me with your safe word."

"I know."

"It doesn't mean we have to stop completely. We can take a time-out for an adjustment."

"I know."

He hesitated a moment longer, but when she didn't use her safe word, he resumed smacking her thighs. She clenched her fists, determined to bear it. He was punishing her for her dishonesty. Until he finished administering the punishment, the anger he'd felt toward her would remain. Only by accepting the full dose of pain would she be able to match the pain she'd caused him. Only then could their relationship start fresh.

Next, he traded the riding crop for the rubber flogger he'd used earlier. The lashes struck her shoulders and back, over and over again. First, it felt like a vigorous massage. Then, as the skin grew more tender, it felt like a massage over a muscle cramp. Finally, it lost any semblance of a massage, and began to burn.

Sassy welcomed the pain. Her breathing deepened, her body relaxing beneath the onslaught as she focused on each blow. She deserved each and every one. By taking the pain into her own body, she removed it from his. She could not offer him a greater gift. That he accepted her gift was a joy beyond measure.

The lashing ended. Michael glided his hands over her body, barely touching her skin. He hesitated twice, probing those areas lightly with his fingertips, and she realized he could tell if he'd inflicted any damage by how hot her skin was.

"You understand submitting to punishment," he said, his voice rough with emotion. "Now you'll learn to submit to pleasure."

Sassy blinked, not certain what response was required from her.

"Get up." He ripped the Velcro straps open, releasing her.

"I...don't think I can stand."

Gently, he lifted her from the table, setting her on her feet, careful to hold her by her underarms or the part of her waist near her kidneys, where he hadn't hit her. He took his hands away, hovering nearby in case he needed to catch her. She swayed, but didn't fall.

Leaving her standing beside the table, he arranged one of the chairs and the cube that had held his toys so they formed a flight of stairs up to the leather sling hanging from the ceiling.

"First, I need to gag you." He held up a thin band of black neoprene, with a neoprene-covered foam ball in the center. "Open your mouth."

A frisson of fear disrupted the blissful haze clouding Sassy's mind. "But then how will I say my safe word if I need to?"

Michael held up a pair of silver balls, shaking them so that she could hear the chimes inside them. "You'll hold these. Let them go, or throw them against the floor, and I'll take your gag off so you can tell me what's wrong."

Nodding acceptance, she opened her mouth and let him stuff the gag inside. He fastened it behind her head with another piece of Velcro. The ball pressed against her tongue uncomfortably, but not painfully, flooding her mouth with saliva. She struggled to swallow.

"Up you go," he directed. "Get in the sling, your ass against the edge, and grab the chains above you."

Sassy clambered up the makeshift stairs, then awkwardly leaned back and half sat, half fell into the sling. The leather slapped her tender ass and burning back, and she yelped in pain, the sound completely muffled behind the gag. Obediently, she reached up and grabbed the chains nearest her hands.

"Good." Michael scooted her a fraction further over the edge, then wrapped thick cuffs around her wrists and fastened her to the chains. He followed with even thicker cuffs for her ankles, lifting her legs to fasten her ankles to the bottom pair of chains. Finally, he pressed the promised chime balls into her hands, so she could stop him if she wanted.

Her sex was spread wide-open before him, and she wondered if he intended to make love to her like this. But the height was all wrong. She was too high for his cock to reach her, and too low for his mouth.

He moved away, and she heard the rip of condom packets being opened, followed by the wet spurt of lubricant being applied. When he returned, he held two condom-covered vibrators shaped like realistic cocks—if cocks were made of glittering purple plastic. One was at least an inch thick through the shaft, and even broader across the head, while the other was only half an inch wide its entire length.

She watched, eyes wide, as he turned the bases of the vibrators, and they started to hum.

He pressed the broad tip of the wider vibrator against her clit, circling it until she moaned in pleasure, then pushing against her entrance. She was already wet and wide-open, her time on the table priming her more than she'd realized. Michael slid the vibrator inside her.

Sassy's eyes drifted closed, the better to concentrate on the feeling of fullness inside her. Then she felt the tip of the second vibrator pressing against the opening of her ass.

She tried to bolt upright, but only set the sling twisting from side to side. Michael caught the chains, steadying her.

"Relax. This won't hurt. I promise."

Trusting him, she lay back in the sling. The tip of the vibrator slipped inside her ass, but Michael made no effort to push it deeper inside. Slowly, the vibrations of the unit relaxed her ass muscles, and he eased it further.

Sassy trembled. Having something up her ass was a completely unfamiliar experience. But he was right. It didn't hurt. She wasn't exactly sure how it felt. Mostly, her brain was sending her a very confused signal that she really needed to go to the bathroom.

Then he pushed it to its full depth, forcing the first vibrator partially out of her vagina. She gasped, then struggled not to choke on the foam ball filling her mouth.

Michael pushed the first vibrator all the way in, and the second popped halfway out of her ass. Sassy cried out at the unexpected pleasure.

Expecting his next action, she moaned as the second vibrator filled her ass, and the thick head of the first one stroked over the muscles of her inner chamber. Without pausing, he thrust it back inside, freeing the second one to slip most of the way from her ass.

She screamed, a harsh cry of pure satisfaction pulled from deep within. No wonder he'd needed to gag her. Even with the foam ball muffling her screams, she was noisy. If he hadn't gagged her, his neighbors would think he was killing her.

He was. Killing her with pleasure.

Soon she was beyond thinking, able to do no more than incoherently beg and whimper as the vibrator filled her ass, then bellow as the other vibrator thrust deep into her vagina and the one in her ass slid almost all the way free. Her cries grew louder and more frantic as she chewed on the gag. This wasn't anything like the escalating pace of sex she was used to. If anything, Michael seemed to be slowing down. Or maybe it was a figment of her imagination, her awareness stretching and time expanding, even though in reality it was moving faster and faster.

She screamed again, broken, begging and pleading. He couldn't understand her words through the gag. Hell, she couldn't even understand the words in her head. They were a senseless jumble—please, now, no, Michael, harder, more, oh, please. Finally, she settled on the two simplest—please, oh, please, oh, please, oh, please—over and over again until they lost all meaning.

And still Michael pumped the two vibrators in and out, filling first her vagina, then her ass. Sassy was crying, tears of frustration streaming down her cheeks, as she whipped her head from side to side, begging him to finish her. But he kept the pace just slow enough that he wouldn't trigger her release.

She couldn't breathe, couldn't think, could only feel the glorious sweet rush as the vibrators slipped in and out. She trembled uncontrollably, her entire body shaking, the chains holding her rattling as she bounced and jangled beneath them.

Her eyes rolled back, her cries morphing into a single long wail that flew up the scale.

Recognizing that she'd reached her limit, Michael stopped teasing her and pumped the vibrators vigorously, slamming each one home before it had done more than moved halfway out. The climax hit her. She threw back her head and howled behind her gag, a primal scream of pleasure, pain, frustration, and triumph.

Dimly, she heard Michael's sharp gasp, followed by a low groan of satisfaction. All she knew was that he'd removed the vibrators, leaving her empty but yet somehow complete.

Something tore loudly by her ears, and he tugged the sodden ball out of her mouth. Belatedly, she realized he'd ripped open the fastening that held the gag in place.

He undid the catches on her wrists and ankles next, her limbs flopping uselessly when he released them. Somehow, he pulled her from the sling and carried her to his bed, her limp and unresponsive body just so much dead weight.

She roused slightly when he laid her down on top of the comforter, whimpering until he lay down beside her. She curled against him, wrapping her arms and legs around him and shivering in the aftermath of her climax.

"Michael," she whispered. "Oh, Michael."

"Shhh." He stroked her gently, soothingly while she sobbed against his chest. She didn't know what was wrong with her, but she couldn't stop and he didn't seem to mind. So she cried. She cried until she was completely spent.

Eventually, she stopped shaking and her tears dried. She felt like every bone had been replaced with spaghetti, and every muscle replaced with Jell-O.

She sniffed, blinking to clear her eyes. Michael was smiling indulgently at her, his fingers sliding through her hair in a soothing caress. His shirt was soaked with tears, and she realized that although she was completely naked, he was still fully clothed.

"I'm sorry. I don't know what came over me."

"I do." He rolled her onto her back, leaning over her to press a soft kiss to her lips. "You understand what it means to submit to pleasure, now."

Sassy nodded. If he'd asked her, she'd have said she'd submitted before this. But now she knew what true, complete submission entailed. It went beyond giving up her will to his. It took her to a place where she had no will at all, simply existing as an extension of Michael's desires.

"Is it going to be like that all the time, now?" she asked hesitantly.

His chuckle reassured her. "I don't think either one of us could take something that powerful all the time."

"I didn't think so, either. But I was willing to try."

He laughed. "You are an amazing woman. Have I told you that recently?"

"Uh, you might've. I wasn't really listening too carefully."

He laughed again, and pressed another soft kiss to her lips. "Wait here. I have something for you."

He pushed himself upright, and hopped out of bed. She waited. She wouldn't have been able to work up the strength to move, even if she'd wanted to. A short time later, he was back, a long, thin box in his hands.

Kneeling on the bed beside her, Michael opened the box to reveal a silver collar, embellished with curling lines of red and blue. "Is it pretty enough for you?"

"It's gorgeous."

"It gets better." He pressed a concealed stud at the base of the clasp, activating the battery, and the curls lit up. The red line cycled slowly through red-violet, to purple, to blue, while the blue line cycled through blue-green, lime-green, and finally yellow.

Sassy smiled up at him. "I love you."

He fastened the collar around her neck. "It's my job to keep you happy, satisfied, and in love. I do so willingly and without reservation."

She blinked. His words sounded strangely formal, as if he was reciting part of a ceremony. Then he bent and kissed her, and all questions flew out of her head at the warmth of his lips on hers. Later, when the kiss finally ended, he finished his declaration.

"I love you, too."

She brushed her fingertips across the metal collar, already warm from the heat of her body. "This is more than just pretty jewelry."

"Yes. It's a badge of ownership. It tells the world that I've taken responsibility for you, for ensuring your health and happiness, and so long as you continue to wear it, you promise to honor and obey me."

"Love, honor, and obey? That sounds like a wedding vow." Sassy tamped down the rising panic that threatened to consume her. He *had* sounded strangely formal. Dear God, she hadn't just gone and gotten married to a man she'd known less than a week, had she?

"Sounds like." Michael nodded sagely, then could no longer maintain the facade and chuckled. "But don't worry, it's not. It's a promise, not an obligation. You can end the relationship at any time by removing the collar."

"You mean I have to wear it *all the time*?"

"Well, not in the shower—the battery shouldn't get wet. I can get you something more discreet if you like."

She grabbed the collar, as if he was likely to try and take it away from her right then. "Don't you dare! I love this collar!"

He laughed, and began tracing the edge where the metal met her skin with kisses. "So what's the problem?"

"I was just wondering how I'd explain it to the people at work."

"Sweetheart, your first article is coming out in tomorrow's paper. I don't think you'll have to explain anything."

Sassy braced herself for the anticipated rush of heat to her cheeks, but it didn't happen. Instead, she felt a warm glow in her chest. Wonderingly, she reached up and felt her cheeks. They were cool to the touch.

"Sasha? What is it?"

"I'm always embarrassed when I'm the center of attention. You know that. Usually just thinking about a situation will make me blush. But I'm not. Why not?"

He continued kissing his way around her collar, pausing to answer, "You don't mind being the center of my attentions."

"That's different."

"Why?"

"You love me. That's the way it should be."

"Then maybe that's why you're not embarrassed to let everyone see the collar."

She nodded. That made sense. "Because it's right to wear it. It's what I should do."

"What you should do is stop talking, and make love with me again."

Sassy laughed. "That, too, my love. That too."

Trademarks Acknowledgement

The author acknowledges the trademarked status and trademark owners of the following wordmarks mentioned in this work of fiction:

Armani: GA Modefine S.A. Company

Armani Exchange: GA Modefine S.A. Company

Aspire: Ford Motor Company

Automatic Slim's: The Dream Team, LLC Ltd.

Back Door Bamby: Creations Production and Management Group, Inc.

Dramamine: Pharmacia & Upjohn Company

Elmer Fudd: Time Warner Entertainment Company,

Expedition: Ford Motor Company

Food Network: Television Food Network

Ford: Ford Motor Company

Hair Glove: Michael J. McROBERTS

Jell-O: Kraft Foods Holdings, Inc.

Jet Ski: Kawasaki Corporation

The Miami Herald: Knight-Ridder INC.

Moschino: Moonshadow, S.P.A. Company

NordicTrack: ICON IP, Inc.

People: Time Inc. Corporation

The Phantom of the Opera: Really Useful Group Ltd,

Polo: PRL USA Holdings, Inc.

Ralph Lauren: PRL USA Holdings, Inc.

Tantra: Tita's Inc.

Time: Time Inc.

Velcro: Velcro Industries B.V. Ltd.

Vera Wang: V.E.W., Ltd. Corporation

Versace: Gianni Versace S.P.A. Corporation

White Star Line: R.M.S. Ltd. N.Y.C. Corporation

Yoda: Lucasfilm Ltd. Corporation

About the author:

Jennifer welcomes mail from readers. You can write to her c/o Ellora's Cave Publishing at 1337 Commerce Drive, #13, Stow, Ohio 44224.

Why an electronic book?

We live in the Information Age—an exciting time in the history of human civilization in which technology rules supreme and continues to progress in leaps and bounds every minute of every hour of every day. For a multitude of reasons, more and more avid literary fans are opting to purchase e-books instead of paperbacks. The question to those not yet initiated to the world of electronic reading is simply: *why?*

1. *Price.* An electronic title at Ellora's Cave Publishing runs anywhere from 40-75% less than the cover price of the <u>exact same title</u> in paperback format. Why? Cold mathematics. It is less expensive to publish an e-book than it is to publish a paperback, so the savings are passed along to the consumer.

2. *Space.* Running out of room to house your paperback books? That is one worry you will never have with electronic novels. For a low one-time cost, you can purchase a handheld computer designed specifically for e-reading purposes. Many e-readers are larger than the average handheld, giving you plenty of screen room. Better yet, hundreds of titles can be stored within your new library—a single microchip. (Please note that Ellora's Cave does not endorse any specific brands. You can check our website at www.ellorascave.com for customer recommendations we make available to new consumers.)

3. *Mobility.* Because your new library now consists of only a microchip, your entire cache of books can be taken with you wherever you go.

4. *Personal preferences are accounted for.* Are the words you are currently reading too small? Too large?

Too...**ANNOYING**? Paperback books cannot be modified according to personal preferences, but e-books can.

5. *Innovation.* The way you read a book is not the only advancement the Information Age has gifted the literary community with. There is also the factor of what you can read. Ellora's Cave Publishing will be introducing a new line of interactive titles that are available in e-book format only.

6. *Instant gratification.* Is it the middle of the night and all the bookstores are closed? Are you tired of waiting days—sometimes weeks—for online and offline bookstores to ship the novels you bought? Ellora's Cave Publishing sells instantaneous downloads 24 hours a day, 7 days a week, 365 days a year. Our e-book delivery system is 100% automated, meaning your order is filled as soon as you pay for it.

Those are a few of the top reasons why electronic novels are displacing paperbacks for many an avid reader. As always, Ellora's Cave Publishing welcomes your questions and comments. We invite you to email us at service@ellorascave.com or write to us directly at: 1337 Commerce Drive, Suite 13, Stow OH 44224.

Discover for yourself why readers can't get enough of the multiple award-winning publisher Ellora's Cave. Whether you prefer e-books or paperbacks, be sure to visit EC on the web at www.ellorascave.com for an erotic reading experience that will leave you breathless.